PRINCE ALEXIUS, HIS CROWN AND HIS CURSE

By

Virginia Ann Work

"POWER TENDS TO CORRUPT.
ABSOLUTE POWER CORRUPTS ABSOLUTELY."

John Dalberg-Acton (1834-1902)

PREFACE

I, Basil Christopher Xavier, on this fifteenth day of June, Year of Our Lord 1229, set myself down to write the story of Prince Alexius and the events that changed the world in 1205 AD when the Fourth Crusade from Europe besieged the Queen of Cities, Constantinople.

Niketas Choniates, the Greek historian, senator and logothete, has written his version of the events, but he was not as close to the prince as I.

To my surprise, joy and anguish, I became Lord Keeper of the Royal Child shortly after Alexius' birth, his mentor and teacher, and so, a first-hand witness to all that occurred.

I admit to some bias, but are not all accounts of history written from the chroniclers' viewpoint, tainted by his experiences, outlook on life, and background? I would wager that a thousand stories could be penned of the siege of Constantinople and all would be different.

This, then, is my humble perspective of what happened to the young prince and God's sovereign hand in it all.

CHAPTER ONE

The Prince

Year of Our Lord 1187

"Your Majesty! Stop! No!" The scream echoed against the ancient stone buildings in the city of Constantinople.

I froze, terrified, for I recognized immediately that it was the voice of Nurse Amanda who was in charge of my student, Alexius Angelus.

I sprang into the crowded street, shoving people aside. My legs seemed to be made of wood, and time stopped, then stretched into eternity, each second a year, an age.

"Get out of my way!" I yelled. I meant to bellow, but the words seemed to come out as a squeak.

The noise on the street at that moment was almost unbearable – people screaming, horses neighing, horns blaring. And then I saw him, but only a glimpse, and what I saw froze my blood.

Young Prince Alexius, whose father ruled the mighty empire of Byzantium, had escaped Amanda's hand and darted with characteristic abandon straight across the Mese, the main boulevard that bisected the city. He did not see the chariot barreling down the street, and the driver had no time to stop.

The small figure disappeared in a flurry of horses' hooves, dust, and debris.

The horses reared straight up as the driver pulled back sharply on the reins. I surged forward. He was lying in a crumpled heap beside the road near a carpet seller's booth. How had the horses avoided trampling him? I did not know and could not afford time to think of it – not until much later when my knees gave way, and I had to stop for a mug of wine.

The driver of the chariot leaped to the pavement, his face pasty white as he held the reins and tried to calm his team. He'd seen the white robe lined with gold and the royal insignia. He knew.

Blood pooled on the stones beneath the prince's head. Evidently, one of the hooves had clipped him and sent him flying. I felt for his pulse. It was strong. His nurse arrived as I turned him gently to his back.

He moaned.

I leaned closer. "Prince Alexius! Can you hear me?"

He was small for his age, five years a few weeks ago, and possessed blue eyes and a mop of dark hair. Strong and angular with a patrician nose, he had a regal posture that must have been in his blood, for he adopted it as soon as he could stand and walk.

He groaned and opened his eyes, reaching for my face. "Christo? The horses ... they were grand, no?" His eyelids, rimmed with luxuriant lashes, fell shut.

I lifted him into my arms, nodding to his nurse. "He will live, yet we must see to his wound."

She smiled tentatively, sparing me a glance. I knew how she felt, for my heart was still doing acrobatics in my chest.

The same expression blanketed the prince's whole entourage, a mixture of relief and fear, for we knew we may all die for this. Not a pleasant thought, for my people, the Greeks, are keen on torture and violent death when it pleases them.

I shoved those thoughts aside and carried him to a litter.

Whether he was the prince or not, I loved him, even though he was often stubborn, strong-willed and difficult. I'd been with him day and night since he was a babe and considered myself fortunate to serve him in this way, even on bad days when nothing we did seemed to please him.

He called me Christo from the first. I was christened Basil Christopher Xavier, and when they told him my full name when he could understand, he reached toward me and said, "Christo."

I swear it is true. He was only one, nearly two, but he was smart and could talk before other children his age. Everyone laughed, of course, and so it was sealed in that little head. I became Christo.

That day in Constantinople had begun like all others in the royal household, the palace Blachernae that perched in regal splendor on the northern end of the Golden Horn strait.

His servants, including myself, rose before dawn to prepare for the day and break our fast with bread and tea. When His Royal Highness awoke, we spent every minute tending to his needs.

When a child has ten adults looking after him, he becomes over-indulged, selfish, and prideful. He learned at an early age, for instance, to command.

"Get sword! I 'mand you!" he would say, pointing at his play sword that lay only a few feet from him.

And three would spring to obey him.

We took the prince on an outing every Wednesday. The places varied— downtown to a market, or to visit a church, or on a sailboat excursion in the Bosporus Sea. He looked forward to these jaunts, yet for those who cared for him, it was stressful.

How he escaped from Nurse Amanda and the others that day remained a mystery to me, and I never found out, for the nurse and several other servants were dismissed immediately, and I never saw them again.

Thankfully, his father was away on one of his frequent wars, or else we would have all been marched without much ado to be hanged.

We returned to the palace where the court physician attended him. The man peered in the prince's eyes and felt his forehead, saying we should let him rest.

Another visitor was announced. My heart fell when I saw who it was: Euphrosyne, the wife of the emperor's brother, Alexius III. She flounced into the room, attended by her servants. She imagined that she had skill in healing, but she practiced only spells and potions, as far as I could discern.

I did not want her near the prince, but she approached his bed where he slept and laid a hand on his cheek. After a few moments, she said to me, "You have done well. His body and his mind are at peace. He will heal."

He opened his eyes, surprised to see the woman so close. "Aunt Euphrosyne? What are you doing ..."

"Hush, prince," I said, soothing him. I turned to the lady. "He needs rest. If you..."

But I got no further, for she was taken with a fit. She threw a hand to her forehead and fell to the floor, swooning. I rushed to her, as did her servants. She groaned and opened her eyes.

"A curse!" she screamed, sitting upright and gazing with glazed eyes at the ceiling. "This child will die. I see it." She riveted her eyes to him and pawed at the blankets.

I tried to pull her away from him. "What do you see, my lady? What harm will befall him?"

"The crown. He must flee the crown or he will die!"

She seemed to faint again, but recovered quickly. With my help, she stood, casting bewildered glances about as if she did not know what she was doing.

"Are you all right?" I pressed a glass of wine in her hand which she took. She drank, throwing it back in one gulp.

"Yes. Yes, of course, you fool. What do you think?" She gathered her robes, lifted her chin, and made for the door. As she exited, she looked over her shoulder and glared at me.

"You have been forewarned. He must not attempt the throne, for he will die. The crown and the throne are cursed. Cursed, I tell you..."

Muttering, she left. Alexius drifted back to sleep, thanks to the poppy juice I gave him for pain.

I wondered at her so-called vision. Was it authentic or did she want to warn the young prince away from the throne? If his father died, he was heir to the throne of all Byzantium, leaving the woman's husband as a mere officer of the court.

A little later, I was called to an audience with the Overseer of the Royal Children, Lord Stephen Kastmonities. As I went, a monk from one of the monasteries joined me, promising his help. He had been there on the street and gave me advice when I first administered assistance to the prince.

When we arrived, the monk bowed low. He said, "My lord, I am a physician at Christ Pantokrator Monastery and was there when the prince was struck by the horse. This man, your servant Basil Christopher Xavier, arrived at the boy's side before I did. He carried the prince to a litter and administered aid, the best that could be done for the lad on the street." He mopped his brow for it was very warm in the room.

"He did what I would have done. He calmed the lad, examined him, washed the wound, and bound it with a clean cloth. After I examined the child, we determined he could be moved to the palace and tended here. This man saved the young prince's life. I swear."

Lord Stephen leaned forward and impaled the monk with a fierce glare. "How much did he pay you to say this?"

The monk returned his stare steadily and calmly. "He paid me nothing. Not all men are dishonest, my lord."

Silence greeted his words. My heart sank because I thought he had spoken too bluntly to one who was extremely dishonest and corrupt. But with flick of his hand as if he was bored, Kastamonities dismissed the monk.

I nodded my thanks to the monk and turned to my inquisitor. Falling to my knees before him, I prayed for mercy.

"It is as he declared, my lord," I said with a dry throat. "I did all I could to save Prince Alexius and regret that he came to grief. He rested well this afternoon and when he awoke, his first words were of the grand horses he saw. I take that as a good sign. He suffered only minor injuries, scrapes and bruises, besides."

The Overseer bent his sharp eyes on me for several seconds and then nodded. "Very well. Your salary shall be suspended for one month, for you should have been closer to your charge to prevent this from happening. Take note of this for further expeditions in the city. That is all. Leave me."

I thanked him and nearly ran from his presence, a great weight lifted, for as much as I liked my monthly stipend, I lived in the palace and had need of nothing.

It was time for the prince's story, his snack, and bedtime. He fussed because he wanted Nurse Amanda, but he knew Nurse Maria, too, though not so well, and allowed her to wash and dress him for the night.

I continued a story I had devised for him – one of knights, distressed maidens, wonderful horses, and great derring-do. He loved it and watched me with great fascination, his eyes sparkling at the funny parts and shouting with glee when the hero knight won over the evil man. He had to get up with his little sword and play act it, but then his head hurt, and he cried.

We got him to bed, at last, and to sleep. I watched as he lay curled on his vast bed, all his beloved toys gathered close, and his father's scarf, the one he clutched to himself always when he needed comfort, tucked under his chin.

I loved him and prayed nothing would ever happen to hurt him again. I did not know it then, but something evil lay just around the corner for my little prince. A curse, the woman said. Could it be true?

Yet I could not see into the future or protect the prince. My only path lay in doing the best for him, praying for him and leaving the rest with God.

CHAPTER TWO

The Queen of Cities

Year of Our Lord 1187

I leaned on the balcony early the next morning and gazed at the city spread below me with the eyes of a man pardoned from death, as if seeing it for the first time. The sun made its grand appearance over the horizon, lighting the rippling waters of the Golden Horn.

Constantinople, the Queen of Cities, spread below me like a fantastic tapestry, growing in colors and intensity, in light and noise. It was waking up – if, indeed, it slept at all. I loved it from the first moment I saw it, when I came here as a lad, barely fifteen, in the company of my uncle.

I was raised on a small farm in Macedonia, the north-eastern part of Greece, not far from where our illustrious king and leader once lived, Alexander the Great. My parents owned a bit of land near the sea that we put into a vineyard, and so between the farm and the wine, we made a modest income.

When I was ten, my parents fell victims to a plague that swept our town, and both died within a matter of weeks. I was left with the farm and servants, but it was too much for me, and soon Father's overseer stole the house and the land, and I found myself running for my life.

Retrieving a stash of gold that Father had hidden, I headed south, for I had an uncle who lived in Athens.

Mother had spoken of him once. "Your Uncle Alesandro lives in Athens, Basil. I only saw him once when we went there after we were first married. Your father pointed him out to me in a crowd. He is quite wealthy, but we have nothing to do with him. He and your father had an argument when they were younger and neither has ever bent to make it right."

When I saw the city of Athens, I was amazed, for I'd never seen so many houses, churches and buildings scrunched together so tightly in my life. When I finally found the estate of my uncle, the servants received me with hesitation, for he was away on one of his frequent journeys.

The overseer studied me critically and nodded. "Very well. You may stay until he returns, but we do not allow people to live here who do not work for their bread. Can you work?"

"Yes, sir," I replied, my voice cracking. "I... I know vineyards, was raised on one. I know how to make wine. I can do about anything. I am a good student and can teach children." I looked around, hoping to hear the voices of youngsters at play.

"Very well," he said again, motioning to a man servant who stood behind him. "Philip here will take you to your room. I shall give you labors at one of our vineyards. Meals are announced with a gong. You will find soap and water to bathe. Be on time."

For several months, I was happily employed in the vineyard of my uncle, and as I worked, I learned much about him. They boasted he was one of the wealthiest men in Greece, but his house, while it was large and airy and pleasant, was not filled with gold and silver, nor even precious treasures from other lands. He had married twice and divorced one wife and lost another to death. He had grown children whom he detested, and to whom he had given a legacy and sent away.

Yet for all his personal problems, his people seemed to love him and serve him with loyalty and faithfulness, so I thought him to be decent person.

The children of the servants drew my attention, and I spent many happy hours with them. Having had no brothers or sisters of my own, I adopted a big brother policy to the small ones. They flocked to me whenever I sat down for a rest, begging for stories. I always managed to find little treats for them, too.

One day as I worked in the hot sun in one of my uncle's many vineyards, I heard a chariot arrive. I did not look up from my pruning job, for I assumed it would be Michael, the overseer, or some other servant. It was not until I heard heavy footsteps approaching down the row of trees that I climbed down from the ladder, dusted off my hands, and looked up to see who hustled toward me.

I knew him from the first moment. He was larger, broader of shoulder and more florid of face than my father, yet he had the same dark, snapping eyes, the same square jaw, the same forcible stride. I wondered if he would hold the old grievance against me, but he did not.

"Basil! So, it is you! Welcome, my boy! Welcome!" He threw his arms around me and kissed me on both cheeks. When he released me, he said, "They told me you had come and that you are a good worker like all Xaviers are, no?" He laughed. "Come back to the house. We will eat and talk, and you shall tell me of your parents. Ah, you are the image of your father, do you know that, son?"

He sobered when I told him my parents were dead, but cheered up again when we arrived at the house. We sat in his garden near the fountain and talked. Dinner came, and we talked. Evening came, and we talked. I'd never talked so much in my life.

But he never mentioned the trouble he'd had with my father.

I continued to work for Uncle. He often spoke of Constantinople, for he went there on business and was a guest in the palace of the emperor.

One evening, he said, "Ah, Nova Roma. New Rome, they call it. You think Athens a great city?" He laughed when I nodded. "You could put ten Athens on the eastern flank of Constantinople with ease. Or ten Londons. They call it the Queen of Cities and say most of the wealth of the world is there – in churches, vaults, beneath the Hagia Sophia church, in the Imperial Palace and in Blachernae. Oh, you should see it, Basil!"

"May I accompany you next time you go, Uncle?" The words popped out of my mouth without my thinking, and I dipped my head in embarrassment for I knew how impertinent they sounded.

But he seemed to like the idea. "You know, that might be good for you. It would show you the world. And you would see what great influence I have in the city. Yes, I will see. In the meantime, I want you to study. The library here is one of the best in the world, second only to Alexandria. Go there. Study about the world. About the Greek and Roman city of Constantinople. About everything. There is so much for you to learn!"

I was relieved of my duties in the vineyard, which I didn't like because I'd taken a fancy to one of the maidens who worked there. But there are other maidens, I told myself, and only one chance like this – to be educated in the library of Athens.

He didn't take me to Constantinople right away. I waited two full years, and during that time, I learned much, for I met a teacher, an older man, who granted me a few hours every day.

It was early in the year of Our Lord 1182 that Uncle Alesandro told me we would be leaving soon on a ship, one of his, of course, that would carry us across the Adriatic Sea to Constantinople.

I could hardly contain my excitement. I'd learned much about the city and the emperors that ruled the once-mighty kingdom of Byzantium, and I was not impressed.

While the city was a thing to see, no doubt, the government had fallen into disrepair and disrepute. I suppose it is the same for all mighty and powerful nations – their rulers begin with great zeal, with wisdom and moral strength, yet they fall into rivalry, greed, jealousy, hatred, and murder all too soon.

Emperor Andronikos I Comnenus was on the throne at that time. Uncle told me that he was very wicked. With a shrug of his shoulders he said, "But he allows commerce from Greece, and so he cannot be all bad."

I had heard rumors and read accounts from those in the area under this man's leadership of Nova Roma, and I saw *bad* written all over the man. When he first ascended to the throne, he killed all the Italians in the city, 7,000 of them to be exact, because he feared their wealth and control.

We came to Constantinople as the sun was setting. Lights glimmered on the seven hills and shone from the church steeples and along the walls. I could not believe my eyes.

The vast skyline of towers, walls and castles – a kingdom within a kingdom – towered over us. Glistening like a jewel over the Marmara Sea, it held ten major monasteries and hundreds of churches, palaces, markets, and gardens. Uncle said it had an amphitheater, a river, bridges, and, of course, homes – both palatial and humble. He did not know how many dwelt there but supposed the number was well over four-hundred thousand, more than I could even imagine.

The city was enclosed by the Interior Seawall that had never been breached in nearly one thousand years. The wall bristled with fortifications, towers and embrasures. I discovered later that there were interior walls, too. Several of them. The Greeks repelled attacks from the sea by pouring Greek Fire on the ships which burned like brimstone and refused to be put out with water.

As we sailed past the city, Uncle Alesandro pointed out the main points of interest – the giant dome of the Hagai Sophia Church that was lit as if from within from the last rays of the setting sun, the Imperial Palace complex near the Sea of Marmara, and many other buildings.

We entered the strait called the Golden Horn, and I gawked at the sailing vessels. I'd never seen so many and so varied – I, who had been raised near the sea. On the left, my uncle named the docks of the people who lived behind the massive walls adjacent to them. There was the Genoese quarter, the Pisan quarter, the Amalfitano quarter, the Venetian quarter.

"All Latins," he affirmed with a shake of his head as if they were despicable. "Italians. They live cramped together in the smallest area you can imagine. Don't go there at night, my lad. They would kill you as soon as look upon you."

"Why do they live so tightly, Uncle? Surely they would have more room if they moved inland."

He snorted. "They want the sea trade, Basil. Every inch of that land is taken up with shops, silk warehouses, markets. The ships that land there bring them trade. Money, lad. And they aren't below fighting their neighbors for more of it. Riots and squalls break out there all the time."

He turned and pointed to the right. "There is the Galata Tower. If there is a threat to the city, they will suspend a great chain between those two," he indicated another tower on the left bank. "The chain is supposed to keep out any vessel that comes to invade the city. Especially this part of the city, the heart and life of it, the Golden Horn. It is well named, for most of the gold in the city comes from and flows into this place."

We sailed up the strait. After a while, he pointed to a white structure high on the upper cliffs on the left, a large complex of buildings that was enclosed with its own walls.

"That, my boy, is Blachernae Palace. The emperors used to live in the south at the Imperial Palace, but that got too crowded, so one of them, Manuel I, built this monumental pile of stones. He put it in the north of the city so he could control the Golden Horn and go hunting with ease."

"Will we... stay there?" I could barely force the words from my constricted throat so much in awe was I.

"Aye. I have a villa on the Fifth Hill near the Christ Pantokrator Monastery, but the emperor has invited me to stay in the palace. We are to sail with him on his imperial barge tomorrow." He grinned. "We will remain a week. It will give you time to look around."

I loved the city from the first and used every waking moment exploring it. The days flew by; it was more than a week that we lingered. We moved to his house on the Fifth Hill, where my uncle dealt with his business matters, but I sensed he wanted to return home.

"Well, Basil," he said to me one night over a glass of wine, "we must think of our return journey. One of my ships is in harbor preparing to sail. I spoke with her captain today and said we wanted a berth. He is sailing in two weeks." He glanced at me, gauging my response.

I shook my head. "Two weeks? Why, I've only just begun to see the city. I haven't spent more than a few hours in the Imperial Palace, and one could spend ... weeks, years there."

Straightening, I tried to look my most grown up. "I've learned more in these two weeks than in all my studies before, even though the library in Athens is a grand one." I hurried to append the last phrase for I knew he was a major contributor.

He chuckled. "I knew you would say that. In fact, I have news for you." He paused, swirling his wine, a slow smile curving his mouth below his moustache. "You are not the lost, forlorn country boy like you were when you first came to me. I have seen you work and study. You are level-headed and a hard worker, like your father."

I sat back, amazed, never expecting to hear such words from his mouth.

He stood and strolled to the windows that allowed in the cool evening air. The sweet scent of magnolia blossoms drifted in to me. For the rest of my life, I would associate the city of Constantinople with that smell.

After a long silence, he spoke again. "I am aggrieved that we never amended our quarrels, but it is too late for that. Still, it is not too late to show kindness to his son." His voice broke. He did not turn from the window.

Finally, he said, "Would you like to stay here?"

"You would allow me to, Uncle?"

He nodded and swung his gaze to me. "Yes. I spoke to the Lord Chamberlain. He is, as you know, in charge of all the domestic arrangements in the royal household. It seems there are children who have need of a tutor. A tutor and a physician."

I stood and paced the room, picking up a trifle here and there and setting it down again. "But I am not a physician, even though I studied in Athens on the subject."

"Ah. But you can learn. There are people here you can work with, who can teach you. You may begin at once in the palace. The Lord Chamberlain will assign you tasks, and you will proceed from there."

He pierced me with a bright glance. "Do you want this? The palace is a dangerous place, they say, and the nearer you get to the throne, the more dangerous it becomes."

I would never forget that moment – the popping of the fire in the fireplace behind me, the sweet scent of flowers on the evening air, the music someone was playing nearby, a low lullaby. I thought of my mother and father. How pleased they would be!

But could I do this? Was this something I really wanted? I knew he spoke the truth of the danger, but it did not faze me at that time. No. It wasn't the danger that stopped my heart and choked my throat.

It was my own self. Could I do it? I was only a humble farm lad from Macedonia. But in that moment, something turned in my heart. I felt a Presence dawning on my consciousness.

I felt it was God. I had given my heart to Him years ago in the small church my parents attended. He was with me. In that moment, I knew He had planned all along to bring me to this city.

I straightened my shoulders and faced my uncle. "Yes, I want this. You say there are children? I will go, then, and do my part." I raised my chin. "Maybe there will be some great task I am destined to perform. The Lord has sent me here, given me a great love for this place, and I trust His wisdom to lead and guide me further."

He laughed. We clinked our glasses together.

When he saw I was well and truly housed and employed in Blachernae, he took his leave of me and the city.

It was five years before I began teaching children or practicing any kind of medicine in the palace, even though I worked many hours in the monastery and was beginning to have some small skills in repairing broken bodies.

A year after that, they gave me the charge of the young prince, Alexius IV.

In those six years, since Isaac Angelus had taken the throne, there had been two insurrections and three attempted palace revolutions against the emperor while he was off to one of his wars.

Riots occurred constantly, for the city was always in an uproar about something. Palace intrigue and gossip was deadly and swirled constantly like an evil cloud over my head.

Dangerous? Oh, yes. But I loved it.

CHAPTER THREE

The Madness Begins

The Year of Our Lord 1189

The prince grew to a lanky youth, all elbows and feet, yet he was agile, intelligent, and quick in his movements and decisions. If there was one thing that characterized this child, it was that nothing daunted him. He had no fear in his heart, and he would try anything that came to his mind.

Like the time I found him when he was just past his seventh birthday dangling by his hands from the balcony railing, the garden twenty feet below. The door to the balcony was open.

Stay calm! I urged myself against the violent pounding of my heart. I noticed his nurse asleep and wondered if he'd drugged her wine. He'd been known to do that.

When I got out on the balcony, I asked in what I hoped was a calm voice, "Where are you going, Your Highness?"

"Down there," he said, nodding toward the ground.

I stepped closer to him, wondering if I could grasp his wrists. "How will you do that?" I guessed that he had clambered to the top rail and slipped off, grabbing the rails on the outside to halt his fall. But he did not want me to know it.

"It is easy. I will... just find... a rope and swing down."

"But there is no rope."

He thought about that. "No. But there is a vine. Over there. Climbing the wall. I shall go... and get down it." He proceeded to switch hands on the railing, each switch making my heart crawl into my throat.

"Alex. Look at me." I rarely used his shortened name and even less seldom the deepened tone to my voice.

He glanced up. The strain was wearing on him, and he suddenly realized his danger. "Yes... Christo?"

I crouched down beside him and put my hands on his. "Listen. The vine would not hold you because you are a big boy now. You would fall and land very hard on the ground down there. It would hurt a lot. I don't want you to be hurt."

He started to sob. "I want a rope!" he cried. "I want to swing like that man did on the rope!"

I reached through the rails and grasped his wrists firmly, remembering in a sudden flash the show on the street we went to last week and how a man fairly flew through the air on a rope that was fastened from above.

"There. I have you, prince. Now, we will move your hands to the top, and I shall lift you over. When I count to three, move this hand." I squeezed his right hand. He did not want to let go, for panic was setting in, but he shut his eyes and relaxed his grip.

I moved the hand up and so we went to the next hand until he was at the top of the railing. Then it was difficult, for I had to switch my hands from through the rails to over top of them. I told him to hang on tightly, and I managed it.

By this time, the rest of his staff was at the door and window, watching and calling suggestions. I lifted him over, and with a gasp of joy and relief, he circled my neck and hung on like he would never let go.

I carried him inside, motioning to Nurse Maria that she should close and lock the balcony door. I set him down and handed him a hankerchief to wipe his face.

"When you have recovered, I have a surprise for you. That very same man you saw down on the street is coming here! We have a rope set up, and he will show you how to swing on it. Would you like that, Your Highness?"

Forgotten was his fear and tears. He dashed about the room, telling everyone what he was going to do and how he would fly through the air on a rope.

Rope. I rubbed my chin and stared at the balcony door. There were no steps on the outside from any of the windows or balconies in the palace. We would bar the young prince from using this balcony again, but it might not be a bad idea to stow a rope out there. Coiled, ready to be used in an emergency.

Like for a fire. *Or a palace take-over.*

I didn't like to consider the threat of the present emperor being killed and someone taking over the throne, but it was there, always at the back of my mind like a panther about to spring.

The prince's life was always in danger, too. Any of the emperor's relatives or servants might rise up and supplant him, and usually the family and servants did not survive if the rebellion was successful.

The prince had his own Imperial palace guards who were loyal to him. They stood outside the door of his apartment day and night, carrying their heavy axes like they knew how to use them. Which they did.

Yet something could happen. These men could be swayed. It had happened before.

By this time, I knew the palace like the back of my hand, even though it was a labyrinth of halls, large rooms and small rooms, and apartments. I mainly kept myself to the children's wing, but occasion took me at times beyond – to the great assembly rooms and halls where state dinners were served to half the population, it seemed, with such splendor and wealth that it took away my breath.

The Prince's birth dates were celebrated in such a manner. I accompanied him, staying always in the background, as he appeared to the people – an erect, stern-faced little boy dressed in the fine apparel of the kings of New Rome, a slim circlet of gold on his dark head.

I was sad that he was so distant from his father and mother and two older sisters. Every week they allowed him an audience that lasted no more than ten minutes. He would rush to them, hug their legs while they combed their fingers through his hair, asking him disinterested questions and dismissing him without a second thought.

No wonder so many royal sons thought so little of killing their fathers for the throne.

Isaac Angelus, Alexius' father, had deposed the former emperor, Andronikos Komenus, a cruel man who was hated by the citizens. Isaac, a military leader, championed the common people, eased the taxes and gave leniency and mercy to many. He proved himself an able leader of men on the battlefield – he could ride, fight, and swear with the best of them.

Yet now he could barely walk on diseased feet. He complained incessantly and seemed unable to rise to the challenges of governing that he was so eager to address earlier. His brother had made two unsuccessful rebellions to take over the government, but Isaac allowed him to live and the freedom to pursue his agendas.

The palace was a beehive, no, it was a thousand beehives of gossip, slander, and politics. It was like a small city, and every evil under the sun festered in the halls of opulence.

The more I understood it, the less I wanted anything to do with it. The people of the palace led miserable lives, pathetically enslaved to greed, lust for power, and jealousy. The poorest beggar on the street down below lived a happier life by far. I knew that, for I'd made some friends of them.

As Prince Alexius grew, his education developed beyond what I could teach him. He took classes in sword play, horsemanship, history, and politics. He learned economics, trade, the sea and sailing, and many other things.

I had more free time, and so went often to my uncle's estate and helped with his business of trade and sailing. He kept warehouses full of goods that came in on the ships. These items must be recorded and stored until they were sold and shipped elsewhere.

Taking over this task of bookkeeping detail, I found I liked it. I must admit, though, my favorite thing was to walk the streets of my beloved city and learn of her, meeting her people, and drinking her ale.

It was in this way that I met a young girl in a tavern in the Old City near the Million where the Mese ended or began, depending on which way you were going. It was The Golden Bull, and had the best ale and mussel stew in the city.

That day, I explored the old city – past the Million, the Hippodrome, the Zeuxippus baths, and Chalke prison. It was once Chalke Gate, the entrance to the great palace built by Justinian I. The brass doors, for which the gate was named, were removed by the emperor, who turned the rooms beneath the ground into a loathsome prison.

At the Golden Bull, I met Basil, a man I'd become acquainted with at the warehouse when he came to purchase supplies for the garrison under his charge. When people saw us, they called us the Two Basils.

We found a seat in the dim interior, and before long, a girl came to serve us. Despite the poor light, I saw she was slim and very pretty. Her face was flushed, for it was warm inside.

"Yes?" She asked, arching her brows. "Ale for you two?"

She had fair skin and long, dark hair caught behind her neck except for a tendril that curled lovingly on her smooth brow. Her eyes flashed in amusement at us two loafers sitting there.

"Aye. And mussel stew, please," Basil said, grinning. "It is nice to see you, my lady. This man, he is another Basil."

"Yes. Pleased to meet you, sir." She nodded and gave us a smile, displaying a pair of the cutest dimples I'd ever seen.

My tongue seemed frozen to the top of my mouth, but I managed a weak, "I am pleased to meet you, too."

She swung away, balancing a tray on her hand like it was glued there.

I had been going to suggest that we take our refreshment outside, but suddenly I was content with the stuffy air and the crowded, noisy room. I watched the girl as she disappeared through the door that led to the back room, hoping she would hurry and return.

I must have sighed, for Basil snorted. "You like her? Join the crowd."

"She's new. I've never seen her in here before." I smoothed my hair. "I wonder what sort of man she likes. One like you with plenty of fat on his waist and a gold chain about his neck, or one like me, young, bright, and good looking."

He laughed. "I was in here yesterday, and she refused the attentions of a soldier. A handsome soldier, at that. Cool as snow, she shut him down with a sassy reply and a curt nod. No, I do not think she fancies any sort of man right now. Give her time. I bet she hasn't been here more than a week."

I leaned back and crossed my arms over my chest. "And give another man the lead? I think not, my good friend. Now, watch as I charm my way to her heart. It will be educational for you."

Surveying him critically, I decided I did not like the way he wore his fine linen garments, nor the chain about his neck that spoke of authority.

"I shall pray for you," he replied with another chuckle.

The girl returned with the ale and plunked it down unceremoniously on our table. "There. The stew will come." She turned to go.

I stood and moved into her way. "Wait! Please." I touched her arm and smiled my best. "I am Basil Xavier. What is your name, please?"

She stiffened. No smile, only a quick glance over her shoulder as if to see if someone would come and rescue her. She stepped back, her blue eyes blazing with indignation. Her face was flushed, her eyebrows arched, her lips in a pout.

She pulled away from my touch and wiped her arm.

"Yes? You want to talk? Can you not see that I am busy? Run off my feet? I cannot chat with you on this day, nor with any other."

"But... I just wanted to..."

She sighed and rolled her eyes. "Very well. I will save you time in answering your questions and maybe you will leave me be. My name is Tania. I arrived a week ago from Thessalonica. My uncle owns this tavern. I must tell you, as I tell all, I do not care to walk with you, go to the games with you, or drink with you."

She stopped to draw breath and seemed to relent when she saw my crestfallen face. "I am sorry, sir. Basil." She flounced away.

I sat down. Soft laughter exploded beside me. I longed to punch the other Basil in his pudgy face.

"Yes," he said when he could talk, "that was very educational."

I went frequently to the Golden Bull after that, and eventually Tania deigned to sit with me outside on the patio and drink a glass of wine.

She was more than just a pretty face. She was intent and purposeful, even driven. She said she wanted to learn medicine because her father had died recently, and she felt that if he'd been given proper medical aid, he would have lived.

I recounted how my parents had perished in a plague, and I, too, was interested to learn how to help people who were ill or injured. Her statement surprised me because women did not go into that field of learning. I tried to dissuade her, but she was insistent about it.

When I told her about my own studies, and the monks I worked with at the monastery, her interest grew. I took her one day to Boukoleon, the old palace, which was not far from where she lived and worked, yet she had never been there.

We wandered the halls, chapels, rooms of state, banquet halls, and dwelling places of royalty, talking and shaking our heads in bewildered amazement at the gold, jewels, precious stones and mosaics which decorated every flat surface we saw.

The gardens were not as well kept as they had been formerly, but it was a joy to discover quiet little nooks with fountains and flowers. We ate at a vendor's stall and then strolled along the Marmara Sea, watching the ships coming in and out of port.

It was evening when we finally turned toward home. She slipped her hand through my arm. "Thank you for a wonderful day," she said. "I will never forget it." She lifted her face to me.

I paused and kissed her cheek. "Thank you for coming with me, Tania. It has been a special day for me, too." I wanted to say so much more, but I knew she wasn't ready.

I continued, "There are many other places we could explore. Blachernae, where I live, the monastery, my uncle's estate, the Hippodrome. Will you come with me again?"

She chuckled as we started walking. "Of course, my friend. I would like to explore all of this city with you."

But we could not do any more exploring, for it was about this time that the boiling kettle of unrest and conflict erupted in the palace.

The mood in Blachernae those days could only be described as threatening. I imagined a giant thundercloud hanging over it every time I approached. The gossip, hatred, and intrigue that swirled through the corridors and laced conversations was evident in every look, every relationship. Being in the children's wing, I tried to avoid it, but slowly I was drawn into it, for everyone wanted to know how the prince fared.

What they really wanted to know was if he could rule. He was only thirteen that summer of 1195 AD, yet they watched him, for the people had grown tired of his father's incompetence and excesses. I liked Isaac Angelus, yet he was not a strong leader, and many people in the government saw that as weakness.

Weak people did not survive, especially when they had a contender for the throne in the form of a brother, and in this case, one who had already tried twice to wrest the government from Isaac's hands. Alexios Angelus III constituted the largest threat to the emperor. I could not understand why Isaac allowed him to live and walk free, yet he had a large following and many admirers.

The emperor left on one of his wars in Bulgaria where the kingdom's hold was weakening and in danger of falling. The prince wanted to go with him, but he said "next time" as he usually did and rode out of the city with his troops.

Yet the expedition did not go as planned. When he left the military camp in Bulgaria on a hunting trip, his brother declared himself emperor, and the troops rallied to his side. When Isaac returned to camp, he was arrested and brought back to Constantinople.

The prince and I rode to the gates to welcome him home, but we saw no sign of his father. Alexius Angelus III led the procession. The prisoners were brought in at the last of the line of soldiers, but we did not tarry to see them. No one spoke of what had happened to the emperor. Perhaps he had been delayed? Was he mopping up resistance with some of the troops?

We discussed it, but finally, with a shrug of his shoulders, the prince turned his mount, and we headed back to the palace with his characteristic aplomb and speed. He did everything for show. His handsome horse was bedecked with enough gold on the bridle and saddle to feed the city for a day.

I thought it a great pity.

The crowds lined the streets to gawk at the young prince who threw coins to them. He laughed as they scrambled in the muck to retrieve them.

When we arrived at the palace, his mood turned dark and sulky. He stepped out on the balcony, for now we trusted him with it. I stood behind him, holding his festive robe, for he was to attend a feast tonight with his mother, the Empress Maria, and his sister, Anna. His older sister, Irini Maria, had married Philip of Swabia, the Holy Roman Emperor of Swabia, and moved to the kingdom of Germany two years ago.

The prince looked out over the city and made a grand sweep with his hand. "I shall rule it one day, won't I, Christo?"

"Yes, Your Majesty," I replied. "You shall rule all of New Rome after your father."

It was a great empire, stretching from Italy and Greece to the Balkans, from the Adriatic Sea and across Asia Minor.

I was surprised that this reminder of his destiny did not lift his mood. If anything, he became even more depressed. I sighed, noting his clenched hands and the hunch of his shoulders.

"Come, prince. You will rule nothing at all if you do not dress for dinner. We must be ready for your father's grand appearance. Remember? It is his birth date."

Running into the other room, he flung himself on the huge canopied bed, suddenly a spoiled child and not the king he liked to play.

"I do not *want* to go to that boring old dinner, Christo! Say that I am sick. Say anything. I want to... I want to ride with the wind and catch the sun in my hand!"

He'd been reading too much Greek literature and fancied himself a god.

I sighed and held out his robe again. "Come. Get dressed, and when you are ready, you will be as grand as the sun in its splendor. And I will get you a pomegranate, if you will heed me. I found some in the market today."

He was inordinately fond of the fruit, and as it was hard to get this time of year, he seldom had it. "Truly?" He stood. Then froze.

Someone pounded on the massive doors that led to the hall. No one ever did that—the guard would take their head off if they tried it.

The booming noise came again. Someone was yelling.

My heart fell. *This is it*, I thought. The end has come. *The guards have been killed, and now they have come for the prince.*

CHAPTER FOUR

A New Emperor

April 8, Year of Our Lord 1195

I stared at the door. I think Alexius screamed. "Christo! Answer it!"

Striding to the door, I unlatched it.

As it swung open, a man fell inside, followed by two Varangian guards. It was Montage.

Montage Komenonos had replaced Stephen Kastamonities as Lord Protector of the Children. He was an older man, the cousin of Theodore Kastamonities who co-ruled with Isaac Angelus. His long grey hair was braided neatly. He wore a golden chain about his neck that bespoke of his office.

I liked Montage, but felt sorry for him, for he should have had a higher position. His cousin constantly berated him, for there was bad blood between them, and gave him only tidbits of authority. I think this title of caring for the children was a slap in the face to a man who could have ably governed the province.

He fell to his knees, his body shaking. I had never seen him in such a state and rushed to help him stand. Blood stained his usually impeccably clean robe.

But he hardly saw me. He leaped to Alexius, falling to his knees again, his hair askew, his face whiter than any linen I'd ever seen.

"Prince! You must flee! Now!"

Prince Alexius stepped back. "Montage! Why do you do this? What happened? Tell me!"

Montage could barely speak so intense was his terror. Then the words erupted from his mouth.

"The emperor, your father, was attacked at the army camp when he went for his hunt. They brought him back here and blinded him. I tried to help him, but they shoved me aside. They laughed at him. The army captains, the officers, all his friends, deserted him. They put him in chains! Like a criminal. Took him to Chalke Prison."

He cradled his face in his hands and wept.

I swear the earth trembled beneath my feet. I could neither think nor react – only stare in dumb disbelief. I reached for Alexius as he stumbled toward me. Terror stared from his eyes.

Before we could say anything, booted feet thudded heavily in the corridor. Harsh cries echoed down the hall.

"Bar the door!" I shouted.

The Varangian guards slammed it shut and let fall a heavy metal beam across it.

The prince shook himself and reached for his sword. "Who … would dare?" At thirteen he was a young man, not a child. His voice shook.

My heart went out to him.

Montage wiped his face with his sleeve and stood with great effort. "Your uncle, sire. Alexius Angelus. He wears the royal buskins now. They are crowning him as I speak. It will not be long before they come for you. You must flee, Prince! They will surely kill you."

Alexius drew himself erect and grasped his sword with whitened knuckles. "I shall not flee, Montage. No! I shall fight them to the death!" His lips were drawn back in a snarl.

Under other circumstances, we might have thought it a brave effort, or at best courageous, but it was neither now. It was his death sentence.

"No!" I came between them, falling to my knees in front of the prince.

They stared at me as if I'd lost my senses. Behind me, I heard the other servants murmur in fear and concern, for we would all die this day, those who held allegiance to the prince.

I focused on the prince. "Alexius, you must listen to me. To me, your friend and teacher. You must submit to the Imperial Guards and the other Varangians who are now swearing allegiance to your uncle. They will arrest you."

He shook his head and gripped the sword tighter. "Do not come near, Christo! I will fight them! I swear it!" He swished the weapon through the air.

I rose, stepped back and bowed respectfully, trying for the soft approach. "Yes, Your Majesty. You will fight, but you will die."

That surprised him. He gave me his attention.

I tried to modulate my tone. "You must go with them tamely. Yes, they may imprison you, but I do not think your uncle will kill you. You will get free, I promise it. We, your friends here and in the city, will free you."

"But, Basil, he must escape!" Montage grasped my shoulder. "It is his only chance. Go over the balcony with him now! I will delay them!" Fine sweat beaded his upper lip.

I shook my head. "He cannot escape. He would be stopped at the gates. They will have them closed by now. We could not hide him in the palace, and there is no way to escape it. If he resists, they will kill him before the hour is out. But if he goes with them meekly and pretends to cooperate, well, then he may have a chance."

Boom! Boom! Something that sounded like a beam crashed into the door. It shuddered but held.

I turned to the prince and took the sword as he handed it to me. Replacing it on the wall, I knelt again before him. Fear darkened his eyes, but he would not allow it to overtake him.

"Prince," I said in a low tone, "submit to them. Pretend to love your uncle. He will free you soon, for he has the mind of an ass. We shall rescue you. This is the only way. Believe me."

He reached for me. "What of you, Christo?"

"I shall go over the balcony on the rope." I managed a smile. "Do you remember when you tried to fly through the air without one? Ah, but now we have one there. Montage and I will take the rope down to the garden and through the underground tunnels. You know where you used to play? Yes. We will get out of the palace, and we will wait. I shall write you. I promise."

He hugged me, a child again, and as I felt his frantic heartbeat, I wondered how I could do this. How could I leave him? *Will they truly allow him to live?*

His hold tightened around my neck. "Do not leave me, Christo!" His voice broke and the last word ended on a high note. "I shall beg for your life! Please do not go!"

"I must, Your Highness." I shot a glance at the door that splintered under the blows it received. Wrenching his hands away, I stood and bowed to him. "Show them that you are a fine prince. Be like the heroes of the Greek legends. Like Jupiter, Ares and Apollo." I smiled. "Be brave and fool your uncle, yes?"

He returned my smile and wiped his face. "Yes, Christo. I shall show them."

The door shuddered again. "Very well. I must flee. Montage? Follow me." I glanced at the others. "I do not believe they will kill you. Pledge your allegiance to the new emperor immediately, and you will be spared."

I climbed down the rope with Montage grunting behind me. As I landed in the garden, I glanced up and saw Prince Alexius peering over the railing. He untied the rope and waved to me, a ghost of a smile playing on his mouth.

I hesitated, wondering what last word I could say to him.

"He will be fine," Montage said in my ear. "You have taught him well. Come, my friend. They will not deal so gently with us."

I exchanged a final wave with the prince and followed him.

He led the way through the garden, always keeping under-cover. I was surprised at his agility and struggled to keep up. We came at last to a hidden door that was in a wall behind a bank of shrubbery. The door squeaked open, and we ran down a series of steps that led to the labyrinth of tunnels under the palace.

He picked up a torch and lit it from the lamp he had snatched from a hallway inside the palace. Water dripped eerily. I expected any moment to hear the heavy trod of booted feet in pursuit.

But none came, and we made our way through the tunnels to another stair that led to the outer wall of the palace near Anemas Tower. The guard on duty knew me by sight. When Montage thrust some coins in his hand, he grunted and opened a small gate for foot traffic.

"I hope your memory fails you tonight, good sir," I said in a low voice. "You saw no one and heard nothing."

"It is as you say," he replied. "Good luck out there tonight!"

The city was in chaos. Montage and I tried to get through the clogged streets, but it was like a game of cat and mouse, for we had to hide and run and dodge flying rocks. The populace seemed to have gone mad, for mobs attacked one another, a church was on fire, and I heard the unmistakable cries of agony and terror from a woman's throat, along with the throaty yells from the soldiers who were looting.

"Anarchy like this always erupts when there is a palace revolution," Montage said. "People figure they can get what they want, and fighting factions take the opportunity to gain more ground."

I shook my head and wept. "It is such a waste, Montage! All this —" I waved my hand to the buildings burning, the gangs running through the streets, "for what?"

He shrugged. "Greed. Hatred. Come, let's not tarry."

We took off again, aiming for my uncle's estate. We found it, to my relief, well-guarded and undisturbed. The guard let us through the gate and locked it sharply after us.

"Do you have relatives in the city?" I glanced at him as we hurried up the walk.

He shook his head morosely. "No, only in the palace. I am afraid I will have to impinge on your uncle's hospitality for a time."

I nodded and showed him into the spacious rooms. "You are welcome to stay. But what can you do for employment? My uncle has often said he will not feed a man who will not work." I grinned, the first since I learned that the emperor had been deposed by his traitorous brother.

He laughed outright and accepted a glass of wine. "Thank you, good friend. Give me a task, and I shall do it to the best of my ability."

I admit freely that I did not sleep much that night. I paced the garden, prayed, and drank Uncle's excellent wine. I heard war-like cries in the city below, and then when the bells from the churches rang midnight, it seemed to give up its riotous ways and settle down for the night.

Evidently, the city guard had quelled the uprisings and something like peace descended, although I knew that hot spots still flared throughout the night. I blew out the candle and sought my bed, but I could not sleep.

After a time, I relit the candle from a smoldering log on the fire and unrolled an ancient scroll I'd received from the monastery as a gift for my help there.

It contained a portion of the Old Testament written in Hebrew, but I had learned the rudiments of the language and liked to practice reading it.

I opened to the Psalms and slowly read, "The Lord Jehovah is my strength and my shield; my heart trusts in Him, and I am helped. Therefore, my heart exults and with my song I shall thank Him."

Comforting words, yet they did little to assuage my fears for the prince.

The next day, I took Montage to the warehouse and taught him to catalog and arrange the items that came in from the ships. He seemed to like this work, but he seemed ill at ease, ever looking over his shoulder and jumping at the least sound.

On the fourth day after the Alexius III deposed his brother, April 13th, early in the morning, Montage told me he wanted to visit the palace and see how things went there. I cautioned him against it, but he was determined to go.

"Pray for me," he said. "If I do not return, then you will know I did not survive. But I cannot sit here and wait any longer. I have to know."

I grasped his arm. "Bring me word of the prince, please."

He nodded. "Yes, I will."

Because the new government was still forming, I had little fear of being seen and recognized, so I went to the warehouse and got busy.

But I could not keep my mind on my duties that morning. A visit to the Golden Bull to see Tania produced little results, too, for they said she was not there and would not divulge where she had gone. That concerned me.

I left word for her and made my way back to the estate, trudging up the steep hill, gnawing on my worry for the prince and for Tania. The sun was high when I approached the house.

Montage met me in the Great Hall, a glass of wine in his hand, his face wreathed in smiles.

"It went well, then?" I received the glass he handed me.

"I am going higher, Basil," he said. "I was escorted to meet the new Emperor, Alexios Angelus III, and was awarded for my loyalty. I will now be the Lord Under-Chamberlain. What do you think of that?" He chuckled. "And here I thought they would take my head from my shoulders."

I slapped him on the back. "Only one step further, and you will be Lord Chamberlain, no? A position much sought after, I understand. I congratulate you and wish you the best." I lifted my glass, and we clinked them together.

He laughed. "Thank you. But I do not want their high positions, only a job that suits me." Then he grew pensive as he strode to the windows over-looking the city.

"I did not need to ask about the prince, for all are talking of it. He was taken to the prison in Anemas Tower, which is closer to the palace. His accommodations are not bad, they say. Yet he is under constant guard and may not emerge. Not for a time. His old care-givers are with him."

My legs suddenly went weak, and I flopped on a low couch. Anemas Prison was an evil-smelling under-ground dungeon. The prince's cell would be an awful place.

I dredged up a smile, for he seemed to think all was well. "It is good news the emperor did not kill him. Yet he will fret being confined like that. He will need his books, his writing. I hope they provide that for him. And he will pine for his horses, for riding." I rose and joined him at the window. "Did they ask of me?"

"I did not speak with any of his servants, and none else in the palace mentioned you. I am sorry."

He lifted his satchel that contained his belongings. He said, "There are ways to get messages in and out of the palace. I shall send you a letter and give instructions. If I can, I will see the prince and deliver any you send to him."

"Thank you, good friend!" This relieved my mind a great deal, for I had no idea how to contact the prince. "I will try to get into Chalke prison to see his father."

He nodded. "Well, I had better be off. Thank you for your kind hospitality."

I walked with him to the palace gates and bade him farewell. As the gates clanged shut, and the guards eyed me in an unfriendly manner, I turned and started back down the hill. I wanted to go inside, but I dared not. Not yet.

It was time to start planning for his escape.

Sauntering down the Mese, I kept close watch on my back trail, and sure enough, it was not long before I spotted him. A spy. And what was even more interesting, I knew him.

He was a Varangian guard, one of the prince's personal guardians, named Michael Trent that I'd befriended. He was a big fellow from England.

I knew he was loyal to a fault to the prince and was surprised that he wore no uniform. Maybe he was not a spy, after all. But why did he hang back and follow?

What could he want from me?

I had learned the rudiments of sword fighting with the prince, but I wore no sword and could not fight one such as him, in any case. As a fine sweat beaded my brow, I wished I had a guard.

A good one.

CHAPTER FIVE

The Plan

April 13, Year of Our Lord 1195

At one of the many little alleyways leading off the main street, I stepped aside, and when Michael Trent approached, I caught his eye and beckoned. Without turning to look back, I led the way to a tavern I knew, not my favorite, to be sure, but they served good ale and fried fish.

Michael Trent followed me inside and sat at the bench across the board table. A serving girl brought ale, and when I ordered the fish, his eyes lit up. I'd noticed his clothes tattered and a hungry look on his face.

"So, Michael, my friend," I said when we received our ale, "how do you fare? I see you are not in uniform. Did you leave the guard?"

He nodded. "Yes, you surmise correctly, I'm afraid. I would not bend the knee to the new emperor, the traitor, we call him. There are others who would not, who fled with me the night Emperor Isaac was taken."

We dove into the fish and bread and occupied ourselves happily for a time.

"How do you fare?" he asked as we drank the ale. "I heard you fled with Montage. Did you find employment?"

"Yes. I am fortunate for I have an uncle who is wealthy, and I live on his estate. Yet he dwells in Greece and has not come to Constantinople, so I know not where his loyalties lie." I grunted and chewed on a chunk of bread. "With his pocket-book, I wager."

He dipped his head in agreement. "Yes. All men are alike."

"How are you employed? Where are the other guards of which you spoke?"

"They are in hiding and making plans to leave. But I have a wife and a child and find it difficult to leap on a boat and quit the city. I find jobs to do that require strength of arm." He lowered his voice. "Have you seen the prince?"

I sighed and straightened, glancing around, checking to make sure no one was within earshot who could possibly be a spy. "No, but Montage went to the palace and became the Under-Chamberlain under the new emperor. He heard the prince is held in Anemas prison. His old servants are with him. I imagine they will release him soon or allow him an apartment in the palace. He swore allegiance to his uncle."

He blew out his breath in relief. "That is good to hear, and I am glad he has friends like Montage in high places." He leaned closer. "And what of his escape from the city? Any word on that?"

"No, we must wait." I paid the serving girl and stood. "Come, walk with me. It is a pleasant day, no?"

We stepped outside and started out for the docks in the Venetian quarter, my favorite place to spend an afternoon. My other haunt these days was the Imperial Palace on the other end of the city. But I did not want to go there today, not with Michael, not with what we must discuss.

We passed vendors who sold every type of merchandise under the sun. Michael Trent stopped now and then to look at a child's toy or a beautiful lace tablecloth. But he passed them all with a rueful shake of his head.

After we'd wended our way through the Venetian quarter and arrived at the dock, I said, "We need to get organized and make a plan."

"Yes, I agree," he replied.

We watched the bustle of men as they loaded and unloaded ships. It always fascinated me, the continual demand for goods and the hurry and scurry of those who met those demands. Commerce, they call it. It makes the world turn.

Or does it?

I shook myself. No time for philosophical contemplation now.

I turned to him and said earnestly, "We must meet at the Haggai Sophia church. There are many rooms we can use. We must spread the word to all who support the prince. We need all who can help, especially those of strong arm who know how to use axe and sword."

He nodded. "Yes, I hear you. Yet it will put us in peril. We have to be careful, for the new emperor has spies everywhere."

"Peril or no, we will proceed with great caution. It must be done. Let us say we will meet on next Sunday? At noon? Mass will be said and people will be milling about. Meet in the forward courtyard near the fountain. Gather all those who care about the prince. Can you do this?"

After a long pause, while a massive Athenian Trireme slowly left the quay, he said, "I do not know if I can do it, Basil. Mayhap Montage?"

"Montage is in the palace. He has little contact with those who have not bowed the knee to the new emperor." We turned from the water and headed back to the city. "No, it must be someone outside. Will you do it?" I paused on the Mese where our ways must part.

"I would, but I have a child. A wife and a child."

I could not fault him for his fear. He was as courageous and strong as any man I'd ever met, yet I knew that his heart trembled when he thought of his family. I waited and bought an orange, telling him to take it to his wife.

Finally, he nodded. "Very well, my friend," he said in a low voice. "I will help you. Meet me here in two days, and I will tell you if we have any who would join us in this work. It is all I can do."

"Thank you, Michael," I said, gripping his large hand. "God protects those who serve Him. Farewell."

I wondered as I made my way up the hill towards home if he would do it. And if not, then what? I could not do this task on my own. In fact, if it were not for my uncle's estate and the employment I had there, I could not move a fly to free the prince.

The estate bustled with activity when I arrived. In the outer courtyard, my uncle greeted me. But not with affection. By this time, after knowing him for the better part of ten years, I could ascertain his moods. He was not in a good mood this day.

"Uncle!" I cried, stepping towards him. "I had no word that you were coming. Did you just arrive?"

He turned from giving instructions to one of the servants, a glass of wine in one hand. His face, florid as always, was drawn into a frown upon hearing my voice and seeing my face.

"Hello, Basil. I came when I heard of the palace rebellion."

"But that was only a four days ago."

"I was in Zara." He drank the wine and handed the glass to a servant. "Why are you here? Why are you not at the palace?" His glare pierced me through as if I was the one who had caused it all.

"I fled. They would have killed me. What did you expect me to do?"

"Bow the knee to the new emperor." His face darkened as he approached me. "Did you? Did you pledge your allegiance to him?"

"But he is a traitor. You could not think that I would..."

"I do not only think it, but I command it. We need to be faithful to the man who sits on the throne of the New Roman empire, whoever he is. We cannot afford, Basil Christopher Xavier, to throw away our properties and our future in silly thoughts of loyalty. You are an idiot if you think Isaac Angelus will ever regain the throne. He is blinded, unable to rule, and cast into prison. He is finished, and I will not have you plotting to rescue the prince from wherever they have placed him."

When he used my full name, I was indeed in trouble, for he'd never used it before. I backed slowly away from him, but he followed me relentlessly until I was pressed against the fountain and thought he might toss me into the water.

"Yes, sir. I see your point, sir." It was all I could manage from my dry throat. I wondered what he knew about my promise to Prince Alexius. Had any of the servants told him what I hoped to do?

He held his riding whip, as usual, and now he slapped it against his leg. "So, you will not object to coming with me right now to do just that."

"To do what, sir?"

"To pledge your allegiance to our new emperor, Alexius Angelus III, and forget your loyalties to his insipid brother."

"I... uh, I am busy, sir. Perhaps another time?" I knew a delay would not work, but in the meantime, I was able to slip away from the fountain and head for the closest door to the house. Anywhere to get away from him and give myself time to think and plan.

"Stop him!" He thundered and motioned to a servant. It was Elijah, a large man from Egypt, who blocked the door, staring at me as if inviting me to try to get past him.

My uncle continued, "You will come with me now. Elijah, bring him."

"Wait." I turned to him with what I hoped was a genuine smile. "I will go with you. You have convinced me, Uncle. Please let me wash and change as I've been working, as you can see, and I cannot appear before the emperor in this garb."

He nodded. "Go. But come back quickly. I sent word ahead that we are coming, and you do not keep an emperor waiting."

I hurried to my room with Elijah trotting behind me. He was my favorite of all the servants. I went with him often to a little gathering of true Christians and enjoyed their worship, a simple service so unlike the grand Haggai Sophia ceremonies of the Greek Orthodox Church.

Catching my breath, I paused at the doorway to my room. My heart beat heavily in my chest, and my mouth was dry. I had to make a decision, and I had to make it quickly.

If I fled, I would leave it all. My uncle's patronage, employment, care, and protection. Everything I was and had built up over ten years would disappear in the flicker of a heartbeat.

On the other hand, I could not in good conscience turn from the prince's plight and my promise to him. If I went to the palace with my uncle, I knew I would not return.

Uncle Alesandro, I mused, had probably already communicated with the new emperor, told him he would give him his allegiance, and promised him I would appear and be his servant. They would give me a position in the palace – that way they could keep an eye on me and hinder me from engineering the defection of the prince.

For they must know he would try to escape.

Elijah shifted behind me. "Time is running out."

I turned and met his eyes. He knew what had been going through my mind.

"I don't know what to do." I looked around the room again. It was appointed with a canopied bed, wide windows that looked out on the city, lush carpets on the floor, tables, lamps, everything a person could desire. "Where will I stay? I cannot flee to the monastery. He knows I would go there."

Elijah grunted. "Hurry, young sir. Grab what you need for this night. I will say I went on an errand, and you bolted. Go to my brother's house where we meet for church. You know it. They have extra rooms where you can stay." He nodded, urging me forward.

I could not take everything, all the treasured possessions I had accumulated during my time here. Grabbing up a leather satchel, I dashed into the room and snatched up clothing, the scroll of the Bible that was my chief treasure, and the bag of my collected coins, saved over the years.

Turning, I nodded. "I am ready, Elijah."

"Go swiftly. The back gate. I will see you later and bring more of your things."

I grasped his hand, thanking him. I then fled from the room, ran down the hall, and descended the stairs in the back. Outside, I trotted to the lower garden, then through a small gate. After a short spurt down a lane, I emerged on the street some hundred yards from the main gate to the house.

It was nearly sunset when I arrived at his brother's house. Judah and his wife welcomed me in, heard my predicament and offered me a room.

"For only a little while," I said. "I hope to find other lodgings soon. I can pay you for what I use in the meantime."

His wife, Birdie, a woman in her sixties, reached up and patted my cheek. "Oh, no, you will not pay, dear heart. Now, get settled and rest. Then come for our meal. You are welcome here as long as you like."

I discovered I was not the only waif they sheltered. Two others, a man and his wife, emerged from a side room at dinnertime, and five people came to the meal from the street. The food was plentiful, hot, and tasty, but I hardly noticed it as I ate.

True to his word, Elijah appeared the next day with some of my belongings. I greeted him heartily, and we went to an inn not far away.

"Was my uncle in a rage when I did not appear?"

He smiled, flashing a set of white teeth in his black face, and settled his bulk on a bench. "At first, he paced and yelled, but when I said you escaped, he gave it up and went alone to the palace."

"And what happened there?"

"I do not know all, of course, only what I heard him discuss with the seneschal. He said the new emperor seems a big improvement over Isaac who cared for nothing but his earthly comforts. This man is taking a grip on the government, and the master feels we will benefit from his leadership. He is giving money away to all, even to the master. I wonder where the emperor, Alexius Angelus, gets it."

I snorted. "From the treasury, of course. He will next raid the churches, and after that, tax the people." I wiped my forehead. "Did he mention me?"

"Not at all. He went to his room early and left this morning at dawn. I readied his horse for him, but he did not speak to me as he mounted."

"Yes. He was probably going out to the farm." I sighed. "Well, I shall have to find employment and a place to stay."

"You can stay with Judah and Birdie as long as you want."

We parted outside the tavern, and I made my way down the Mese to the center of the old town. It did not take me long to arrive at the Golden Bull.

Inside, I searched again for Tania, hoping she had returned. When another girl approached me, I asked about her.

She sniffed as if a bad odor had reached her. "Oh. Tania. She is gone. Disappeared like a vapor." She waved her hand in the air.

"Where did she go? You must tell me!" I gripped her arm.

"Please." She disengaged my hand and moved a step away. "Someone, a palace official by the looks of him, came here after a chariot race. Tania served him, and they talked out on the patio. I overheard some of their conversation. The man said how beautiful she was, and that she would please the new empress as one of her maids. Next thing I know, she was toting her satchel out the door."

"Did he take her against her will?"

She cast me a glance like she thought I was an idiot. "Against her will? No, sir. She went of her own accord, or so it seemed to me. And she's never come back. How do you like that for gratitude to her uncle who sponsored her to come and gave her lodging and employment? Please excuse me. I have work to do."

I found her uncle in the kitchen. Sweat covered his body as he kept the fire going and the kettles full. He turned when I called the third time and gave me the barest of glances before tending a leg of lamb that was turning on a spit over the fire.

"I am looking for Tania," I shouted above the din.

"She's gone, Basil. She went up to the palace. That's all I can say."

"Did she go willingly? Will she return? What is she doing there? Surely she left word for me."

He stepped from the fire and mopped his brow, frowning. "I know nothing more than what I said, young sir. She has not sent any word. It's like she's vanished from the face of the earth. Them's that go up there, they never return. That's what I say. Keep it under your hat. It's not healthy to inquire about such things."

He went back to the lamb. "We will hear from her one of these days, I reckon." He cast me a disparaging glance. "She's prob'ly a high and fancy lady by now, serving Her Highness, the Empress Euphrosyne."

I left, my mind in a whirl. I had to think of planning the escape of my protégé, Prince Alexius, and now I had the task to find and hopefully free Tania from those who had stolen her.

For I knew beyond a shadow of a doubt that she had not gone of her own free will.

Haggai Sophia church was nearby. I approached the enormous structure, struck anew with its beauty and grandeur. To call it a church was a vast under-statement. Perhaps a temple. Cathedral. Palace.

Yes, all of that and more. The name means Holy Wisdom. As it was erected on suspending arches, the building seems to float in air, and the domes above it let in light from all directions.

I had been there many times, and each time, I reveled in the glory of it, making new discoveries that delighted my sense of beauty and precision. Even the great golden dome above my head thrilled me, for it let in light from every angle from windows all around it.

I proceeded to the large center room, found a bench, and bowed my head to pray.

Which of the tasks set before me should I do first? Free Alexius from the emperor and the city, or find Tania? And how could I, an outcast as I was at the moment, accomplish either?

But even though I prayed and sought God's mind on this, nothing came to me. I stood.

It seemed as I strode from the great church that the greatest need was to locate Tania, if she was in the palace or no, and ask her if she was forced into the service. I could not imagine that she would want to serve the Empress Euphrosyne. Everyone in the kingdom, from the beggar on the street to the highest court official, knew that our new queen was mad.

There had been rumors of her eccentrics before she became queen, and now with the power and authority of the throne at her finger-tips, she was out of control. She had the insane desire to destroy all the splendid statues in the city, stating that they must come down or the gods would not bless her.

I don't know how many she destroyed.

She lived in the nether world of spirits, spells, and potions. Raging one moment and weepy the next, I suspected she took some of the drugs she demanded for her religious rites.

It was unthinkable that a gentle soul like Tania was engulfed in the chaos, danger and craziness that swirled around the throne. I gripped my fists tightly and wondered if they'd promised her money or education. Or had her uncle sold her? It happened all the time.

I remembered the crafty gleam I'd caught in his eyes just as he turned from me when I asked him about her. Was it my imagination or had he profited from the sale of his niece?

But what could I do? It seemed hopeless, for I was banned from Blachernae. Would they let me in or take my head if I attempted entrance?

I sighed. Well, there was only one way to find out – write to Montage and march into the palace like I owned it.

CHAPTER SIX

The Girl on Daphne Street

April 15, Year of Our Lord 1195

I could not march into Blachernae like I owned it.

But I wrote to Montage the next day, giving him the location of my new lodgings. I took it to the gate of Blachernae and waited for the next courier to come by. When he received it, I tipped him nicely and asked him to deliver it to Montage.

After some time, the man reappeared and gave me the reply. I took it back to my little room in the back of Judah and Birdie's house.

Montage wrote, "Basil, I cannot do as you asked me concerning the Empress's maidens. I would be putting myself at deadly risk if I were to inquire about this friend of yours, even though I am Under-Chamberlain and in charge of the household affairs in the palace. As you well know, life is precarious in the palace."

My heart fell.

I shoved open the shutters to get more light. It was raining. The smell of bougainvillea drifted in to me. I moved to the fireplace where a meager flame promised more heat than it delivered. I continued reading.

"The prince will be released soon and allowed freedom of the palace, but I am not sure how much outside activity he will be given. He wants to see his father, but that will be denied him. I have seen him once, and he asked about you and wondered if you could come to visit. I said I would find out about it. If it does, indeed, transpire that you can meet with him, before you come to the palace, he wants you to go to the prison and see his father. I will send documents that will allow you entrance. I am sorry about your friend, the girl, but you must be aware that I walk the knife's edge here. I am not free to do as I wish and often regret returning to this place. Please keep me in your prayers. I am, as always, your devoted friend, Montage."

I waited to hear from Montage for three weeks. It seemed a lifetime when I wanted to be doing something towards my goal of freeing Tania. And the prince. But I reminded myself that nothing in the palace moved swiftly. It was like watching molasses move on a cold day.

As I was dressing one day in May, a courier brought the documents from Montage. In the leather packet was a letter from the prince to his father. I knew it was dangerous to be the messenger between them, for this could be construed as treason, yet I knew if I wanted to see the prince, I must do this.

Dressing in one of my finest robes with the Romanesque style toga draped around my shoulders and my finest sandals on my feet, I started down the Mese.

It was in its usual chaotic state with people, vendors, soldiers, and sailors crowding the stalls, bargaining, and purchasing goods madly. Children laughed and shouted, reminding me of how much I missed the little ones on my uncle's estate and the others I'd known at the palace.

Every so often, a cry would sound, or a trumpet would blare and the thunder of hoofs would echo down the street. Most of the people fled to the side, for those driving the chariots did not proceed with caution. Once in a while, a person was trampled. It was awful to see, and I always helped if I could.

I paused to purchase a pastry from a vendor and a mug of freshly squeezed orange juice. While I was eating, a troupe of jesters entered the square and began entertaining. I was especially intrigued because one of them, a girl about Tania's age, was especially good at acrobatics.

She must have sensed my interest because when the show was over, she came around to collect money, holding out her hat.

"Did you like the show?" She asked, her eyes twinkling with fun. She had dark hair like Tania and was as slender as a willow twig.

I smiled and gave her a few coins. "Yes, I liked it very much." A sudden thought struck me. "Do you entertain at the palace? At Blachernae?"

She dipped her head. "Yes, some of us do."

"Do you entertain the empress?"

"Yes."

"Can I talk to you?"

She nodded. "See the tavern over there? Meet me in a while." She proceeded down the line of people, holding out her hat and making small talk.

I ambled over to the tavern, went in, and order two ales. By the time I was served, the girl plunked herself down beside me on the bench. I'd never known a jester who did not appreciate free ale, and she was not an exception.

After quenching our thirst sufficiently, she said, "My name is Phillipa. And yours?" Her amber eyes were framed with long, dark lashes.

"Basil. Philippa is a beautiful name for a lovely girl." I wished I could see her without her make-up.

"That's a come-on if I ever heard one." She drank her ale and sighed. "What do you want?"

"Is it wrong to pay respects to one who is not only talented but also pretty?" When she laughed and tipped her mug of ale to me, I continued, "Well, there's this girl."

"Ah. I thought there was a reason for this."

"Well, this girl is special. Her name is Tania. Her uncle owns the Golden Bull. She came from Thessalonica several months ago and works in the tavern. She is beautiful, and she wants to study medicine."

Her eyebrows shot up. "Ah. Lovely and gutsy. Nice combination."

"Yes. And intelligent. A couple of days ago, she disappeared. Her uncle said an emissary from the palace came and saw her. He spoke with her, and after that, Tania said she had to go, and left with a few of her belongings. She has sent no word to her uncle, nor to me. It feels like she has vanished from the face of the earth. Have you heard of her? If she went to Blachernae, I suppose she would be in service to the empress."

She lowered her eyes and shook her head, speaking in a low tone. "Were you engaged?"

"No, nothing like that. Just friends. I've been studying medicine and was going to take her to a monastery where they perform surgeries. I can't imagine she went to the palace of her own accord, or if she did, she was tricked and found herself... enslaved."

The other jesters trooped into the tavern and settled down near our table.

Phillipa lifted her somber eyes to me. "What does she look like, this Tania?"

"She has dark hair and is very slender, and she has a wonderful smile. Straight white teeth."

She rubbed her forehead and grimaced like a headache formed there. "I think I know who you mean. They have named her something else, I can't remember what it is, something like Lily or Lilac. Oh! I know. Iris. She is new, and she seems very sad, but of course she does not show it. I can see it in her eyes, though, and in her body language. I wondered about her."

"Could you take a message to her for me?" I leaned forward, for others pressed close, and I did not want them to hear.

She shook her head. "It would be very risky, but I will try it. Do you have the message written?"

"No. I could write it right now, though. Hang on." I began searching through my bag. Surely, I had quill, ink and parchment in there. But I did not. "I see I left my writing equipment home. Can I meet you somewhere tomorrow?"

"I go to the palace very early. If you could bring the message to my house tonight, I could take it in the morning. I live with the other jesters in a large house on Daphne Street near the Great Palace. Oh! I must go. Come tonight! Ask for Horatio."

She leaped from the bench and was gone with the other jesters.

I sat and nursed my ale, thinking and praying. *Oh, God, if only I could contact Tania! Please help me!* But I told myself that I must face the truth when I found it: if she went of her own accord, I must let her go. I couldn't force her to return to the Golden Bull or to me.

And if she did not? If she truly was a prisoner, a slave, in the palace, how could I free her? I had no money, no position, no inside help. Montage would not help me. It would have to be my initiative, yet I had no idea how to proceed.

A commotion in the street startled me back to the present.

I stood and rushed out, wondering if someone was hurt. But it was a royal procession coming down the Mese. I knew because I'd been in enough of them and could tell by the trumpets, the fore-runners, the shouts. They were probably scattering coins to the crowds. It was a favorite trick of the empress and her daughters.

Standing near the tavern on a raised platform used for loading and unloading wagons, I watched as they drew near. The horses and riders were adorned heavily with silver and gold. The Imperial guards marched smartly past in their blue and gold uniforms, carrying their swords. Then came the trumpeters, and finally, the litters bearing the royal family.

The Empress called a halt now and then and tossed coins to the crowd, much to their delight.

Following the litters was the emperor himself, Alexius Angelus III, riding on a fine black stallion. They said he suffered from pain in his legs and could barely sit astride the animal, but this day he appeared relaxed, almost jovial. He was a robust man in his early fifties, graying a little at the temples, yet firm in his saddle with a lusty voice and laugh. He, too, scattered coins to the cheers and applause of the crowds.

It was his favorite trick, I'd been told. He was lavish in his gifts, especially to those high in government, yet he'd already drained the treasury and had resorted to commandeering money from the churches. "God doesn't need money," he was reported saying.

I found myself on tiptoes, scanning the riders at the rear of the cavalcade. Would the prince be in the entourage? Surely not.

But he was.

Yes, there. Prince Alexius rode his tall white stallion, smiling and waving to the crowds like he was already emperor. He was dressed in white with a purple toga, held with a large gold pin, draped over his shoulders. Silver sparkled from his boots and stirrups. A circlet of silver crowned his dark head. He laughed.

My heart stopped at the sound. Up until now, I did not know how much I'd missed him. Tears stung my eyes. I lifted a hand in greeting.

I did not think he would see me, standing as I was back from the street near the building. But he did. He met my eyes squarely. I saw surprise and pleasure in them.

He lifted a gloved hand. "Christo! Come and see me!" He beckoned.

I returned his salute. "Yes, Prince! I will!"

Of course, we could not hear each other, yet we could read lips, and we knew. I wanted to tear into the crowd and grab him into a bear hug, but I could not.

As the royal train continued down the street, I sagged to the platform. Ah, well. He was free. He was re-instated in the family. He was happy. At least he seemed so.

I wiped tears from my eyes and stood again, remembering the errand I had set out upon – deliver the packet and the prince's message to his father, Isaac Angelus.

The sun was shining, and birds trilled happily. Rose, bougainvillea, lilies and other flowers brightened the street. I smiled and hummed a tune. It had turned out to be a good day. I had a lead in finding Tania, and I had seen the prince.

After passing the Hippodrome, I hurried past the Haggai Sophia church. Chalke Gate, the prison, was only a few hundred yards from there. Suddenly a cloud swept over the sun, and a crow cawed annoyingly from a tall pine tree. Sweat formed on my brow. I turned the corner and started for the imposing edifice.

But a burly form blocked my way. It was Michael Trent. He was in uniform. He carried an axe. He was not happy.

"Come aside, Basil."

"But I have to..."

"Now!" He grasped my arm and steered me into a dark alley between two imposing buildings. The pressure on my arm increased. I had no way to escape, for his bulk towered over me.

"Please. You are hurting me." I wrenched my arm away and rubbed it. "What is wrong, friend Michael?"

"You! You are wrong!" He leaned closer. I smelled alcohol on his breath. "I was forced to bow the knee to the new emperor. See? I wear the uniform again. And somehow, they found that I have conspired against him. I nearly lost my life, I'm telling you."

"I'm sorry, Michael. Truly. I do not know how they discover these things." I glanced around furtively, expecting to see a spy duck around the corner. "Did you inquire of those who might help the prince escape? Are there others who would meet with me?"

"Yes." He shifted his feet. "But they may betray you as they did me. I would counsel you not to meet with them. With any of them. They watch me constantly. I cannot even go home to my wife and child. Someone I spoke to must have been the emperor's spy. I can no longer work with you." He gave me the first direct look since we'd met.

"I am sorry. Truly." He hung his head.

I put my hand on my chest. "Go your way, friend. Think no more of it. I do not exist for you any longer."

He nodded. "Very well. I am sorry."

He was gone before I could draw breath. For a man as large as he, I was surprised at his agility. I leaned against the warm stones of the old building and closed my eyes.

So, there was a spy in our midst. I should not have been surprised about that. Did this mean I should not meet with those who wanted to help? What if I were the next to be charged with treason? It was not a pleasant thought. It seemed I was fated to fail at everything I put my hand to.

But I still had to deliver the message to Isaac Angelus.

I shook myself and made my way to the great, imposing gates of Chalke, which means bronze. Isaac Angelus himself had the bronze gates removed and made a loathsome prison of the edifice. I suppose his successor thought it fitting to incarcerate him here.

My papers got me inside, and a guard took me down the steps. The prison was under-ground as most of them were in the city those days.

Prickles descended my spine as we proceeded along the corridor lined with cells. Some of the men were lying unheeding or asleep on the hard bench they called a bed. Some of them were angry, clanging at the bars with their clay dishes, clamoring for food or attention. The smell was more offensive than I could hardly bear.

Closing my nose, I followed the guard, stumbling now and then over an uneven stone. At the end of the hallway, the guard stopped and indicated a large cell, maybe two or three cells put together. Inside were three men.

I knew Isaac Angelus immediately even though his hair and beard had grown. With him was another man, Alexius Doukas, who was related to Isaac through his wife. I'd seen him around the palace but did not know his official position. Tall, stoop-shouldered, he sported bushy eyebrows that earned him the name Murtzuphulus.

Whenever I saw him or was in his presence, I had the urge to grip my dagger and keep him in full sight, never turning my back on him as I would a tiger I encountered in the wild. Why had the emperor Isaac Angelus given him a position of authority? Because he was kin to his wife? I wouldn't have trusted him with a cat.

The third man was Theodore Kastamonites, Isaac's maternal uncle and co-emperor.

All three were sitting on a bed. Theodore, the oldest of them, was reading from a scroll. Doukas was playing a card game. The cell was appointed with a water basin, tables, eating utensils, books, blankets and candles.

When the guard announced my arrival, Isaac came to the bars. I was shocked at his appearance when I saw him closer. His hair hung in twisted, dirty locks to his shoulders. His robes were torn. His eyes were covered with a black eye patch, and his hands shook as he grasped the bars.

I said rather formally, "Your Majesty, I am Basil Christopher Xavier. I once taught your son, Alexius."

"Ah, yes! Yes!" He reached forth his hand. I extended mine, and he grasped it as if it were a lifeline.

I whispered, "Your Majesty, I have never bent the knee to the traitor, your brother. I will be loyal to you and your son to my death."

He chuckled low in his throat. "Thank you, Christo." He sighed. "Ah, it is good to hear the old palace formalities." He paused and lowered his voice. "Do you have word for me? From Alexius?"

I nodded and withdrew the packet I'd been given. "Yes, Your Majesty. Here." I shoved it into his hands. "He has been released! I saw him today, riding with the royal train. He looks hale and hearty and not a whit damaged or downcast."

He received the packet with trembling hands and wiped his eyes. "Thank you, my good friend! What good news you bring me in my present calamity. Can you wait? I want to reply. Theodore will write it for me."

"I do not know how long they will allow me to stay." I wanted to leave straight-away, but if I waited, I would not have to return very soon – or if it was up to me, not ever.

He was going to call the guards to ask permission for me to stay when another party approached down the hall. It was the princess, Evdokia Angelina, daughter of the current emperor.

When the guard announced the visitors, Isaac gripped my hand. "This is a stroke of luck, Christo. Stay here with Evdokia's party. She is in love with Doukas." He shook his head and made a wry face. "Why, I cannot tell, but this will give me time to dictate a reply."

"Yes, Your Majesty." I stepped back.

The princess was dressed in a gorgeous gown of blue silk with flowing sleeves. Jewels flashed from her neck and fingers. She flew to Doukas, oblivious of all in the hallway, and kissed him on the lips through the bars.

I winced, for it seemed so strange. She was not beautiful by anyone's standards, but she was young and had the choice of any man she wanted. Why this evil, twisted man? Did she think he would rise to fame and riches again? I snorted. That was the stuff of nightmares – Murtzuphulus on the throne!

After the kiss, they whispered together and continued in that fashion for some time while a woman jester sang a love song as she played a lute.

I paid attention to this woman, for it was not Phillipa, and I figured she must entertain in Evdokia's court.

I approached her and spoke softly when she completed the song. "Hello. I am Basil Xavier. I spoke earlier with the jester, Phillipa. Do you know her?"

The woman nodded and continued softly playing the lute. "Yes, I know her. What do you want?"

"I want to get in touch with a new girl brought to the palace a few days ago. Tania was her name. I think they renamed her Iris. Do you know of this girl? I am desperate to find her. Dark hair. Very pretty."

She shook her head. "No, I do not know her. I am sorry for your plight, but there is nothing I can do for you." She began to sing again.

I stood, returning to the bars.

After a while, Isaac rolled up a document. He approached the bars. A smile lit his face. He stood straighter and strode forward firmly. "Here, good sir. Please deliver this to my son. Keep it secret, do you hear?" He passed the document to me through the rails.

"Do you have hope, Your Highness?"

"Yes," he whispered. "Hope. Thank you. You have earned my everlasting friendship." He turned, then looked back. "Come again."

I knew what he meant – a reply from the prince. "Yes, Your Majesty. I will try."

The princess was finished her tête-à-tête with the ugly Doukas and her party departed. I trotted down the loathsome corridor and emerged into the sunlight a few minutes later, taking deep breaths of air.

Stowing the document under my robe, I looked around. The weather had changed – again.

They say if you don't like the climate in Constantinople, just go a mile, and it will be different. It was raining hard, and with the rain, came sleety flakes of snow.

I gathered my robe about me and made off for the Haggai Sophia. If I could find some writing materials there, I could deliver my message to Tania and take it now to the jester's house, for I did not relish the thought of another trip down the Mese this evening.

The church was never closed. Priests in small and large groups filled its halls and rooms. After searching for a time, I found a monk sitting at a table making notations on a parchment.

He looked up when I drew near. "Yes?" I could tell from his tone that he was annoyed by my interruption. Perhaps he'd had people all day asking questions of him.

"I was wondering if I could borrow some writing materials from you. I need to write a letter, a short one, mind you, and found I'd left mine at home. It need not be a large piece," I said hurriedly when he looked about the desk. "Just a wee bit. And a quill, if you don't mind."

Well, he did mind, but courtesy and his training to serve won the day. He produced a sheet of real paper and a quill. "Now I suppose you need the desk to write it on."

"Yes, please. I can use this corner."

"Oh, never mind. Use the whole thing if you've a mind to. Excuse me, I have an errand to run."

He did not run, but that was just as well, for it gave me time to pen my message, one that I'd been thinking of all day.

"Dear Tania," I wrote, "I missed seeing you, and when I inquired at the tavern, they said you'd gone to the palace. We, your aunt and uncle and myself, were surprised we never received any message from you. I would like to meet with you, if I could, and have friends who can make it possible in the palace, even if you are not free to come and go. Please send a reply with the person who brought you this. I am forever your friend, B., the man who would teach you medicine."

I rolled up the paper and sealed it hurriedly from a pot of melted wax that sat next to a small candle and a seal. Haggai Sophia Church, it said. Well, that might get it past any who would intercept it.

After making several inquiries, I came to Daphne Street. It was named, I supposed, for Daphne Palace, the dwelling place of the empresses inside Boukoleon. I had explored and admired it several times in my jaunts around the city.

It was not hard to find the house of the jesters, for the door was painted with a bright tri-pointed hat and whimsical pictures of dogs and children dancing.

I knocked. No one came. After waiting for a time, I found a vendor and bought a dish of spiced noodles along with a cup of hot cider. The rain let up and brilliant rays of light escaped the dark clouds. Wet clear through, I was tired and longing to be home.

She said evening. It would be a long wait.

As I sat there slowly drying in the brisk wind that came from the sea, I began to wonder if this was a wise thing to do. What if the girl, Phillipa, was a spy for the emperor, or worse, the empress? Would she betray my trust?

But what else could I do? If I wanted to contact Tania, I had no other means. Montage would not or could not help me. Prince Alexius was in no position to do it, and I had no other close friends in the palace.

Thinking of my encounter with Michael Trent, I shook my head. Spies were as abundant as flies in the city, and I had no desire to end my days at the end of a rope.

No. I cannot do it. It was just too risky. I'd have to wait until we received word from Tania.

I stood, wrapped my damp robe around me, and started off. But I hadn't gone more than ten steps when Phillipa came into view, heading merrily toward the house.

She saw me at the same moment I saw her.

"Oh, here you are!" She bounced up to me. "My, you look tired. Do you want to come in? I can make some tea. Or give you wine. I'm sure they won't mind."

She reminded me of Tania. I shook my head and smiled. "No, thank you, Phillipa. Here is the letter for Tania. You... still want to take it, don't you?"

"I don't know for sure." She received the scroll with a bob of her head and glanced at the seal. "Oh. The Haggai Sophia. This is good. If I am discovered with it, I can say it is an official missal for... hmm. I don't think it would be for the empress. She has little to do with the Greek Orthodox church. I can say for Mistress Sophia. She is in charge of the girls. Yes, I will do this for you."

"I appreciate your help. Where can we meet if there is a reply?"

"Right here."

"How about near Blachernae? I live up that way. It is a long walk down here to the old part of the city."

She nodded, the bells on her hat tinkling. "Very well. At the tavern where we met this morning. Evening bell tomorrow."

CHAPTER SEVEN

The Jesters

May 11, Year of Our Lord 1195

The next morning, Birdie awoke me with a shake. "Basil! Get up! There is a palace courier here for you!"

I sat up and glanced about fearfully, thinking that they'd found out about my conspiring to help the prince and had come for me. "No! I mean, yes. Where? What does he want?"

"Just get dressed!" She hurried from the room with an impatient shake of her head.

I threw on my clothes and went to the front room. A man stood there, shifting from foot to foot, not bothering to keep the impatient and disdainful look from his face. This home was humble and these people were black of skin, something disdained by the Greeks. Yet I'd rather be with them any day than with those in the palace, no matter how sumptuously they lived.

"Basil Christopher Xavier?" He said formally.

I bowed. "Yes, sir."

"I have come to escort you to the palace."

"Can you wait? I have not eaten."

"Hurry. You do not keep royalty waiting."

Well, you do not keep me from my morning meal, either.

I rushed to the kitchen. Birdie, bless her heart, had warm bread, hot milk and fish left over from last night ready for me. I wolfed down the food, grabbed an orange, and patted her shoulder. "Thank you, Birdie."

I returned to the front room. I nodded to the palace official. "To whom do I owe this pleasure?"

"It is not for me to say. I was only commissioned to come and get you." He led the way into the street.

I knew it must be the prince. He was the only royalty who knew me and wanted me to visit. Montage had probably told him about my new residence.

The gates swung open for us. As I trod through the massive front doors of the main palace, and walked those familiar halls, emotions swept over me, for it brought back many memories – some good, and others evil.

My heart was thudding uncontrollably as we approached the prince's apartments.

It was in a different part of the palace than where I lived with the prince as a child. Imperial Guards were posted at twenty-foot intervals in the hall. Alexius did not have true freedom, but at least it was a gilded cage, much better than a dank and foul-smelling prison.

The guards opened the doors, and I walked in.

The prince was nowhere to be seen. The apartment was appointed with tapestries on the walls, carpets on the floor, and low couches along the walls. Light flooded the room from wide windows facing the east, overlooking the Golden Horn. Men and women servants moved quietly about the apartment.

Someone strummed a lute and sang a low song. "Close your eyes, my darling, it is time to sleep. Rest your heart, my dear one, and do not make a peep." It was a lullaby we used to sing the prince to calm him for sleep.

I smiled. "Prince? Where are you?"

"Out here on the balcony, Christo! You know how much I love balconies!"

I stepped out the door. He was seated on a low stool with a lute on his lap, his hair ruffled by the wind, a smile on his lips and welcome in his eyes.

"Don't you remember, my old friend? Me dangling like a fish from the balcony, and you..."

"Oh, yes!" I laughed. "I caught you and hauled you overboard. Prince Alexius! It is good to see you!"

He stood, and we embraced. "Aye. It is good to see you, too, Christo. Here. Take a seat, and we will talk."

He resumed his position on the stool and patted a bench. Without even glancing over his shoulder, he bellowed, "Stephanos! You slow old clod! Bring my friend some wine! The good stuff! And bring me some, too."

"Yes, Your Majesty."

Soon, with our drinks in hand, we sat and looked at each other.

He broke the silence first. "So, tell me how you fare. Montage said you had taken lodgings in the city. Did your uncle throw you out?"

"Yes, yes, he did." I nodded and related my adventures, or misadventures. "I like it where I am, yet I must find employment, or I will be catching those coins you toss out so generously."

"Not I. The empress. They won't let *me* near the money." He went to stand at the railing, overlooking the strait. "She is the one who intoned that dreadful curse over me years ago. Now she throws it in my face. 'It is the curse,' she says. '"You must flee the crown!"'"

"And do you believe her?"

He shook his head and laughed. "No. Life is what you make of it. Right, Christo?"

"Life is what God makes of it for you when you trust Him." I looked at the small space where we sat. "I see there is no rope on this balcony."

"No. They won't allow that, either." He turned to me. "Do you have something for me?"

I nodded and glanced behind us. One of the servants stood at the window. Since there was no glass, he could hear every word we said.

"I have an orange. Would you like that?"

When I took it to him at the railing, I whispered, "I have the other, too, what you are looking for." We faced outwards. Shielding my hand with my body, I drew out the rolled parchment and handed it to him.

He knew my meaning and hid it adroitly in his robe. "Ah. It is a good orange. I don't get them very often."

As he peeled the orange and shared it with me, I said, "How are you faring, prince? You look fine. And happy."

He made a wry face, one I knew so well. Yet he kept his voice low. "How can I be happy when my uncle rules the land that I was meant to rule, and my father sits in a dungeon, blinded? I must get free, Christo, and garner help. I need friends. Friends with money. Have you... done what you said you would..."

"No, not yet, Alexius. We cannot hurry these things. Read what your father wrote. I will watch the servants."

I turned and faced the house as Alexius unrolled the parchment and read his father's message.

He expelled his breath sharply and hid the roll again. "It is as I thought. He wants to free me, but he has no way, no means. What can we do?"

"Leave it for now, prince. Don't hurry. I will work to free you. I promised, and I will do it. But it may take time. Worm your way closer to your uncle's heart. Gain more freedom every day. In time, he will allow you all that you desire. Then, when that happens, I shall have a plan, and we will work it. Do you hear me?"

He grinned and swiped at his eyes. "Yes. You remind me of the old days when I was your student. How long do you think it will take?"

"I know not, prince. But I know this, that God is on our side to right the wrong done to you. One day you will sit on the throne."

He lifted his head, the old posture of royalty coming back to his spine. "Yes! It is true. One day, I will be emperor. And my enemies will pay for what they have done, I swear it!"

Chills descended my spine as if someone walked on my grave. Glancing over my shoulder, I saw the servant, Stephanos, leaning out the door.

I laughed and slapped the prince on his back. "In your dreams, Prince Alexius. You must do all you can for your uncle. Do you hear me? For your uncle." I spoke loudly and lifted my eyebrows, for the prince looked at me as if I'd gone insane.

He nodded, understanding immediately. "Yes, I know. Perhaps my uncle will give me a high position. Perhaps I shall be Lord Treasurer! I am good with figures."

Stephanos was called inside.

I breathed again and patted Alexius' arm. "Very well. Be careful. The spies of the emperor are here, in this very room. They report to him every word you say, even in your sleep. Did you want to reply to your father?"

He nodded. Stepping inside, he called for quill and paper, and soon had a message written. Rolling it up, he sealed it and handed it to me.

"Come again, Christo. It was good to see you. I hope you find profitable employment." He laughed loudly. "And women to wench."

I joined his laughter. He walked with me to the door and leaned close as I tapped on it.

"Let me know."

"I will, prince." Giving him a one-armed hug, I left.

After making many inquiries, I found Montage's apartment, but he was not there. Servants directed me to another part of the palace.

Montage sat in a little office, a corner only, with a small desk and a candle. Shelves holding rolled parchments lined the wall above him.

He looked up and stood. "Basil! It is you! Did you find the prince?"

"Yes, thanks to you. A courier came for me this morning. How do you fare? Is this your office?"

He glanced around disparagingly. "Temporarily. They are remodeling the one I shall occupy soon. I would ask you to stay, to sit, but…"

"No, I must hurry. The prince is well and is in good spirits. He has hope that buoys him up."

"Did you also see his father?"

"Yes. Chalke is horrible, but they have allowed Isaac some comforts, at least. He sent a letter to Alexius, and the prince sent a reply, which means I have to return to the prison."

Montage nodded. "Go carefully. These are dangerous times. I wish I had never come back here." He sighed. "If we thought the government was corrupt before, well, it is ten times worse now. Greed, lust for power, and every kind of evil drips from these walls. I can almost hear the demons cackling at times."

He glanced around as if fearful the old timbers could hear him. "Pray for me, will you? I believe God put me here for a reason, but I do not know what it is yet."

"Yes, I will pray, and so will the others. I am staying with Judah and Birdie, Elijah's kin. Do you remember the large black servant on my uncle's estate? His brother and wife. They are teaching me about the Christian faith. The true Christian faith."

"I wish I had some of the Scriptures to read."

"I will get you a portion, Montage, for all you have done. The next time I come, I will bring it."

He clasped my hand. "Thank you!" He lowered his voice to a whisper. "Did you learn anything about your friend?"

"Not yet. But I found a contact, a jester girl, and wrote Tania a message. I'm hoping she will reply. Pray for me. I have set myself some impossible tasks."

"Nothing is impossible with God."

I nodded. "Yes, that is true. Fare well."

"Fare well, Basil."

After leaving the palace, and to tell the truth, I was glad to get out of there, I returned to the house on the mean little street near the Upper Market and St. Stephen's Chapel.

Elijah greeted me when I walked into the front room.

I shook his hand, and we sat on a wooden bench as Birdie brought cups of mead and two of her freshly baked sweet rolls.

Elijah told me my uncle left the week after I departed. "I received a letter from him. He hadn't even gotten home before he regretted losing you. The manager he put in your place at the warehouse was a thief and took off with a fair amount of goods. Your uncle instructed me in the letter to find you and beg you to return to the estate and your old job."

He showed me the parchment. "See? I have never known him to admit to a wrong, yet here he points out that he shouldn't have tried to force you to bow the knee to the new emperor."

I nodded and took the missal. "Well, I have found no other employment, so I suppose I can return." I sighed.

Elijah shot me a surprised glance. "I thought you would be doing cartwheels for joy. This place isn't as comfortable as the mansion."

I laughed. "No, it is not, yet I find it more to my liking." I smiled at him. "But I will come back. It will give me a place from which I can work."

"Work? You mean, oversee the warehouse?"

"No. I mean my real work." I glanced around the room to make sure no one was present who could overhear our conversation and lowered my voice.

"I promised the prince to help him escape, and now it seems I have become a courier between him and his father. I also want to contact Tania, and if she is in the palace against her will, then I must free her from that place." I had told him before about my search for her.

He nodded slowly. "It is a lot to do."

"Yes." The weight of the world seemed to settle on my chest as I thought about the impossibility of both tasks. "Pray for me, will you?"

"Of course." He stood. "Will you come now?"

It was almost dinner time, and we could both smell roasted chicken and freshly baked bread from the kitchen.

"After dinner."

He stayed and then helped me lug my things back up the hill to the estate. It felt good to be back in my old room, yet as I looked down on the city, my heart went out to the people who lived like Judah and Birdie and the friends I'd made on the streets. They seemed so innocent, so unaware of the looming disaster that threatened with a corrupt government and poor defenses.

The empire that had once boasted of the finest navy and the best defensive walls in the world had sunk to a mere shell of its former glory. Now the nation proudly called New Rome could boast of only twenty ships that could float and not enough manpower to use them. And the walls? They could be breached. A traitor from the inside could open the gates to the enemy.

The nation was dying from within of horrible rot, evil and greed.

The servants' children swarmed me with shouts of glee when I appeared. I chased them through the fountain and the garden, then told them a story.

About an hour before vespers, I returned to the tavern on the Mese where I promised to meet with Phillipa. I wondered what the girl had found out – had she news of Tania? My heart pounded when I entered the low door, nodded to the serving girl, and plunked down on the hard bench.

It was past the bell by a half an hour, I surmised, when she appeared. At first, I did not know her, for she had scrubbed off her whiteface and wore boy's clothes of hose, tunic, and short cape with a hat perched on her head. Her dark hair was caught behind her neck, and her face was stained with tears and a smear of mud.

She was lovely with finely chiseled cheekbones, high forehead, and bright eyes. She panted heavily as if she'd been running hard.

Leaning close, she whispered, "I am sorry, sir. I did not find the girl. You see, I dropped your missal in the hall, and a guardsman picked it up before I could retrieve it. I had to flee. They know me. I had to change clothes, but I think they still follow."

"What are you going to do?" I glanced behind her to the door. "Will you come with me?"

She shook her head. "No! You don't understand. They must know it came from you. Your life is in danger, too."

"But I did not sign my name." Slowly, I stood. "I used only an initial for my signature. But you are right. I must take care. What are you going to do?"

"I don't know. I will try to get to the house and collect my things, but it is hard, I have nowhere else..."

I grasped her arm. A Varangian guard had passed by the window. "Come with me. Now!"

Pulling her along, I found a rear exit, and we entered an alley. Fleeing in the opposite direction of the Mese, we came to another street and saw a church. There are literally hundreds of churches, large to tiny, in the city.

This one I noticed, in the midst of my fear and distress, was The Church of St. Jude, a tattered excuse for a place of worship, yet it met our need. She followed me inside. It was not the perfect refuge, for the Varangians had no fear of God, only fear of the emperor, and in this case, the empress.

"Kneel," I whispered as a tonsured monk peered out from a curtain at the front.

I dropped several coins into the offering box. He nodded, then disappeared.

We knelt for a time and when no one came searching, I stood. "Come. I will walk with you to the jester's house."

"But they will have spies watching it by now," she said, dusting off her knees.

"We must try." I started down the alley toward the Mese, watching carefully those who passed. There was no sign of guards, whether Varangians, the city patrol called the Vigla, or the Imperial guards. But I could not ascertain whether there were spies about.

A storm was brewing over the Bosporus. The wind picked up, carrying stray pieces of trash and straw, and the first drops of rain pelted onto the flagstones on the road. My first concern, of course, was to get the girl to safety, yet my mind raced ahead when I thought of Tania.

Would they find out who wrote the note? Despite my fears for my own safety, I realized with sinking heart that they would surely tighten security around Tania, or maybe even move her, possibly to one of the other mansions the emperor owned. I wanted more than ever to free her, if she was indeed a slave, but my chances for that seemed to be dwindling.

Maybe the only way was to get a position in the palace.

At the jester's house, we paused before we crossed the street. I bought hot cider drinks and sweet rolls for both of us as we watched the house. There seemed to be no one about. As we waited and ate, three people approached the house and entered — a man and wife and a dwarf.

"Horatio," Philippa said quietly. "And that's his wife, Patience. The dwarf is Virgil."

"I think it's safe. Let's go." We hurried across the street just as the storm hit, bringing with it the smell of the sea.

Phillipa entered first. In the large common room past a narrow hall, the group of jesters looked up in surprise.

"Phillipa? What's wrong?" the man named Horatio asked.

"I must explain," I said, stepping forward.

Phillipa introduced me to the group, which included, besides Horatio and his wife, two tall, broad-shouldered men named Silas and Mason, a young woman named Varda (the lute player I'd seen in the prison), and a giant of a man named Hector. I couldn't keep their names straight but bowed to each.

They invited me to sit while Patience and Phillipa brought drinks. I told my story of how I'd asked Phillipa to take a message to Tania in the palace. Phillipa admitted to dropping the missal and how she fled the palace.

"So, you can no longer entertain there," Horatio said in a low tone. "And what of us? Will we receive a visit from the Varangians soon?"

He had no sooner spoken the words when a sharp rap came to the door. Phillipa and I fled to the kitchen. She led the way out the back door to a shed in the back. We crawled up a ladder to the loft and pulled the ladder up with us.

They came searching, but they did not see the loft. Awhile after they left, the dwarf, Virgil, came into the shed and called to us.

"They have gone," he said. "Come back in, and we will talk."

The mood seemed to have lightened. I heard laughter in the other room, and Patience smiled and nodded to me as I went through the kitchen.

Horatio grinned and motioned for me to sit. "We said the girl had gone, that she gathered her things and didn't tell us where she was going. Which is true." He flashed a grin in my direction.

"Yes," I said, telling my heart to stop beating so hard. "We didn't say where we would be hiding."

"They wanted to search, and we allowed them. Who can withstand the Varangians? They delight in killing. But now they have gone, and we must consider what to do."

"Are you free to return to the palace?" I asked.

"Oh, yes. Virgil here is a favorite of the emperor, and the empress loves both Varda and Phillipa. Phillipa may have to go somewhere else for a time, unfortunately."

"I am very sorry for involving her in my plan."

He glanced up. "We want to help you, Basil. No doubt of that. And we will. They may have taken the girl to another location." He thought for a time. "Yes, I heard they are entertaining at the palace at Scutari, across the sea. I will go with them and see if I can locate the girl."

"Very well. I will write another..."

"No." He held up a hand. "I do not think that is wise. I will speak with her if I can find her. If she is held there by force and wishes to be free, I will find out, and I will say you want to meet with her."

"And that I miss her very much," I added.

Standing, he said, "Wait. I have a better thought. How would you like to come with us? As a servant, one who carries our props? No one would be the wiser."

I rubbed my forehead. "What if they recognized me?"

Patience laughed. "Then you must wear whiteface. We can make you part of our act." She glanced at her husband. "What do you think? Could he do it?"

He nodded, giving me an appraising look. "Oh, yes. We will give him the idiot's part." They roared with delight when they saw my expression.

Virgil spoke up, "I think it fits!"

"You can scrub it off in a hurry if you see the girl," said the woman called Varda.

I tried to join in the amusement, but my laughter fell flat, for I felt out of my depth, and I was not used to smiling in the face of death. "When are you going?"

Horatio walked me to the door. "On the morrow. Meet us here, and we will rehearse. Then we join the emperor's party aboard his galleon."

I didn't want to do it, yet it was a way to find Tania. I gulped and nodded. "Very well. Tomorrow."

"Early."

"Yes, my friend. Early."

I had the pass from Montage for Chalke prison and the letter from the prince, and since I was in the old part of the city, I decided to deliver it. If I was apprehended, I certainly didn't want a letter from Prince Alexius to his father on my person.

Once again, I was admitted to the prison without much ado and taken down the foul aisle between cells to Isaac Angelus' cubicle. He rose when his companion jabbed his ribs and spoke in his ear.

Eagerly, he came forward.

"It is me again, Your Majesty, Basil. I have seen the prince, and he sends you this." I shoved the parchment between the rails, hoping to discharge my duty and flee the loathsome place as soon as I could.

He nodded. "Thank you, my faithful servant, Basil. Will you stay to receive my reply?"

"Yes, Your Majesty. Of course." I wanted to hurry him, but I could not say it. One did not demand things of royalty.

In his rush to return to his bed, he stumbled and fell. Alexios Doukas, the tall tufted fellow, rushed forward and tried to help him stand. But he could not. The former emperor was wailing piteously as if in great pain.

I pressed my face to the rails, wishing I could reach him. My little knowledge of medicine might aid him some. But I could not go in.

They called for the guards. Between Doukas and two guards, they lifted him to the bed. He moaned and sometimes cried aloud.

Doukas approached the rails when they left. "They are fetching a physician. I do not think he will be able to reply today. Please come back."

I nodded, relieved. "Yes, I will. Tell him my prayers are with him."

The man seemed to see me for the first time. His eyes gleamed as he lifted his hands and placed them on my head almost as if I were a child and he a priest blessing me.

"I thank Thee, O God my Father, for this faithful servant of Thine," he intoned. "Go with him and bless him and bring him back soon for the comfort and help of my lord and master. Amen."

I squirmed away from his hands, for I held such dread of him in my heart that his touch seemed to burn.

"Thank you," I managed to say and fled down the hallway.

CHAPTER EIGHT

Tania

May 12, Year of Our Lord 1195

When I arrived at the jester's house the next morning, I wondered what they would have me do. After we spent several hours in rehearsal, I was relieved, for it was mainly falling, allowing them to fall over me, and taking the brunt of their jokes. Which I could do with little talent.

In fact, it seemed I'd been doing that most of my life.

The Imperial Palace at Scutari was not built for defense. It was built for pleasure. Situated on a wide tract of land beside the sea, the palace was surrounded by acres of lush gardens. These contained not only pathways, flowers of every description, and ponds and waterfalls, but also a menagerie. The haunting cry of peacocks and the roar of lions echoed from the trees as we disembarked and made our way to the palace.

Carrying their gear, I followed behind the jesters, keeping my head down. They had painted my face white and given me bright green diamonds below each eye. I'd watched the people who were onboard the galley, but the empress kept to herself and her girls were veiled.

Her youngest daughter, Evdokia, kept up a lively conversation with the captain of the galley. I had learned that Tania had been given to the princess as a gift from her mother.

She had a couple of girls with her, but I could not see their faces as they, too, were veiled.

The thing that bothered me was that if Tania was one of the veiled women, she would not recognize me under my whiteface disguise.

At the palace, the dinner, show, music, and wine were all that you would expect from the emperor of the greatest kingdom in the world.

I played my little part during the jester's show and thought perhaps I did it well. I took my bows when they applauded and helped them gather their gear.

After we had eaten in the kitchen with the other servants, I went looking for a *necessarie*, and upon my return, made a wrong turn. I trod down a hallway, and eventually, after what seemed miles of corridor, I heard giggling and feminine voices.

Maybe not a wrong turn.

An apartment was just ahead. The door was open, for the evening was warm and a breeze from the sea was a blessing. I hesitated outside it, listening. Then I screwed up my courage and stepped inside.

In fake alarm, I cried, "Oh! I am sorry! I did not know this was the apartment for the lovely women of the court!"

A dozen or so ladies lounged on couches or chairs, fanning themselves, eating a light lunch. Some held golden goblets. I was surprised there were no guards around.

I went on, moving back a step, "I must go. Please forgive me."

"No, come in, sir jester. Perhaps you can make us laugh," one girl said. She was far gone in her drink and probably did not know what she said, only that she thought it was funny.

They all giggled and pled for me to stay.

I bowed. "If someone will point me in the right direction, I would appreciate it. This place reminds me of the Great Palace and all the fountains there. So lovely, don't you think? Especially in the evening. A stroll through the gardens in the evening is wonderful."

I hoped with this statement to give a hint to Tania if she was there. Most of them did not wear their veils, but I did not want to seem rude by staring at them.

One girl leaped up. "Oh, yes! I will do that, sir!" My heart leaped, for in the quick glance I gave her, I saw she had long, dark hair.

I bowed to her. "I believe your name is Iris?"

"Yes. How did you know?" She fluttered her eyelashes.

"I guessed because you are as beautiful as the flower. Let us walk."

"Don't be gone too long," a woman called to Iris. "The empress may call for us soon."

We walked several paces from the door before I spoke. "Tania, I have found you at last."

"Yes, my dear Basil." She sighed, stifling a sob. "How did you do it? And why are you in jester garb? I would like to see your face."

"I will take it off in a moment, dear one. I knew you must be with the empress' waiting women. I met a girl, one of the jesters, who came to entertain, and she thought she'd seen you. She told me the name they gave you. I determined to come and try to find you myself."

I led her to a side door and out to a small garden. There, I washed off the whiteface in a fountain. Then, clasping hands, we sat on a bench.

"Tania, tell me what happened. Why did you leave the inn?"

She stood and turned away. "I am so ashamed, Basil. It was my fault, really. I should have known. I should have fled."

"Was it your uncle? Did he..."

"I do not know!" She whirled back to face me. "I only know that a man came. He offered me money. He said my duties at the palace would be light, and that any time I wanted, I could return to the inn. I thought about the money I need to learn medicine, to travel to the great schools which are in Alexandria and other places, and I wanted that more than anything. And so, I said yes, I would go with him. I left a note for you. Did not my uncle give it to you?"

I shook my head. "No, he did not. That's why I'm suspicious that he received money for you. He did not want me to know very soon, not until you were there and confined."

She sat beside me. "I am sorry for the grief I have caused you."

"Do you want to... escape? Leave the palace?"

She nodded. "More than anything. Once I got to Blachernae, I realized I was not free. I could not return to the inn any more than can those poor beasts over there return to the wild."

"Yes. I figured as much. Well, we need a plan to free you. That's all there is."

She shook her head and paced to the fountain. "That is impossible, Basil, as you well know. You cannot free me, and you would die if you tried."

"So, you are content to live in the palace as a serving maid to the empress for the rest of your life?"

She whirled to face me, her eyes blazing. "Content? Did I say that? No, I will escape, but I must wait for my chance. It may take me years, but I will do it."

"Tania, listen to me." I lifted her chin and gazed into her beautiful eyes. "You cannot wait years. Something inside you, your free spirit and passion for life, will die. I cannot allow that to happen. Believe me that I will come for you."

Someone called.

Her eyes widened in fear. "I have to go back. I don't want you to get into trouble."

I kissed her cheek. "I love you, Tania, and I will come for you."

She nodded, sobbing a little. "Yes, Basil. Be careful."

With that, she ran through the doorway and down the hall. I listened until her footsteps faded, then returned to the jesters who were finishing their packing. Horatio re-painted my face hurriedly.

"I thought we'd lost you," he said. "Did you find what you were looking for?"

"Yes, I found a little flower who is wilting in this stuffy palace, and I vowed to set her free."

He shook his head and motioned to the boxes of gear. "That is a big order, my friend. A big order."

After our return trip across the sea, we docked below the Great Palace. I helped Horatio with the gear and stayed for a light meal Patience prepared at the house. Then I bade them good night and returned to my uncle's estate on the fifth hill.

Elijah met me at the gate. His forehead was creased as he opened it for me. "Ah. Basil, at last. I wondered where you'd gotten to. You have a visitor, and it is good you came when you did, for he said he had to leave soon."

I found Montage in the library where a fire crackled in the fireplace and two glasses of good wine sat ready for us. Elijah bowed and left as I entered.

"Montage! It is good to see you."

"Aye, and you, my friend."

We drank, and I motioned to a cushioned chair by the fire. "What brings you here?"

"You will not like what I am about to say." He turned to me. "I left the palace. Resigned. They demoted me. Made me Keeper of the Horses, can you believe? I guess I did not play their games. The new emperor has emptied the treasury, and now he proceeds to raid the churches for money."

"I am so sorry, my friend."

He shook his head. "I just walked out. They will probably kill me for it, but I do not care."

"And you've come to me for help? I could have used your influence in the palace." I leaned forward. "I found her, Montage. The girl. She was with the empress' women, her serving women, at Scutari Palace. I was right about how she got there, too. Her uncle sold her. I talked to her, and she wants out. I have to devise a plan to rescue her." I paced to the window where I could see the lights from Blachernae.

"Basil, you cannot do that. It would be suicide. You are in enough trouble as it is, trying to help Prince Alexius escape. What are you thinking?"

"I am thinking that a young girl needs my help, probably more than the prince. I promised to free her, and I shall."

There was silence, and then I said, "What are you going to do?"

He sighed and leaned back, gazing into the fire. "I do not know."

"You can stay here for as long as you want."

"No, I have my own place, but I wonder if it is safe for me to be there. Perhaps I shall accept your offer. For a fortnight? Could you put me to use?"

I nodded. "Oh, yes. You are good with figures. You can help down at the warehouses again. I must say with all my other activities, I am rather behind. The books are in a mess."

"Well, it will be better than keeping the imperial horses." He grinned. "Yes. I will do it. It will be a fine change from the mess I have had to put up with in the palace."

I took him the next day to the warehouse and showed him my bookkeeping system. It did not take him long to learn, and I left him after our midday meal.

The next day, he and I went we went to see Isaac Angelus in Chalke prison.

Isaac was in bed. It was the creepy Alexius Doukas who came to the bars when we arrived. He knew Montage and nodded to him.

To me, Doukas said, "You see that my master is ill. He has been abed since you came last." He lowered his voice to a whisper. "Do you know what it is they write to each other?"

"Yes, sir, I know." I wanted to edge back because if anything could be worse than seeing the man, it was seeing him up close. But I stood my ground, for I sensed he was an important ally in the plan to free the prince.

"Prince Alexius must be free," he continued. "The emperor wants him to go to his sister who is married to the Holy Roman Emperor, Philip of Swabia. They are talking of a new crusade. Perchance the rulers of Europe and those who are financing this crusade will find the prince's plight interesting. Do you understand?"

"Yes, Doukas, I understand, yet I do not believe the crusaders will be dissuaded from attacking the Muslims in the Levant or Alexandria, as was their plan. Why should they help the prince?"

He tapped his nose. "We will see. We will see. Here is the missal the emperor dictated to me." He shoved a rolled parchment through the bars.

We took our leave of him. On the way back up the Mese, Montage wiped his face as we made our way through the crowded streets.

"What was Doukas whispering to you about? The new crusade?"

I nodded. "Yes. I do not know who is leading it, but the sailors who come from ports in Europe talk of nothing else."

"And how does this forward Isaac's plan to put his son on the throne?"

We paused while I bought some figs from a vendor. "All I know is that the prince must escape Constantinople. The plan is to get him to his sister in Swabia. There he can work toward overthrowing the traitor, Alexius III." I sighed and wiped the sweat from my forehead. "It is more than I can conceive. I can only try to do what I promised the prince."

I was tired. It seemed I'd been running up and down the Mese, from Blachernae to the Great Palace on the other end, in a frantic race to accomplish both of my goals.

He gripped my arm. "Take some time off, Basil. Between trying to free the girl and helping the prince escape, you are running yourself ragged. Neither the girl nor the prince is in any immediate danger. Please, Basil. Help me out at the warehouse. Take care of your uncle's estate. Go out to the farm. Write. You have a story to tell, having tended the prince all those years."

I shook my head and wanted to brush off his hand. So intense were my feelings about both tasks that I did not want to heed his warning. "I feel an urgency about this, Montage," I said, shifting so he dropped his hand. "Very much so."

He sighed. "I know. Yet you may do more damage if you hurry it. Please consider."

"Very well. I will work with you and try to get some semblance of order at the warehouse. I owe it to my uncle."

I did as I said, yet it was a trying time for me.

Five years went by in this fashion – I tended my uncle's farm and estate, worked in the warehouse, and visited both Blachernae and Chalke prison. Montage found he was not in danger from the emperor, so he returned to his own home on the fourth hill just below the Church of the Holy Apostles.

My uncle did not visit Constantinople in all that time and only corresponded with the head servant, a man named Alexander, whom he trusted. He gave me instructions through Alexander, and I sent him reports.

Twice a month, I visited the former emperor and the prince and carried letters back and forth, never once being intercepted. The jesters kept me informed of Tania who continued in service to the princess Evdokia.

Prince Alexius was, as I predicted, given more freedom as time went on, riding freely about and joining with the excursions of the royal family. I heard that he trained with the army, leading a contingent of men. He would like that, I thought, remembering the times I had to carry him on my back while he pretended to joust.

He was affianced to a princess from Cappadocia who had come with her father on a state visit to the capitol. The emperor asked them to extend their visit, and the deal was set. It was advantageous to both rulers, for it sealed trade between them.

Every time I visited Isaac Angelus, he asked for my advice on their plans to free Alexius from the clutches of his uncle. They had devised many strategies, but there were problems with them all. We were at an impasse, and the letters between the two dwindled to only one a month.

Just before Christ's mass of that year, Alexius called for me. He was eighteen, in the prime of life, handsome, talented, intelligent. Strutting about the apartment, he reminded me of a young rooster.

"I have news for you, Christo," he said as I entered. "My esteemed uncle has gotten me a wife." He bowed and swept his hand in a grand flourish. "How do you like that?"

I nodded. "I am pleased, prince. Did you meet her?"

"Yes, I did." He grinned. "She is not unpleasant to look upon, but she is very young. I will be her teacher in all things, and she will look fine as the em… I mean, as my wife."

"Come. We must talk." I went out on the balcony where we always met, for it afforded us a little privacy.

"When is the marriage to take place?" I asked him, leaning against the rails while watching a rain storm beat its way across the strait.

He shook his head. "They left, returned to Cappadocia. No date has been set. I would like it to happen soon, but my uncle, the emperor, dodges the issue and will not give me an answer."

I noticed he named his uncle *the emperor*, and I wondered at it, for previously in private he always called him the traitor.

"Where would you go if we are able to free you?"

He shrugged. "Father says if I can make it to Germany, I must go to my sister, Irene, and her husband, Philip of Swabia. From there, I can raise the support I need. He says the leaders of the new crusade have made a treaty with Venice to take them to the Levant by ship. If I can persuade them, they may aid me in my bid to retake the throne."

"That's a lot of ifs."

He turned to watch the storm as it approached. "Yes. I am not sure I want to leave. Look at me. I have everything I need here. My uncle will die one of these days, and I shall be his heir."

I raised my brows. "What of his daughters? They will surely have a child, and if it is a male child, you will not be the next emperor."

"I know that, Christo! That is why I must escape. Leave me now. I am getting bored of you."

His mercurial changed of mood and arguments astounded me, as always.

He stomped away without further conversation. Our interview was over. He had given me no letter for his father, for his head was full of his own importance.

I didn't like this new Alexius. Something was happening to him, and it was not good. But I could not change it, nor could I change him.

My plans to free Tania had come to a standstill, too. Philippa gave me reports of her and carried our letters back and forth. She was careful when doing so, for she did not want to be caught twice.

I despaired of both my endeavors and spent some time feeling sorry for myself, blaming God for the ill events of my life. I should have been blaming myself, for I am most often my own worst enemy.

That next spring, I was called to the palace. It was the occasion of the prince's nineteenth birthday. He wanted to talk with me, but when I arrived, I found he'd gone to the staging ground for the army and was not available. The army was being deployed to a war the emperor wanted with Thrace.

I walked back to the warehouse and consoled myself with the books for a time. At mid-morning, I sat on a bench outside the warehouse in the warm spring sunshine, drinking a cup of tea and watching the great ships come and go on the Golden

Horn. They never ceased to amaze me, for I could not get the lure of the sea from my head and heart. I'd made friends of the captains and crews who came to the warehouse.

Hearing a light patter of feet, I looked over my shoulder.

It was Philippa, wearing her whiteface, motley and cap, skipping up to me. She held out a rolled parchment tied with a ribbon. I took it eagerly, for I knew it was from Tania.

"How is she?" I asked as I rubbed my finger over the neat words on the outside.

Philippa perched on the bench beside me and nodded, the bells on her cap tinkling. "She is fine. Did you know the emperor is throwing a huge feast for Prince Alexius?"

"I thought he would. Coming of age? Or is it his marriage?"

"No, not marriage. I understand that agreement was broken." She chuckled. "The girl ran off with one of the servants. It is his birthday, you know."

"Yes. I know." I answered abruptly for I wanted to read Tania's letter in private. "I am sorry for him. He seemed to like her. But such is the way of the world. How are you this morning?"

She bobbed her head, setting the bells jangling merrily. "I am doing well, sir. Morning is my favorite time. At this great feast, the emperor wants the whole jester troupe to entertain. We thought perhaps you would like to join us as you did when we went to Scutari Palace. Remember?"

"How could I forget? What do you want to do?" Last time, it was merely to find Tania, to see her. This time it might mean much more.

She glanced around. "I cannot say here. May we walk?"

We strolled the short distance to the quay.

A giant Pisan merchantman had docked this morning. The captain was a man with the unlikely name of Sir Oswald St. Johns. His crew called him Cap'n Os. He was a veritable mine of information. I passed these tidbits of information to Isaac

Angelus who wanted to be kept abreast of the affairs of the world.

I pointed her out to Philippa. "See that ship? She is scheduled for a new bowsprit and main mast since she got damaged in a storm on the way here. Her keel needs scraping, too."

Philippa studied the ship for a moment, but turned with impatience and yanked on my sleeve. "Basil, listen to me! We have little time. The feast is tomorrow night. You will have to practice, and you must, too, if you want to join our act. Can you come now? The others are at the house."

"Very well. Let us return to the warehouse. I have a few details I want to finish. Then we will go."

We hurried back. I gathered my things into a rucksack and read Tania's letter.

"Dear Heart," she began as always, "it seems forever since I have seen you or talked to you, yet you are ever in my thoughts. You have brought hope to my dreary world and the reason to carry on. Philippa will tell you of the recent developments that may bring my hope to a reality. Whatever you decide to do, please be careful, dear one. I do not want to lose you. I will keep you in my prayers and hope to see you again soon. Your own, Tania."

It was short and oblique, as always, never mentioning people, times, places or events. Yet this letter held more mystery than any of the others. Decisions. Momentous events unfolding. Danger.

Has the time finally come? Am I ready for this? Can I do it? Oh, God! Please help me!

CHAPTER NINE

The Feast

April 14, Year of Our Lord 1201

I practiced with the jesters for the best part of the day. When I was thoroughly covered with sweat and dust from my many falls onto the hard ground, I sat on an upturned barrel and accepted a mug of excellent wine.

Varda, the young girl who entertained the Princess Evdokia, was not there. They said she had only a minor part to play in the act and she had been called to Blachernae early that morning.

We trooped into the house where Patience had prepared a nice dinner. I helped them put it away – turkey, beans, fresh bread, and fruit. Quite a feast for me, as I was used to grabbing cheese and bread from the house and eating on the run.

Outside again, Horatio explained their plan. He showed me a cylinder they'd built for one of their magic tricks. It was maybe five and half feet long, made of light wood and covered with fabric. The diameter was two and a half feet. It lay on a table outside.

"She will fit in here," he said. "In fact, two will."

I was interested, for I'd seen the woman-cut-in-half trick done before and often wondered how it was accomplished. "There are two inside?"

He nodded. "Yes. I don't usually tell anyone, but you must know. One woman is already in the tube. It's usually Philippa and Varda, for they are both small. Of course, they only occupy half the tube. Philippa moves her feet out as Varda gets in, and then Varda leaves her head showing. There is a partition inside. We make a big ordeal of it with smoke and silks, and then we cut the tube in two."

"I see." Scratching my head, I perched on the top of a barrel. "And Tania will be selected to be the second woman?"

He nodded. "She has been instructed to sit close by. We have silks to form a curtain. She disappears behind the curtain, then when the trick is finished, a cloud of smoke goes up, prepared by Virgil here," the dwarf nodded with a pleased grin, "and Tania reappears and takes her bows. As we go into another routine, Tania slips behind the curtain and gets back into the tube. When we finish, we carry out the tube with her inside."

"Can she breathe in there?"

"Yes, she can breathe. But it will be very cramped, a tight fit, I imagine. It is the best we can do. You will help carry the tube."

"What if they ask to inspect it?"

He shook his head. "I doubt if they will. The guards will be lax. I am going to provide the ones who will be at the gates with wine. They are not allowed to drink while on duty, but I think I can persuade them. Besides, we will stuff the silks in top and bottom so it looks as if we are only using it for the material."

I didn't like it and could see a hundred ways it may backfire. But if it was the only way to rescue Tania, then I had to go along with it.

"Has she been instructed?"

He sighed and finished packing their equipment. "Yes, Basil. She knows what to do."

"Well, then, I guess..." My words were cut off by someone bursting into the back yard where we had all collected to finish preparations.

It was Varda, her hair standing out on end like she'd been in a lightning storm. "You must come," she said, running up to me, panting. "Now. The emperor ... wants to see you, and the... guards said they would only allow us only... a short time."

"The emperor?"

"The deposed emperor. Isaac Angelus. The one in prison. Come!"

I wanted to pull away from her grasp, but she seemed so intent on her purpose that I went along with her.

Horatio followed us to the door. "Come tomorrow morning, Basil," he called as I followed after the girl. "Early!"

"Yes, I will! Tell Patience thank you for the meal!"

I found I could not keep up with Varda and had to stop to catch my breath. She glanced back with an annoyed look on her face.

I rejoined her. "Why does he call for me?"

"You will have to ask him yourself. If we make it in time."

"I will make it to my grave, more likely."

She laughed.

Thankfully, it was not far, and the guards allowed us entrance, yet they were uneasy and paced back and forth.

Isaac Angelus was waiting by the bars when I rushed down the aisle to his cell. He seemed more disheveled than I'd ever seen him. Doukas hovered near him, his face twisted anxiously.

"Yes, Your Majesty?" I grasped the bars. "It is I, Christo. What would you have me do?"

He nearly collapsed. "Ah! You made it. Oh, Christo, just the sound of your voice cheers my heart. Now. There is no time for courtly manners." He pulled me to my feet when I would have knelt. "They will not allow you to stay long, so listen carefully."

"Yes, Your Majesty. I am your servant. Say on."

"You must go with haste to the captain of the Pisan merchantman ship that is docked in port. You know him. Captain Os. He is sailing with the tide, I am told. You must see him. We have a plan." He glanced around with his sightless eyes and lowered his voice, pressing his face close to mine.

"I will not give you a letter, for they may suspect something and search you. No, you must go and talk to the captain. We are ready with a plan to help the prince escape. The captain will sail his ship around to Thrace. The present emperor, my brother, plans to march there tomorrow morning. He is trying to win back that country. The prince is riding with him."

He made a grimace. "It will be a grand parade when they leave the city, to be sure. He loves pageantry. But the main thing is this: the prince goes with him. At a certain juncture, Alexius will escape from the army camp and ride to the coast where our friend, Captain Oswald, will pick him up. From there, he will sail to Italy and on to Germany." He took a breath. His knuckles were white where he gripped the bars and sweat ran from his face in rivulets, yet he made no effort to mop it.

"You have planned well," I said, my voice a bare whisper. Behind me, the guards moved restively. "I will do as you say." My knees felt weak, and I prayed I would not faint, so much did the news fill me with dread.

"One more thing, Christo," Isaac said in a whisper.

"Yes?"

"You must go with him. You are the only one I trust."

"But I..."

He gripped my hands as the guards approached. "Listen to me!" His breath hissed in my ear and was foul in my nose. "You must go with him. He is... not capable of doing this on his own, and there is no one else I trust. He will return soon. Surely you can spare me a few months for this important mission."

"Yes, Your Majesty. I will do it. But..."

"Time!" The guard yanked me from the bars. "You must go, or we will clap you into a cell of your own!"

"Yes. I am going." I dusted myself off and beckoned to Varda, who had been standing back by the wall, her eyes the size of saucers. "Come, my friend. We must go."

I do not remember how I made it out of the prison or back to Horatio's house, but Varda helped me. I told her what Isaac Angelus wanted of me.

"I must go tonight to see the captain. Tell Horatio I may not be able to practice in the morning. I will meet you at the palace."

She sighed. "Oh, Basil. I hope all goes well tomorrow. I hope it for your sake. And for Tania's."

"Thank you. Say a prayer for me, will you? I feel... without strength. My legs are hardly able to hold me upright." I drew a deep breath. "But with God's help, I will do what I must do."

She squeezed my arm. "Very well. We will pray."

I made it back up the Mese as the sun set and evening enveloped the grandest city in the world. Yet tonight, I did not think of it as special, only that it was large and a long journey from one end to the other.

The ship was battened down for the night, but I knew the night guard, and he allowed me to come on board when I stated I had an important message for the captain. I mounted the gang plank, and he escorted to the captain's quarters.

Captain Os was an older man who had seen many voyages. He hailed from England, yet he was an educated man and well versed in several languages.

He looked up from a book he was reading and smiled, standing to receive me. "Ah! Basil Xavier! To what do I owe the pleasure of your company on this night?"

"I must speak with you. It is very urgent, and..." I glanced around at the first mate who was setting up a chess board. "Very private."

The captain did not blink an eye. "Mose! Out!" he bellowed. "We can play later, you lubber!"

The first mate rose, saluted, and left.

"Sit, Basil. Wine? Some of the best." He poured a glass.

I received it with thanks and sat opposite him.

"Now. Tell me your news. I see it on your face. It has to do with the prince, does it not? Out with it, man! Time is wasting!"

I took another drink of the wine and set down the glass, not to be hurried now that I had arrived and was comfortable.

"Your guess is pretty close to the mark, Captain. I would make my own guess that you have been corresponding with the former emperor, Isaac Angelus, he who sits in Chalke Prison."

He nodded but said nothing, his eyes glittering like the gems on his fingers.

I shifted. "I spoke with Isaac. He wants to spring his plan and rescue the prince from the clutches of his brother." I smiled. "Which may or may not please the prince, if I may be so bold to say."

He made no comment, only nodded again for me to continue.

"The former emperor has commissioned me to tell you that you are to sail on the morrow for Thrace. The army is marching out, too, with the dawn. You will arrive before them. You are to wait in the bay north of Athyras, on the Thracian coast, and he will come." I cleared my throat. "I should say we will come."

He grinned. "Ah. You are going on the grand adventure, then? I thought as much. I saw that on your face, too. And it does not please you?"

"Well, there are other things I would rather do," I confessed, wondering at the transparency of my face. Maybe I should wear the whiteface of the fools all the time.

I rose. "I promised Alexius six years ago I would help him escape, and I promised Isaac just now that I would see it through and accompany the prince, so I am committed. Do you sail at sunrise?"

He shook his head. "I will sail in a few hours with the tide. I did not get my keel scraped, but we got a new bowsprit and main mast. We are loaded and ready to go. Too bad you can't come with us. It would be much easier than riding with the army."

"I know. But Isaac does not think his son is capable of doing what he must. And so, I will ride as you sail." I held out my hand. "I wish you the best, Captain."

He stood and shook my hand. "I will see you in a fortnight. My prayers are with you."

I was a little surprised, for I did not think him to be a religious man. "Thank you, sir, and mine with you."

All I wanted after I left the ship was to get a good night's sleep in my own bed, pack a few belongings, and rise ready to face the new day. But I discovered I would get few very of the things I wanted that night.

Elijah met me at the gate. I was surprised for the second time that evening, for he usually retired early and rose before the dawn. His forehead was creased in a worried frown as he let me in.

"Basil! I was worried for you. They are here. You must go with them." He wiped his forehead and shook his head. "They are not happy to wait for several hours."

"Who is here, and why do they wait for me?"

He did not have to answer, for behind him three men approached, two of them in the garb of high palace officials, and the third, a Varangian who looked, as they all do, serious and intent.

The oldest of the officials, a man I knew by the name of Antonio Chrystoniphis, was a pompous man who was eminently aware of his importance and enjoyed igniting fear into the hearts of lesser beings. A deep scowl was embedded on his flabby face.

"Basil Xavier!" He said my name as if it were an accusation. "Why have you arrived so lately? Do you not know it is illegal to be about the city at this time of the evening?"

"I have a pass," I said, "for my business takes me abroad. Do you want to see it?"

He waved away my offer and drew himself up proudly. "I am on an official errand for the prince. He wants you to attend to him. Now."

"Now? But..."

"There are no excuses. Come with me!" He made a grab for my arm, but I evaded him and stepped back, closer to Elijah.

"I must get some of my personal belongings. It will not take long." I didn't wait for him to press his demands but fled into the house, Elijah covering my back. When I glanced over my shoulder, I saw they followed part way, but then stopped, glaring at me.

"I warn you! Come quickly!" Antonio yelled.

"He will arrest you if you tarry," Elijah warned.

I dashed into my room and with his help, gathered up what I thought I would need for the next several months.

"I'm not going for the night only," I explained breathlessly. "The prince is escaping, riding with the army on the morrow, then fleeing to a Pisan ship off the Thracian coast. His father wants me to accompany him. Please take care of the estate while I am gone."

"For how long?" He held the door for me.

"I know not. I hope not long. I will try to send you a letter, but you know how hard that is."

He nodded. "Yes, Basil. Go with God."

I stopped and looked up at him, sad to leave, yet excited that our long wait was over. I shook his hand. "Thank you, Elijah. I shall return."

With the Varangian guard prodding me along with his sword and fierce demeanor, I found the strength to dog-trot along with Antonio and his friend to Blachernae, thanking the Lord it was not the Great Palace on the other end of the city.

I thought of the jesters and wondered what they would do without me. Would Tania be able to escape? Did they really need me to accomplish the rescue, or would they abandon their plan if I did not show?

It was a worrisome thought, but I did not have long to chew on it.

Antonio led me to the prince's apartment, then departed without a word. I knocked. The door opened immediately by an Imperial Guard, Toledo Espandia, a Spanish man. I had met him before and was impressed with his strength of character.

He bowed, stepping aside. Two Varangian guards moved back to allow me entrance.

"Christo!" Alexius bounded over to me. "It is my birthday tomorrow! I am glad you could come."

"Yes, prince, I know." I wanted to ask him why he wanted me this evening, but I did not, for I knew he would not give me a straight answer.

"You do not sound impressed," he said, going to sit by a chess board that was set up on a small table. "Come. Play with me. They are making preparations in the palace. Everywhere. It will be a grand time." His eyes glowed with pleasure.

I sat across from him. I had taught him to play, but he could beat me now, for I had grown slow and dull from little practice.

He dismissed the servants, and we played. He won all the games, even though I did not let him. At last, stretching, he said he would go to bed.

In a low voice, I said, "What are you plans for tomorrow, Your Majesty?"

"Tomorrow?" He yawned. "I am going to have my birthday feast."

"I mean after that."

"Oh. I am riding with the army to Thrace, Christo. Are you coming with me?"

"If you desire it, sire."

"I desire it. In fact, I command it." His eyes gleamed as he leaned forward, speaking in a low, fervent tone. "It is my chance for the throne. It shall be mine. That, and all of New Rome."

I drew back, for there was something odd about his demeanor. I'd noticed it throughout the evening, but now it was so much in my face I could almost smell it.

He has gone mad, much like King Midas and his golden touch. It is the gold fever. I'd seen it before, not only for gold, but the insane lusting for the throne. For power.

"Yes, prince. I know." I sighed.

He stared at me intently as if he expected me to crown him emperor at that moment. When I did nothing but stifle a yawn, for it had been a long day, he shoved back with one of his sudden moves and stood.

"You shall sleep where you have always slept. Good evening."

"Good evening, prince. Sleep well." It's what I always used to say to him. I heard him chuckle as he called for his servants and went to his bedroom. I stretched out on the couch and covered myself with a blanket for the evening was cool.

Despite the fear that haunted my every waking thought – fear for Tania, fear for the prince, fear for what might and could happen – I fell asleep almost immediately and was shaken awake when it seemed I had just closed my eyes.

"Christo! It is time! Get up!"

April 15th, 1201. I shall always remember the date.

It was the prince who woke me. He was clad in black and gold. His hair shone from the oil they put on it, and he played nervously with a long golden chain that hung from his neck as he paced the apartment like a caged lion. Rays of early morning sunshine slanted on the walls from the eastern windows.

I rubbed the sleep from my eyes and availed myself of the hot water and towels that the servants brought.

They proffered a tray that held hot tea, a glass of wine, bread warm from the oven, dried fish, figs, and an orange. I ate ravenously, for I did not know when I would eat again. Yet I wondered if I would keep it down for my stomach twisted at the thought of what would happen this day.

Alexius strode to the balcony to stare out at the awakening city, and then stomped back in again, shouting commands of every sort to his beleaguered servants.

Later that morning, under the pretext of setting up for his birthday party, I managed to slip away. It was good that I had spent so much time in the palace, for I knew my way around, and even after six years, there were servants and officials who remembered me.

I hurried to the kitchens, glanced at the fevered preparations, and then went to the grand hall where state affairs and dinners were held.

Servants stood on ladders, festooning the hall with garlands of flowers and greenery. The finest golden goblets and other eating utensils rested on the tables along with platters of nuts and dried fruit.

"Which way to the *necessarie*?"

I whirled. It was the dwarf jester, Virgil. I laughed and leaned down to shake his hand. "You know where it is, sir. How are you?"

"You were supposed to be at practice, Basil." He pulled me to a side room near the dais where the other fools were assembling their props for that evening.

Horatio came over.

I nodded to him and said, "I am sorry I missed practice. I was detained by the prince who wanted me to dance attendance to him. He forced me to stay the night in his apartment." I shifted and glanced around, wondering how long it would be before the prince sent someone to find me.

Horatio shook his head. "It doesn't matter. Are you still going to perform with us? And help us with our task?"

I knew he meant Tania's escape. I rubbed my forehead where a headache formed. "I hope so, my friend. I will try to convince His Highness that I must be absent from his feast for a short time. On the morrow, he rides with the emperor to Thrace to engage in battle, and from there," I lowered my voice, "he plans to escape."

Horatio raised his eyebrows. "I did not know. Are you going with him?"

"Yes. I promised when the rebellion happened six years ago. He wants me with him, has commanded it, and so does his father."

He snorted. "Ah. The command of a boy who wants to be emperor someday. You also promised something to Tania."

"I am hoping I can fulfill both."

"And if not, which will you chose?"

"It will mean my life if I refuse Alexius. He is no longer a child. He is giving commands as if he were emperor and all obey him from least to greatest."

I paused, hearing my name. A servant trotted down the hall with an anxious look on his face. I caught his eye and waved. "I am coming. Wait a moment, if you will."

Moving back into the room, I glanced at Horatio. "I will join you before the show."

"Another promise?" He lifted a box of props to the table.

"No. A hope."

I had no more time. The servant said the prince was beside himself with concern for me. *Yeah, right,* I thought. *More concern for himself and his grand plans.*

Hurrying behind the man's stiff back, I reviewed my promises and wondered how I could keep them all. My knees felt weak with the responsibility. It seemed I'd dug a pit that was too deep to fill.

But it is not me, not my strength. I remembered a verse from the book of Zechariah that Elijah shared with me the other day. It seemed to echo along with my footsteps down the tiled hall.

Not by might, nor by strength, but by My Spirit, says the Lord of hosts. I sighed. It was very true. I could not do this on my own.

Oh, please, God, help me this day! Give me guidance. Direct my mind and my feet. This I pray in Your Name. Amen.

CHAPTER TEN

The Trick

April 15, Year of Our Lord 1201

The prince's rage exploded when he saw me. He used every foul word in his vocabulary, stamped his feet in his worst tantrum ways, and shook his fist.

I endured it meekly, nodding my head as I used to do when he was a boy.

When he paused for breath, I apologized. "I am sorry, Your Highness. I thought you knew I must attend to the details of your party tonight."

He flopped down on a cushioned bench, his face red and dark hair askew, calling for wine.

"You must dress, Christo." He clapped his hands and without consulting me, ordered my wardrobe.

They brought out a white tunic with gold at the sleeves and necks, sandals embedded with jewels, sash of yellow, a blue silk cape lined with fox trim, and a dashing Roman-style toga over all.

As I was dressed and combed, I watched the prince with concern. He could not stay still for more than a few moments and seemed agitated and angry, flinging things around, even valuable urns that smashed to the floor.

He was not the Alexius I knew as a small boy. Now he was a spoiled and indulged child in a man's body. He had inherited not only the name of his fathers, but their disposition, as well.

Worst of all, he had allowed his passion and lust to control him. If I could have stayed with him, I might have been able to stave off some of it, but now all I saw was the corrupted soul and mind in the boy I loved.

Was there hope for him? I did not know and felt perhaps God had sent me to him for saving grace. Maybe if I got him away from the palace, from the city, and from his uncle he would change.

We managed to get him ready for the feast, and after much delay during which I fumed silently, I followed behind his retinue. Some of his servants went before, some beside him, and some trooped after. The Imperial Guards were present, as ever, along with the Varangians.

With a blare of trumpets, Alexius was announced, and we entered. It took my breath to see so many people gathered in the hall.

Alexius sat in the very center on the dais. Next to him was the emperor, his uncle. On the other side was his aunt, Empress Euphrosyne. Their three daughters, Irene, Anna, and Evdokia, lounged on either side of the empress, their disdain and outright dislike for the prince showing plainly on their faces.

I was curious to see the empress close up, this woman who made the whole city buzz with gossip and amazement. They said she was crazy, that she was indwelt by demons, even that she could fly.

They seated me at a lower table. The prince was drinking with abandon and laughing loudly at everything that was said. They would bring in the presents later, lavish gifts, no doubt.

The emperor officially opened the banquet. We all stood while a priest intoned the blessing. After we sat, a long line of servants carried trays loaded with food and wine to the tables.

The hall was filled with a bedlam of loud talking, laughter, and music. The entertainment would come later.

I took a sip of the wine, ate a few figs and some cheese, then rose from the table, not looking up at the dais. I hoped the prince was too busy to notice my departure.

Making my way forward to the right, I found the small room where the jesters were making last-minute preparations for their show.

Horatio beckoned me over, a frown creasing his forehead. "Have you seen Tania?"

"No. I looked for her with the other serving women of the empress, but she was not there. I assumed she was with you."

"We do not know where she is." He wiped at his forehead, careful not to smear his make-up. "There is no time to find her. I can only trust that she will appear when we are ready for her. Come, you must get on your whiteface and costume. We are on in a few minutes."

I allowed them to paint my face and climbed quickly into the costume they held for me – white hose, a silky red tunic, motley, and a cap. I hoped the prince would not recognize me, but he might notice my empty place at the table.

Sweat trickled down my face as I waited in the wings, praying that Tania was seated nearby so she could volunteer for her part in the drama. With a fanfare of trumpets, Horatio leaped to the makeshift stage and introduced the troupe. Patience joined him, and the juggling commenced with comedy and laughter.

When my part came, I performed with what I thought was passable skill.

At last, Horatio introduced the magic trick of cutting the woman in half. Drum beats began and increased in tempo and volume as the crowd grew still.

"Who will help me with this?" He eyed the crowd. "I need a willing volunteer who will trust me with her very life. Come along, ladies. Who is a brave soul?"

Silence. I could not breathe.

"I will."

It was a voice I remembered well. I took a deep breath.

Horatio accepted Tania's offer. He took her hand, and she stepped onto the stage. My heart thudded heavily in my ears as I saw her again. She was willow-thin. Her long, dark hair was piled on her head. She wore a flowing gown of saffron silk. A veil of white lace was pinned back to reveal her face.

Horatio and Tania bowed to the audience. The crowd clapped and called encouragements.

"Do not damage my lady!" A voice called from the dais. Some people clapped and some laughed. I did not think the speaker, Princess Evdokia, was jesting.

Horatio bowed to her. "I promise you, Your Highness, that I shall not harm a hair of her head."

The tube was lying vertically, suspended by two work horses about waist high. Horatio assisted Tania into the top of the tube feet first, and as she entered, the feet of Philippa, I assumed, extended from the other end.

With Tania's head showing, Horatio played it to the hilt with silk scarves, music, and white smoke billowing about. Then he took a saw and began sawing the tube in half.

The hall grew as silent as a church. It was so convincing that even I who knew the trick was more than a little worried about my beloved.

The trick ended with the smoke screen. Tania disappeared in it, then re-appeared from behind the curtain and took her bows. There was thunderous applause.

Philippa was still cramped and uncomfortable inside the tube, but they hustled it away and began another routine.

Tania disappeared behind the screens. I stood and started for the side when someone tapped me on the shoulder.

My heart fell.

It was Toledo, the chief of the prince's personal guard. "He is calling for you, Basil. You had better attend him. Wash your face and come with me. Now."

"Yes, my friend." I smiled, trying to cover my disappointment. "Give me a few moments, and I'll be right there." I turned as if to hurry off, but he detained me with a strong hand on my arm.

"Oh, no. You will not escape me. In his present mood, the prince will have my head on a platter if you do not come with me."

"Why is he so out of sorts? I would think his party and presents would occupy his thoughts for a time."

He shook his head. "Forget about cleaning up. Come."

"I need to get this white face off. Just a moment." He watched as I found a basin and scrubbed off the paint. But he was distracted by someone else speaking to him, so I dashed off.

Ducking behind the curtain where Tania was supposed to be hiding, I searched for her. But she was not there. Nor was she in the tube or among the piles of silks.

Philippa came behind the screen from the stage after the last routine. "Basil, help me. I can't..."

I took a step towards her. "Where is she?"

"She's not here?" She motioned to the tube.

"No. I must find her! The prince has sent..."

Toledo's bulk burst into the small area. He did not look happy. "Basil! Come!"

I could not protest, for he grabbed my arm, and I could not get free of him. "Tell her, I will..." He pulled me from the small room. She followed. "Tell her I will help. I promise!"

She had no time to reply.

I was literally dragged through the Great Hall. By this time, so many were drunk that no one noticed my cries for help. And what could anyone do against the bulk and might of Toledo who represented the Imperial Guard?

His arm encircled my neck. I fought with all my strength but could not disentangle myself from his grasp. I had one last weapon to use.

I bit down as hard as I could on the massive arm. He yelped and loosened his hold. I knew it would only be for an instant, for these men were conditioned to pain. I wiggled my head free of his arm and kneed him in the crotch.

I knew it would do little good, for they wore protective gear. Yet I had to try.

To my surprise, he exclaimed loudly and bent over, coloring the air with such language that would make the devil blush.

In that instant, I reclaimed my freedom and fled from the room, knowing I had to really disappear this time, or he would find me again.

I had to find Tania. Had to take her back to the jesters. Help her escape. Halting to catch my breath in an alcove in a wide hall, I looked around, hoping I would catch a glimpse of her. I could see into the Great Hall, could see the dais where the prince sat with his gifts piled around him.

If the Princess Evdokia had seen her onstage, perchance she'd been dragged back much like I had. Yes, I saw Tania now. She sat with the princess, bending her head like she was weeping.

There was so much commotion going on that I could barely think above the din. I had to get her away. Entering that room was like stepping into the lion's den, for by now Toledo would be searching for me, and I ran the risk of Prince Alexius seeing me, too.

But regardless of the danger, I sprinted into the hall, right up to the table where Tania and the other women sat. They saw me coming.

Surprise and alarm mingled on Tania's face. She half-rose.

Just as I approached, I fell, tumbling several times in what I hoped was a convincing tumble. What I hadn't counted on was a low footstool. My head connected with it, and I saw stars.

Pain seared across my head but I did not lose consciousness.

The ladies laughed, some applauded. One screamed. I raised myself up, almost at Tania's feet. Something wet trickled down my face. I mopped it. Blood.

"Please help, my lady!" I implored Tania, crawling over to her. "Help me."

She rose and turned to her mistress. "He has hit his head. May I take him and get him help, my lady?"

Princess Evdokia had been one of those who had laughed at my fall. I was still in the jester's costume, so maybe she thought I was putting on a private show for her.

She drew back as if the sight of blood was too horrific for her delicate eyes. "Yes, by all means, Iris. Take him away. I cannot stand the sight of blood!" She turned her face.

Several of the other ladies rose to help, but Tania assured them she could do this alone. Taking my arm, she helped me stand, saying all the right things one would say in such a circumstance.

Out in the corridor, I wanted to bolt to the jester's room, but she found a laver with water in it and doused my head with it.

"There. That ought to fix it," she said, concern lacing her tone. "Are you okay, Basil? I must say, it's a good thing you stayed in your costume."

I nodded. "We have to flee. Come."

I took her hand, and we threaded our way through the crowded room to where the jesters were still collecting their things. Philippa was out of the tube. There was no time for explanations, for I could almost feel Toledo's grasp on me, and the third time, he would bring several hefty men to hold me securely.

"Quick! In the tube!" I shoved her into it and with the help of the others, covered it with silks.

They were ready to go. Without a backward glance, we headed for the main gates. I wondered if they would search the equipment, especially the tube, but they did not. Horatio hurried ahead and spoke urgently with the chief guard who stood on duty.

The man nodded and accepted something from Horatio. He motioned us out into the street. I helped Tania from the tube, and we embraced. Tears streaked her face.

"Oh, Basil. I can't believe we are free! Thank you, my love. Thank you so much!"

I couldn't believe we'd done it. Both of us now free as the birds of the air. But it was not quite that simple.

The revelry of the prince's birthday feast had spread to the city – at least to the part of the city closest to the palace. What ensued, as it always did, was a riot.

How things could proceed quickly from dancing, drinking, and happiness to violence and murder always puzzled me, but this city was known for it. Anything was an excuse for a riot.

We ran, ducked, ran again, and finally halted in the shelter of a church, scrunched in with ten of us, catching our breaths and trying to avoid being killed.

A gang sprinted past with stones in hand and screams in their throats.

I put my mouth close to Tania's ear. "Tania! I must return to the palace! The prince will look for me and will not quit until every stone is turned in the city! Get to my uncle's estate. Horatio knows the way. I will see you when we return."

She shook her head, tears forming in her eyes. "No, Basil! I need you! Please don't leave me now! I have... no one. I cannot return to my uncle. Surely you know that."

"Go to my uncle's estate. Tell the head servant, Alexander, that I have sent you. Hide there. I will not be gone long. Perhaps a few months."

At that moment, someone in the street spied us. One of the men shouted, "Hie! You jesters, you! Come and dance for us!"

Horatio cast me a glance. "We run!"

"Head for my uncle's estate!" I called to him.

He nodded even as he led out. The men, Silas, Mason, Hector and Virgil, the dwarf, followed readily. I kept close to Tania, watching the back, making sure the women kept up with us.

A mob formed behind us. Another gang approached from up ahead. We would be caught between the two. Buildings formed a solid wall. There was no escape. We would have to stand and fight.

Horatio called back to me, "Women at the back by the wall. Men, form a circle. Fight with what you have!"

Patience, Varda, and Philippa wouldn't stand back but drew their weapons. Tania huddled by the wall. I brought out my only blade, a short sword and was thankful I had that. It had been a prop for one of the acts we did.

Yet my heart sank as the men rushed upon us. I wasn't skilled in fighting, especially hand to hand combat. The ruffians were drunk and fearless. They brandished swords, short blades and daggers, long sticks, stones and other hastily grabbed weapons like tools from a blacksmith's shop.

We gave a good accounting for ourselves, even though we were outnumbered. Once the mob found out we could fight, they tired of it and ran off down the street.

But one of them, a huge burly man, maybe the blacksmith, saw Tania. "Oh, ho, me laddies, don't be so quick to run! Lookee what I'se found here!"

We were all busy with our duels, but from the corner of my eye, I saw him haul Tania from the wall by her hair.

"Now, this'n is somethin' to fight fer," he called with glee.

Two other men wheeled and started back, lust gleaming from their eyes.

"I found 'er first," the giant taunted them. "Now, go git yer own! Lookee over there." He nodded to Philippa. "That one whose fightin'. She's pretty, too."

Horatio ran up and delivered a blow to the head of my assailant. We turned to rescue Tania. Patience, Varda and Philippa were in danger, too. Yet they could defend themselves. They backed up against the wall and held up their daggers, crouching low.

Horatio tried to distract the big man while I dove in to free Tania from his grasp. But the man swatted both of us away with his free hand and called for help. In a few seconds, his friends would be swarming the street.

I thought of kicking him in the crotch like I'd done Toledo, but I knew it wouldn't faze this man due to the leather apron he wore that would turn my blow. I picked up a stone.

But just then a bow twanged, and an arrow flew through the air. The big man staggered back against the wall, the arrow in his chest.

Philippa drew another arrow and took aim. Two men ran towards us, screaming that we'd killed their friend. Someone in the mob had a bow and arrow, too.

"Philippa! Watch out! He has a bow!" I lunged for Tania.

In his last move before he died, the big man grabbed her and brought her in front of him like a shield. The man in the street shot, aiming for Philippa, but she jumped aside in time, and the arrow plunged into Tania's breast.

She screamed.

I caught her as she fell. All the street noises dimmed as I held her. Her blood soaked her gown and my tunic. The arrow would have to come out, but not here, or she would bleed to death.

Horatio urged me to run. He had to pull me from the crouch I was in, else I would have stayed there and wept and been killed. I gathered Tania into my arms and fled.

Philippa covered our backs as we flew down the street. How we escaped, I can never tell, but at one point, I sagged to the ground.

Tania's eyes were closed, and her face was as white as any candle I'd ever seen. I thought she was dead. Hector, the strong man, took her from me. We continued at a loping run.

When we arrived at the estate, I rang the bell and was gratified to see Elijah hurrying across the courtyard.

"It is I, Elijah. Open the gate, please."

He did, but as we passed inside, he said, "I was praying you would not come, Basil. Oh, Lord, I wish I could have warned you." He looked past me.

From the shrubbery near the gate, several men appeared. Large men. In the blue, white and gold uniforms of the Imperial guards.

"Come with us," the tallest of them said. He grabbed my arms and manacled my wrists.

I could only weep. "Get a physician for Tania!" I called to Elijah. "Tell her I will return soon!"

It was all I could manage between my tears and my pain. Something inside me said Tania was dead, for I'd seen her waxen face, her limp body. She'd lost a lot of blood, and she uttered no sound when I gave her to Hector.

With a broken heart and a bleeding body, I returned to the palace that night. The prince had left already with the troops.

They bandaged me as well as they could. I gathered my things and found my horse, setting out with a guard.

Clenching my teeth tightly against the pain and grief, I rode into the darkness. I'd lost my dearest on earth, and I was still in bondage to the prince. Nothing had turned out right. *I have failed!*

The horse's hoof beats seemed to repeat the word. *Failed. Failed.*

Oh, God! Where were You when I needed You? Why have you allowed this to happen? My dear Tania! What has she ever done to deserve this?

I found no answer and no relief as the night deepened and my horse carried me further and further from the city.

CHAPTER ELEVEN

The Escape

April 16, Year of Our Lord 1201

The guards allowed me a brief halt in the early morning as dawn touched the sky. I ate something, I can't remember what, and fell on the saddle blanket for an hour or so of sleep. The men took turns on the watch. There was never a moment when I could escape and ride back to the city.

It was a long three days before we caught up with the troops who were camped on the shore of the Marmara Sea. At the camp, the guards escorted me to the prince's tent. I left my tired horse and walked in, praying he would be in a good mood.

He was not.

"Where have you been, Christo? I have had nothing but trouble since leaving the city! This dratted army, the heat, the flies! I have half a mind to ride back to the palace. At least there I was treated with respect. Here I get nothing but rude comments and the dust from their blasted horses!" He paced the tent like a caged panther.

Troubles? It was I who stood there trembling from exhaustion and pain. It was I who was torn and bleeding inside from grief. It was I who had seen his beloved pierced with an arrow and did not know if she lived.

But Alexius could think of nothing except himself.

"I am sorry I am late in arriving," I said calmly. "My horse went lame, and we had to find a blacksmith. I am glad to see you whole and well, Your Highness. We are only five days' ride from the city. That should cheer your heart."

"Cheer my heart," he mumbled, mocking me. "I have not missed your droll humor." For the first time, he turned his gaze upon me. "By the gods, you look like hell. Go and get cleaned up. Then we will make plans."

I was led to my tent where a basin of water and a cot awaited me. I washed and changed into clean clothes. One of the servants brought me food.

After I ate, I went back to his tent, but he was so far gone in his wine he did not want me. Nor anyone.

I returned to my tent and fell asleep almost at once.

We followed the coastline for several days, then lost it as we headed due west. I had never seen this country before and even though my heart was heavy and my eyes bleary from little sleep, I loved the that land I saw.

It reminded me of my homeland, nestled in a sweet valley that was fed by streams from the mountains. The villages were few and scantily populated. Most of the people owned farmland. I spotted orchards, garden plots, and wide pastures that contained sheep, cattle, horses, and once in a while, pigs.

I took special notice of the horses – fine Arabians – for I loved them and would like to raise them someday if I had the means to buy a parcel of land and stock. Which I didn't. Not now, and not in the foreseeable future, unless Uncle Alesandro softened his stance toward me, and I became one of his heirs.

The moon will turn to gold before that happens, I thought with a chuckle!

I watched the prince carefully but saw no sign of mental instability that I feared in him. He rose early each morning, reviewed his cohort, saw to the care of his horse, and readied himself for the journey. He was the model captain. He conferred at times with his uncle and the other captains. I wondered about that.

Did he truly intend to flee? Or was this a clever act to make them trust him more and loosen the guards? Did he want to stay and cast his lot in with his uncle?

To me, he was distant. I did not mind that at all and made friends readily of his closest servants, particularly an older man who was his physician, Dennis DeWhitt.

Dennis had a sense of humor that he did not use in the presence of the prince, but one which I found refreshing. He covered his bald head with an Arab-like scarf instead of the helmets the army wore, and rode beside me, regaling me with stories of his adventures in the wide world. He wore a sword like he knew how to use it but carried no shield, lance, or other weapons.

We had skirmishes along the way but nothing that the army could not quell in a matter of a few hours. This delayed our progress, and I chaffed at the postponement, for I knew Captain Os would be waiting for us, and he would not wait long for the tides were strong in the bay.

On the tenth day from Constantinople, we rounded a bend in the road, and I smelled sea air and heard gulls crying. My heart leaped, for I was born and raised near the sea, and I loved it.

We camped one night about five miles from the city of Athyras. It was this city that had reportedly rebelled against the rule of Byzantium and refused to pay taxes. Dennis said this was an unsettled area with insurrections arising constantly.

The Thracian people were not warlike, though, I found. They wanted to raise their crops and animals and survive like all the rest of us. Yet when they were roused, they were formidable enemies and could fight skillfully and with great fervor to protect their holdings.

Alexius III desperately wanted a victory so he could return to Constantinople in great honor and glory. This way, he thought, he would seal the adoration and loyalty of the people to himself once and for all.

To this end, he planned his campaign very carefully. The soldiers made camp and went about their duties while the captains met in the sumptuous tents of the powerful leaders, making maps, arguing about methods and means, listening to the reports of the spies.

Prince Alexius was in the thick of it, and never once did he call me to his tent for a private interview. I began to think our plans and preparations, and even my journey, were in vain.

The next morning, I saddled my horse and prepared to ride, only to be stopped by a burly soldier who stood guard over my tent. I had thought in the beginning the guard was set to protect me, but then I realized it was to keep an eye on me.

"Where do you think you are going?" The guard said gruffly, taking the reins from my hand.

"I want to ride up to that hill." I nodded to an outcropping of rock that I hoped would give me a view of the bay. "To look around. You can come if you like."

"Orders is that no one rides out of camp. That means you. Unsaddle your horse. Return to your tent."

I had to do as he said. I joined a game of dice to while the time away and found several jobs to do in regard to my horse. His care was delegated to me, and I enjoyed it.

The day inched by. I wondered that the Thracians did not come out for a parlay or sortie, or whatever, to inspect the threat that had come to their door-step, some twenty-thousand troops. But the city remained quiet, its gate shut tightly, no sound at all. I surmised they were waiting for the emperor to make his first move.

He made it the next morning. Surrounded by his top captains and lieutenants, he rode with banner flying to the city. The prince galloped behind him in rank with the other captains, and I followed with Dennis in case there was fighting, and we were needed to patch up the wounded.

The emperor's herald called out in a strong voice, "Hear ye! Hear ye! Emperor Alexius III calls you out to discuss your insurrection against him and the kingdom of New Rome and Byzantium! Come forth, if you can find a man to speak for you, and speak to answer for your crimes!"

The gates opened. A man rode forth, dressed in white, carrying the banner of the city. Several men came behind him. He stopped within yelling distance of the herald.

I could faintly hear what he said.

"We have done no wrong! Under oath I declare it. You have been misinformed by our enemies. We wish no war with Byzantium and the emperor. Withdraw your troops, or we shall make you wish you had!"

There was further talk, but I caught only snatches. From what I could ascertain, things were not going well. The emperor insisted they were rebellious, and that he must speak with the governor of the province.

After being told that the governor was not in residence, Alexius III declared war on the city unless they could prove they were not guilty of insurrection and that they pay a large amount of back taxes.

They replied they were innocent of any crimes, and that they were unable to pay any money. The deputation from the city made one last effort for peace, and then rode back. The gates shut.

How could they defy the troops assembled against them? I shook my head as we rode back to camp. I did not want to get involved in a battle, but unless the prince called for me, it seemed I would.

I thought of Tania and wondered if she still lived. Perchance we would meet in heaven if I had to fight, for I had little confidence in my skills as a warrior.

The prince called for me that night, dismissing his servants. We spoke in low tones, knowing that the tent walls were thin. The Imperial Guards kept a constant vigil over him.

"We must make our move soon," I whispered. "Tonight."

"Tonight?" he raised surprised eyes to mine as I poured our drinks. "Why, Christo? I thought to fight. To win glory and honor."

"And to impress your uncle." I sat close to him but did not touch him. He didn't like to be touched.

When he would not speak, I continued. "You know it to be true. You have lost sight of our true mission. Remember, Your Highness, we are doing this to get you away from Byzantium. Clean away from your uncle. Nothing can be done to free your father or restore the kingdom to your family unless you are willing to stop this ... this play-acting and start thinking about your future."

I knew the mention of the kingdom, of his father, would jolt him out of his lethargy.

He sat upright. "I know, Christo! But is it the proper time? I would..."

"Hush!" I put a finger to my lips and glanced at the tent door. "If you value your life, keep your voice down."

He nodded. "Yes." Standing, he paced the small space, sipping his wine, his face clouded. Then he sat next to me, leaning close.

"I would have liked to try my mettle to fight. But I see you are right. Is the ship in the bay?"

"I don't know. They wouldn't let me ride out to see. The captain said he would wait a few days, but we arrived late, and I fear he will not tarry."

"Is there a signal? How does he know when we will arrive at the beach?"

"We will ride to that knob of a hill over there and start a small blaze. That will be our signal. By the time we get to the beach, they will be there."

"And how do you propose to get out of the camp?"

I rose and spoke loudly. "It is a fair night out. I would take a stroll. Would you like to come with me, prince?"

"Yes, I would." He took my cue.

We stepped out into the night. Two Imperial Guards stood stiffly not five feet away. There was no moon, and for that I was grateful. A small wind played with the tent flap and lifted my hair from my damp forehead. Men played dice not far away. Someone strummed an instrument and sang a love song.

The salt breeze brushed my face. I pulled my cloak around my shoulders and led the way along the lane.

Glancing over at his hunched figure, I smiled. "There. That's better. Now we can talk. Not loudly, though, not even here."

We walked to the edge of the camp. I nodded to the guard who stood there. We started back.

In a low voice, I said, "I have bribed the guard, that one there. He will look the other way when we ride out. I hope. I will get our horses and ready them. Meet me down there by that stand of trees when the gong sounds for lights out. Midnight. Have all your things."

He nodded, his face hidden in the fold of his hood. His voice cracked when he spoke. "Christo? Are you sure we can do this? I don't want to die. I don't want the curse of the crown to fall upon me." He shuddered. "It will not, will it?"

"You will not die. Pray to our Father in Heaven. He will give you courage and strength. He is stronger than any curse. Once we are onboard, all will be well. That I promise you."

He faced me, and we stopped walking. "Very well, Christo. I trust you. Do not fail me."

He sounded as he had when a small boy, and I wondered at it. All his pomp, bluster and craziness seemed to dissipate on the night air as he stood before me, unsure and afraid.

But it only lasted a moment. He squared his shoulders, shoved back his hood and glanced around.

"This camp is a pig sty!" he yelled with curses. "Hey, you! Get over here and clean this mess! I cannot even walk without stepping in muck! Now! Do you hear? I will have you whipped to an inch of your life, you miserable scupper!"

I grinned. The old Prince Alexius was back. It was a show, of course. All was a show. But now we could proceed, and I hoped that when he left his uncle, I could reach him again.

I stole from my tent later that evening. The guard was gone. I found the horses and saddled them, watching with bated breath for the sound of booted feet on the hard-packed ground.

But my bribes held good, and no one came near.

I rode to the hill above the camp and started my little fire, shielding the tiny blaze with my hands. When it flared up, I went back to my horse and rode down the hill, praying it would be seen by those on the ship that anchored out in the water.

I found the trees I had pointed out to Alexius and dismounted. Waiting was hard. The moon made a late appearance, playing hide and seek with the clouds, and a low mist rose from the creek. My nerves were raw, and I jumped at every sound – the hoot of an owl, the rustle in the bushes of a small rodent, the call of a coyote out on the hills.

I paced the perimeter of the small area, eyes intent on the road that led to the camp, ears aching for the sound of a hurried step.

And then I heard it. Footsteps approached.

He appeared as a wraith on the road, hunched and stumbling at times, his black cloak flapping in the breeze from the sea. He carried a pack on his back and seemed a waif, a beggar.

He hesitated and looked about.

I stepped out onto the road. "Alexius! I am here."

He gasped with relief and hurried to me. I took him to the horses. Without a word, I tied on his pack behind the saddle, and we rode off.

Dawn was peeping over the edge of the sea when we came to the beach. Leaving the horses, knowing they would be found and taken back to camp, we trudged through the sand toward a small skiff that had been pulled up on the beach. Two men stood beside it.

I could see lights on the ship out in the harbor. We ran the last few steps, and I thought we had escaped. But when we were almost to the skiff, I heard what I dreaded most. The sound of hoof beats.

Alexius grasped my arm and almost fell to the sand. "They come! Oh, Christo! They will take us!"

"Steady, sire. A few more steps. They cannot see us yet."

Together we sprinted to the skiff. Without a word, we leaped in the water and clambered aboard while the two men shoved off and climbed over the side. They rowed with strong, steady strokes across the surf.

"Get down!" One of them ordered roughly. "You must not be seen!"

We hunkered down the top edge of the boat. Alexius was moaning, praying, crying. I said my own frantic prayers, ones that ran along the lines of, "Help us, Lord!"

The soldiers on the shore shouted out to the men in the boat to stop, to return, but they did not stop, and they did not answer. It seemed a lifetime while we tossed up and down with the waves, and the two sailors pulled with all their might.

Once at the hulking monster of a ship, I grabbed my pack and Alexius shouldered his. I followed him as he climbed a rope ladder to the top rail where hands pulled us over and onto the deck.

"They will search you," I said to the captain who came striding up to us, worry lines creasing his forehead.

"Aye. I know," he replied shortly. He nodded to Alexius. "You. Go below with the mate. They will show you what to do." He looked at me. "And you will get into these. Quickly. They've found a boat. They come."

A sailor handed me clothes that I hastily donned over top of what I already wore – loose-fitting pants, a rough tunic, a rope for a belt, a hat. They daubed some foul-smelling substance on my face to darken it. *Just like the jesters*, I thought. *Well, if it works, I won't mind.*

A brush was thrust into my hands and a bucket of water. They told me to scrub the deck. I thought it was a strange time to do that, but I did not argue and bent with a will to my task. The other sailors grouped around me, shielding me from view.

We did not have long to wait. Soon the boat the soldiers had commandeered arrived at the ship and several of them climbed the rope ladders. They made us stand in a line. I kept my head down and the bucket in my hand.

They did not recognize me.

When they went below, my knees almost gave way for fear for the prince. I resumed my task. It seemed the officers took a lifetime with their search below decks, but at last they reappeared and left the ship, satisfied that neither the prince nor myself was on board.

Later, when we swung in the hammocks they gave us for beds, Alexius told me what had happened down below.

When he went into the hold, one of the sailors opened an empty cask and motioned for him to get into it. He lowered himself into it, folding his legs and squishing down as far as he could. It smelled of rotten figs. They tamped down the lid over his head. He waited, wondering if he would suffocate before they got him out.

Soon he heard the tramp of feet, sharp commands, the sounds of barrels rolling and nails ripped from the wooden lids.

"My heart fairly stopped beating, I tell you," he said with a grin. "And then it began pounding so hard, I swear I thought they would hear it. Another order was barked, and my barrel was upended. I nearly swooned with fright, sure that they would find me. But evidently the barrel had a false bottom and sour liquid flowed out."

He chuckled and lay back. "I heard the man curse. They set it down, and I breathed again. At last they tromped away and the sailors let me out of my prison. Whew! I think I'll never eat another fig in my life!"

The waves rocked me to sleep that night as I prayed for Tania, and for Alexius, and for myself. The low Thracian hills disappeared from sight, and we sailed out into the sea.

CHAPTER 12

The Marquis and The Promise

June Year of Our Lord 1202, Germany

Three weeks and six days later, we arrived in the German city of Stuttgart where the Hohenstaufen castle, home of Philip of Swabia, sat perched on a hill above the valley. The rolling countryside contained forest, rivers, lakes and meadows where small farms and villages abounded.

We were welcomed gladly and taken into the castle.

Alexius was whisked away, and I was given quarters with the other servants. At dinner that evening, a grand feast, he sat next to his sister, Irene, and on the other side was his brother-in-law, Philip of Swabia.

I knew of Philip, for I had followed his career and often wondered how high he would climb. High, indeed. In 1198, he was crowned emperor on the Holy Roman Empire which encompassed much of Europe. That he was married to the daughter of the emperor of Byzantium made his position stronger, even though he warred constantly with the Welf dynasty and their man, Otto of Brunswick, who was also crowned emperor in a different city.

Philip did not look the part of a ruler of a mighty empire. His appearance would denote more of a scholar or the clergy, for he was of slight build, had stooped shoulders, and was of a quiet nature.

As I bowed before him, I caught a gleam in his eyes and knew he was strong willed. Here was a man who knew what he was about and how to get what he wanted.

Formalities aside, I retired early and walked the castle grounds, looking out over the valley to the farms below. There were beautiful gardens in the upper bailey, but I barely noticed them. The moon rose over the German landscape, and my mind flew to Tania. I wondered if she lived, and if she remembered me.

Was that same moon looking down upon her this night? How long would Alexius want to stay? Why was I here? Perchance I could petition him and return to Constantinople.

Shaking my head, I went to my room. I doubted very much if he would give me leave.

In the weeks that followed, I found employment in the infirmary, in the stables, and in the guardroom, sharpening swords or scrubbing the floor. In the evenings, I played dice games with the men.

In company with Dennis DeWhitt, the physician I had met earlier, I worked my way through the inns in the town, drinking, eating and laughing. We discovered that Germans love their wine and make excellent ale. The people were hospitable, generous and kind, yet they grumbled about the nobility, those who sat in the castles on hills and took their hard-earned wages.

The inn was a good place to hear all the latest gossip, if it could be believed.

Preachers everywhere carried the news of the new crusade and appealed to the common man as well as the nobles to join it. They asked for donations to fund the campaign, for it seemed as the summer wore on that they were lacking in money and men.

I shook my head in disbelief every time I heard one of the priests expound on the topic, for they used every emotional gambit in their repertoire – crying, screaming, tearing their hair and ripping their clothes. It always saddened me to see the poorest of the land dip into their pockets and deposit their coins in the offering bags that circulated after such a sermon.

Summer bloomed and faded as fall turned the leaves red, orange and yellow, and the days grew crisp. I loved riding in the forest, yet I longed to be back in Constantinople.

The prince called for me now and then. I dreaded these appointments, for he was so gloomy and ill of temper that I despaired he would survive.

One time, pacing the room, he said, "I have spoken with my sister and her husband many times about my plight, but they seem to take little notice of me. Philip is more concerned with what the Welf people are doing to unseat him and the possibility for war..."

"War?"

He nodded. "Oh, yes. They have been fighting for decades. Philip was crowned emperor, but so has Otto, his rival." He sighed. "I know my case will be heard too late. The crusaders will sail any day now, and my cause will be lost."

"You intend to petition them to help you?" I raised my brows. "It seems they have enough problems of their own."

He disregarded my comment and continued, "If I have to sit here in this miserable castle for one day longer, I think I shall go mad. Philip sent an envoy to Count Boniface of Montferrat, but I do not know how long it will take the courier to get there and to return with a message. I watch the road every day, hoping to see him coming back, but he does not."

"I hear the crusade will be launched next year. There is time, Alexius. Do not fret yourself." It was futile to try to soothe him with this line of talk, and so I suggested a ride.

"It is a beautiful day, and you like riding that fine stallion the emperor gave you. Come with me and forget your troubles for a time."

He acquiesced grudgingly, and we enjoyed our time, especially since he invited a girl to accompany us. Her name was Maria, the niece of Philip, staying at the castle for the summer.

She laughed merrily and paid Alexius the attention he craved.

It seemed to lighten his spirits, but then he was cast down again when Philip said he doubted if Boniface or anyone else in the crusade's leadership would answer his appeal for help.

The days and weeks trudged by like an old man with a huge burden on his back. The old year ran itself out with Christ's Mass. There was feasting, snow, and throngs celebrating in the cathedral.

We waited through the winter and into the spring. Would the crusaders ever hear Alexius' plea and come to talk? What had happened? I felt isolated from the rest of the world. Even the rumors of the crusade faded as talk centered on the weather and the crops.

***

The fleet of the Fourth Crusade sailed from Venice October 1202 with great acclaim, glory and praise. The Army of the Lord they called themselves. We heard about it in Germany and wondered.

The European lords who became the leaders of the Fourth Crusade, Boniface of Montferrat and Baldwin of Flanders, among others, had promised the doge of Venice, Enricho Dandolo, eighty-five thousand silver marks to provide ships for the crusade. When they gathered at Venice, they found themselves far short of the number of troops, and could not pay, thus, they became indebted to the doge.

Dandolo took command of the enterprise. He hated the Greeks of Constantinople as they had blinded him when he was young. Besides his personal vendetta, he lusted for complete control of the shipping lines in the Adriatic Sea.

Because of this, they were deterred from a holy cause to free the holy lands from Muslim control and sailed instead across the sea like an evil dragon, raining horror, death and destruction upon the villages and cities that lay in its path, for they had to make up the money they had promised the doge.

When the army landed at Zara, they ignored pleas from the pope and threats of excommunication and proceeded to attack a Christian city. They razed it to the ground, stealing, murdering, raping.

The Fourth Crusade stayed that winter in Zara while Dandolo planned their next move.

Boniface of Montferrat left to return home and to see his cousin, Philip of Swabia. He also was intrigued by a letter he'd received on behalf of the young prince Alexius Angelus, Philip's nephew. This letter petitioned the crusade to travel to Constantinople to re-instate the prince as the emperor.

Baldwin gave it little regard. The crusade was bound for Egypt and Palestine. Not Constantinople. He would not be deterred. They would go to Egypt as promised and fight the enemy of Christendom there.

***

One day that spring, April 1202, Prince Alexius called me to his apartment in the castle. I washed hurriedly, for I'd been out all day on one of the estate's farms helping with the livestock.

He opened the door to my knock.

"Christo! Come in! Did you see our distinguished guests arrive?" He led me to a low couch, poured a glass of wine for me, and brought it to me.

I was surprised at this new Alexius. He who would have never deigned to do anything for himself in Constantinople, much less serve anyone, was now giving me wine.

"I heard about it," I said. "But I did not see them. I was out on the farm. Who is it? Why are you keeping me in suspense?"

He cocked an eyebrow at me and grinned.

I noted that glint in his eye. "Ah. Our esteemed Marquis of Montferrat, Boniface, has arrived!"

"Yes, Christo! And he shall hear my plea this very evening. I want you to be present."

"Yes. I will come, if you desire it. You will make his head spin, will you not? This is the moment you have waited for so long. It is finally here. Have you said your prayers?"

"To every saint in existence, it seems," he admitted with a smirk. "Yet it is I, Alexius the Fourth, who shall pull this one off, not some dead saint. Philip told me they are searching for a cause to draw more men."

"And your cause is to be re-instated on the throne along with your father."

"Of course. What could be nobler? More righteous? More worthy?" He sprang up with his endless energy. "I must dress." He eyed my rather plain apparel. "I see we shall have to give you decent clothes. Those will never do."

I did not complain, for I enjoyed Alexius when he was in this mood. After allowing his servants to dress me and cut my hair, I joined the prince for the dinner.

Marquis Boniface of Montferrat, a baron of a duchy in southeastern France, held himself straight with dignity as we entered the great hall.

The marquis stood beside Philip on the dais as the people of the duchy and castle began arriving. Boniface was a tall, handsome man in his late fifties with dark hair highlighted with streaks of gray, broad shoulders, and a high forehead. His dark eyes were alight with intelligence and command.

The prince was seated next to him while I chose a table below the dais with the other servants. I liked this arrangement because I could hear the conversation from the head table.

Philip introduced Alexius to Boniface. They smiled, bowed, and exchanged a few pleasantries. The meal began. To my dismay, the noise of the hall blocked out most of what transpired between Alexius and the baron, but I noted that the marquis seemed not to accept Alexius' plea, for he kept shaking his head.

Philip joined their conversation and noted that the noise in the hall was so great that they must retire to his private chambers for further talk. Alexius motioned to me when the meal was completed.

I followed the group to the audience hall where the men of both parties stood around a raised platform. Philip, Alexius, the marquis and several of his men occupied the chairs on the dais.

Philip was the speaker for Alexius who sat toying with the tassels on his sword hilt. I wished he would sit up straighter and keep more eye contact with the marquis. Hadn't he listened to anything I'd taught him?

When Boniface heard the appeal, he shook his head. "The crusade has always been bound for Egypt. That was decided years ago by the pope. We cannot veer from our path, not even for the plight of this young prince. It would be wrong."

Philip began pacing. "But you left that path to visit Zara and attack it," he said with a lift to his chin. "The crusade is wintering there. Why do you not sail for Egypt?"

"We are waiting for fair weather." Boniface stood, too. "I am traveling to my home on the morrow. I would suggest you seek audience with Pope Innocent about the crusade. We can do nothing without his approval, as you are well aware. If he gives permission, we will consider Constantinople. That is all I can promise."

Philip conceded with little grace. Written on his face was his dislike for having to appeal to the pope for anything, for he was the emperor of the Holy Roman Empire and held great power.

The prince left the room in high dudgeon, his face twisted into a snarl, his eyes flashing with anger. I figured it was best to leave him alone for a few days and returned to my room.

I felt the prince's keen disappointment and added some of my own. To travel back home to Constantinople had been my prayer and dream for as long as we had been in Germany. Now it seemed we would not be going anywhere soon.

A week later, someone pounded on my door just as I rose. It was one of the villagers who said a girl had fallen from a tree and needed my attention. I gathered my bag and followed him down the hill.

The child had broken her leg. It took some time to set it, give her a draught of poppy juice for the pain, and instruct the parents on how to care for her.

I found several others I needed to visit in the village, and so the day was nearly spent when I started back to the castle.

The church bells pealed out for vespers as I emerged from the village. I thought to join the people in the small church, but a man ran down the path from the castle and accosted me. It was Ulrich, the seneschal of the castle. It was an urgent errand upon which he came, for certes, or he would have sent one of his pages.

"The prince calls for you, Basil," he said. "Where have you been? We scourged the whole castle for you. You know how the prince does not like to wait."

I chuckled. "Yes, indeed. I am sorry for your trouble. A child fell and had to be tended. I was down in the village."

We had time for no more chatter as we needed all our breath to climb the hill to the castle in short order. Ulrich was panting hard by the time we reached the gate.

I left him to hurry into the prince's chambers.

Alexius greeted me at the door, a smile as wide as the sea splitting his face. "Christo! Come in at once!"

There was a great stir inside. Servants hustled around with arms full of clothing and bedding. Higher ranking servants called out orders, and in the general melee, some bumped into others, and things got dropped and retrieved.

He drew me aside. I had never seen him like he was that day. His face was dull purple, his eyes distended, his passion running so high he was nearly jumping out of his skin.

"We are leaving on the morrow," he yelled over the din. "Philip and I and many others. We are going to Rome! Can you believe it, Christo? We are on our way, at last. I have a good feeling about this."

He thumped me on the back. I grasped his hand. "I am glad to hear it, prince. You will have success, I know, if your brother-in-law comes along."

"Go, pack your things. We leave at daybreak." He sprang across the room to attend to a detail of packing.

I smiled. Rome! Well, it was one step closer to Constantinople. I could almost smell the magnolia blossoms and visualize Tania. My dear, dear Tania! Would I see her soon or attend to her grave?

Casting such thoughts aside, I gathered my things, told my friends good-bye, both in the castle and out of it, and met the prince the next morning as we broke our fast in the drafty old hall of the castle.

Philip and his entourage waited outside, mounted on fine horses. The prince and I ate a hurried meal and emerged into the dawn's chilly air a few minutes later.

I bade Irene fare well and thanked her for her hospitality. She had tears in her eyes when she gave Alexius a warm hug.

We rode through wet weather and muddy roads to the Slovenian port city of Trieste, a Byzantium military outpost, which boasted of ancient Roman ruins. We came down from a high escarpment to sea level by means of a snake-like road, intersected at points with booths for idol worshippers and vendors.

Philip engaged a merchantman in the port, and the next morning, we were sailing south on the Adriatic Sea.

Of the journey to Rome I will say little, save that we sailed too early and suffered much from ill weather, running to port often, including to Venice. I saw nothing of the city for it was pouring rain, and I had a cough and aching muscles.

As we rode inland toward Rome, the prince's mood lifted. He had been morose, saying things like he would never be able to return to Constantinople, never be seated on the throne, never see his father again. I tried to cheer him, but when he wanted to be miserable nothing could deter him.

Now he looked about with a bright smile.

Seeing the pope was no easy matter, not even for Philip of Swabia, but at least we found decent lodgings. At last, three weeks later, Pope Innocent deigned to meet with Philip and Prince Alexius.

Why the Roman Catholic pope would bother himself with affairs of a Greek Orthodox Byzantium nation, I could not fathom, but Philip had concocted a list of reasons why the crusade should detour out of their prescribed path to set Alexius on the throne.

One of them was that Alexius promised to bring the whole Byzantium empire under the control of the Roman pope. Again, I could not imagine how he intended to accomplish such a feat, but who am I to question those above me?

I went with them to the Lateran Palace where all official affairs of the church were discussed and waited for them in the anteroom of the audience chambers.

It seemed they were in the audience for a long time, but finally they appeared. I studied their expressions. Both were the same. Anger. Disappointment. Frustration. Philip looked as if he'd eaten a lemon. I could imagine it would not be an easy thing for him to appeal to the pope and have it rejected.

They said nothing to me. I fell in behind them, catching their sporadic comments like tidbits thrown to a dog.

"He had no right," Alexius muttered.

Philip grunted. "Yes, he had right. His mind was made up before we arrived. He knows everything and decides according to his knowledge. Once he makes a choice, nothing moves him. He is pope, after all."

"Not even my plight?"

"He will not be deterred from the crusade going to Egypt."

"What if we petition him day and night? For weeks? That should change his mind."

"His goal from the outset for the crusade was Egypt. Remember how many times he mentioned that?" Philip sighed as we entered the house. "Get used to it, Alexius. Nothing, not even an angel from God, will change his mind. You can wait here until the kingdom comes and petition him until you grow old, but the answer will be the same."

I ventured a question. "The answer was no?"

Alexius stomped off to his room.

Philip sat on a low couch. "I need wine, Christo."

There were other servants about, but I obeyed him and fetched the wine, taking a glass for myself, too. Waiting for them was thirsty work.

We drank in silence – he, sitting with a far-away look in his eyes, and me, standing near the table.

"Well, then, you must go to the source," I said, turning to him.

He raised his brows. He was not accustomed to speak to the servants, other than giving an order, but he recognized me as a person of slightly higher rank.

"The source?"

"Yes, my lord. You must appeal directly to the crusader leaders. In Zara."

"But Boniface would not hear our plea. Surely, the others will not, either."

"Then you must give them good reason to listen. Do you not have a list of the things the prince has promised them?"

He nodded. "Yes. Silver marks. Bringing the nation under the rule of the Roman church." He laughed. "As if that will ever happen."

"Offer them more, then. Make it something they cannot resist, that they cannot refuse."

He rose slowly. I could not read his face to ascertain whether he was pleased or angry. Coming to stand near me, he nodded.

"Hmm. Interesting." Turning abruptly, he said, "Send John in to me. I have work to do."

Smiling to myself, I found the secretary and sent him to Philip.

Since Alexius was indisposed and probably drinking heavily, and Philip did not need me, I strolled the streets and bought a meat pasty from a vendor.

We had been in Rome for three weeks. My whole being itched to be on the journey again. I wondered what the future held. Would the crusader leaders accept the plea from the prince sent by Philip?

Philip of Swabia was not a man to ignore. If it had not been that he took up the prince's plight, I doubt if Alexius would have had any chance at all of returning to his city and his throne.

We did not leave Rome straight-away as I supposed we would. The next morning, Philip and Alexius poured over the documents the emperor had prepared. Alexius argued for more concessions while Philip, ever cautious, wanted to scale back.

They came to an agreement before the sun was high. With the documents re-written by scribes that evening, they were ready to be sent to Zara. Philip petitioned the pope for envoys and got them.

Alexius met with the two men and instructed them carefully about each point. I listened while reading a book from the library in Rome, finding his promises too extreme to hardly warrant belief. But, I reasoned, they would be the lure to the bait. The crusaders could hardly refuse such an agreement.

The first promise that Alexius made was that he would bring the whole of the Byzantium empire under the authority of the pope. The second was the vow to pay the crusaders a jaw-dropping sum of two hundred thousand silver marks. This alone would sway Marquis Boniface and many others, I wagered.

The third was the offer of twenty ships frpm the royal navy to help with their war against the Muslims, and last was the pledge that Alexius would station five hundred knights in the holy land to keep what was won back from the Arabs.

It was extravagant. Extreme. But it might sway them. It might ensure Alexius' bid for the throne.

With the envoys gone, there was nothing for us to do. Philip returned home. The prince and I continued to share our apartment in Rome until we heard a reply from the crusaders.

We waited through the summer and winter. Boniface arrived one blustery night in the wee hours of the morning. It was March 30, 1203.

The prince was getting difficult to manage because of the long wait. I had tried everything I knew but was running out of patience myself. It seemed a time that had no end. I found a church and a small group of Christians to fellowship with, but even this did not lift my spirits when I returned to our apartments.

With Boniface's return, I felt things would move again. He met with Alexius for hours the next morning, discussing the letter that was sent by envoys. He had come from the crusader camp, and was now passionately in favor of helping the prince.

Why? I asked myself. *Ah. It is because of the promise of money.* Two hundred thousand silver marks would sway any man. He also now believed firmly in the right and just cause of helping Alexius regain the throne, and he would stay true to his conviction until the end.

Alexius strode to the window with his endless energy. "What did they say about it? Will they help me? I thought it would be a matter of a couple of months. It has been..." He paused. "Eleven! Almost a year, and I have heard nothing. It is driving me mad!"

Boniface leaned back in his chair and smiled that secret smile of his that I'd come to know. "While you have been fretting yourself to madness here in Rome, much has been happening in Zara. We are planning to sail to Corfu soon."

"Corfu!" Alexius' eyes gleamed with interest. "Why there?"

"The land around Zara has become as bare as a newborn's bottom. In Corfu, we can find a good harbor and food for both horses and the troops."

"What have the other leaders decided?"

"Ah. That is the question. You stirred the bee's nest, for certes, with your letter. Baldwin of Flanders, Louis of Blois and Hugh of Saint-Pol, myself and others were persuaded, but the vast majority objected. Strongly. We had many discussions. Some were strongly opposed, and others just as vigorously in favor. The envoys you sent pressed the issue of your dispossessed throne strongly."

He sipped his wine. "But the majority are opposed to your proposal, mainly because they see it as a deterrent to the goal of the crusade. Both noble and base-born took the cross to help recover the Holy Land for the Christian faith. They cannot envision the army attacking a Christian city such as Constantinople, one of the five patriarchal seats in the world. Not even for a strong appeal such as yours."

"But the crusade can proceed to Syria later, after they have put me on the throne," Alexius said. "It will not take long, surely. Did you tell them that?"

Boniface nodded morosely, downing his wine in a gulp. "Oh, yes. We told them that and much more. Still, they hang on with stubbornness to the thought that we must only go on to Syria. Twelve of us, the leaders of the crusade, were strongly determined to accept your plea. I have the response. We met with Dandolo and swore to an agreement. It is here, the signed charters confirming the covenant. The crusade will proceed to Constantinople."

From an inner pocket on his vest, he removed a leather packet which he laid on the table.

Alexius nearly jumped out of his skin. He gathered it to his bosom. "Oh, praise be to God and all the saints! How can I thank you, best of friends?"

Boniface took a step back as if to avoid being embraced. Who could tell what these crazy Byzantiums would do?

He nodded. "You must prove yourself worthy of our trust. There are still many in the crusade who may leave us. If we lose nobles and their men, the crusade is no more, that which we have labored for over four years. Only a few weeks ago, John of Nesles appealed to us. He had a large contingent of French soldiers who wintered in Marseille. We ordered him to meet with us at the port of Methoni on the western finger of Asia Minor. But he sailed directly to Palestine. Others, like the French knights whose leader was Reynald of Montmirail, begged to go to Jerusalem as pilgrims and pledged on a Bible they would join us in Constantinople for the siege."

He snorted. "I doubt if we will see them again. You can see the serious hemorrhage of our endeavor. If this continues, we will not be in a position to proceed."

"What are you going to do?" I refilled their glasses.

Boniface sighed heavily. "Do? I will leave on the morrow. You will follow and arrive at Zara on April 25th, Saint Mark's Day. We will meet with those who are still there. A large flotilla of the ships have probably already left for Corfu."

Alexius clapped. "Yes! We will sail in a few weeks. Christo, you must find us a ship. Anything else, my lord?"

Boniface pierced him with a bright glance from under shaggy brows. "Say your prayers, Your Highness. We shall need all we can get."

The marquis slept only a few hours and before dawn was gone.

CHAPTER 13

Zara and Corfu

April 25, Year of Our Lord 1203

Three weeks later, we left the little house on the narrow street in Rome and rode to the port city of Ostia. There, we boarded the vessel I had found. We were on the way to Zara, and after that, Constantinople.

It was, as we planned, St. Mark's Day, April 25th when we were rowed ashore at Zara. The lords of the crusade, including Boniface, met us at the dock. The ruins of the city, which had been beautiful and proud, still smoldered.

Rumors of what had happened in Zara reached us in Germany, but none could scarcely believe their ears. I wept when I heard the news.

It was inconceivable that the army of the Lord that had set out so bravely and with such high hopes had become an evil force, attacking without provocation a noble Christian city and destroying it.

As I viewed it, walking with the others in the group, I was overcome with such horror that I could not speak. I could only weep.

What were we getting involved with? Did the prince really want to join with such an enterprise? Evidently, he did.

I watched him with trepidation as he marched into the city so confidently. His old selfish, prideful, bullying ways had returned with the attention he was receiving, for everyone in our party believed he would become the next emperor of the most powerful empire on the earth, and they treated him accordingly.

Except for me.

They received us into what was once the governor's palace built on a knoll above sea. It had been spared the fires but stood lonely amidst the ruins. Count Geoffrey de Villehardouin led the way to the mansion and invited us inside.

The doge of Venice, Dandolo, greeted us in the hall. I'd never seen him before and was interested to view for myself what kind of man he was. He wore a heavy damask robe of green and gold, lined with fur, a tunic of yellow silk, a chain about his neck that I supposed was a symbol of his office, and fur-lined boots. His face was lined with wrinkles, and his gray hair was long.

Although blind, he did not act according to his disability, but came forward eagerly, meeting the prince and embracing him with a kiss to each cheek. After that, he took the time to shake each of the servants' hands, including me.

I liked him. He seemed to me like a lordly king even though he wore neither crown nor sword.

The room I was given was cold and drafty even after I managed to find wood to burn in the fireplace. The elaborate meal that evening seemed to never end. Alexius gave a speech during it, repeating his pleas for help and outlining his promises to the crusaders.

They ate it up.

The majority of the troops had already left for Corfu, as Boniface predicted. The prince was given sumptuous quarters in the mansion. He accepted the Venetian offer of three galleys and crews to sail them with a regal nod. I am sure he was elated, but he could not show it.

We celebrated the feast of St. Mark in the newly reconstructed cathedral with much aplomb and ceremony. The prince was put front and center at every meeting, a tactical move on the part of the leaders, showing that they supported him and already acclaimed him as emperor.

My stomach turned when I toured the gutted city. A few of the citizens, those who survived and remained, were busy rebuilding. They lifted dirty faces when I passed and nodded to acknowledge my friendly greeting.

I was surprised they did not pull me from my mount and murder me, knowing that I came with the crusaders.

We were at Zara four days before we sailed.

The prince's joy was evident for all to see as we took our leave. I was afraid for him, for he was nothing but a pawn in the hands of the powerful barons that had set their faces on conquest.

He was fawning on Boniface who gave him grudging regard almost as an indulgent parent on a child who pleases him for a moment. I sighed. Yes, Prince Alexius would be their champion, their pliable puppet. A little boy king of Byzantium.

He saw it as a way to regain his stolen throne to become Alexius IV, the ruler of the greatest empire on the face of the earth. He envisioned riches, power and all that is worthy and desirable as he set his sights toward Constantinople.

But I saw only the ruin of his soul and disaster. How much better he would have been to remain in Germany, marry into nobility and take a lesser position such as baron or count under his brother by marriage who would have set him up handsomely.

The day after we sailed, the prince called for me. I made myself as presentable as possible and entered his room, the captain's cabin, I noted.

"I have not seen you for some time," he said empirically. "What have you been doing? I would have you serve me faithfully in my new position. What do you say to that?"

I did not know which question to answer first. I bowed and said, "I have been helping on the ship, Your Highness, making sure it is safe for your passage. I have aided the cook in preparing meals and your servants in mending your clothes. What else would you have me do?"

None of this information impressed him. He toyed with a leather purse someone had given him. It jingled with the sound of silver coins.

He grinned and leaped to his feet from the low divan on which he had reclined. "Ah. That is good to hear. But I would have you serve me further. Do you know what this contains?" He held out the purse but did not allow me to touch it.

"Silver?"

He chortled with glee and danced a few steps. "Yes! It makes a lovely sound, does it not? They gave this to me, Alexius, for traveling expenses. Twenty silver marks." He set it aside and laughed. "A mere pittance in view of what I shall one day possess."

He shook his head. "My Latin needs work, they say. I must be able to speak it if I am to rule. You will come every day and teach me. I do not want you toiling on the ship with the other slaves. You are too valuable to me for that. Come after I have broken my fast in the morning."

With a curt nod, he dismissed me before I could reply.

A city on the mainland drew my attention. It was Durazzo, I was told, a post on the north-western edge of the Byzantium Empire. When we landed, the citizens gave their town over to Prince Alexius and swore allegiance to him.

This pleased the prince and the crusader leaders immensely, for it promised that others in the realm would receive him in like manner.

We arrived at Corfu on the evening of May 1st, 1203.

The crusader flotilla anchored in the bay, hundreds of them. They had made a camp on the broad plain near the sea. We were ferried ashore the next morning.

The men lined the beach, jostling to get a good position to see Prince Alexius, for they had never seen him, and they wondered what kind of man he was.

He landed with Boniface and other crusader leaders and clergy. I followed in the second boat with his retainers and servants. Strutting off the pier, he gazed around at the thousands of men who gawked at him. Baldwin of Flanders, Louis of Blois, Conon de Villehardouin, and Hugh of Saint-Pol met him at the beach and escorted him to the camp.

They had pitched a pavilion for him next to Baldwin's and not far from where Boniface's tent stood. He was in the very center of the camp. I helped set it up and unpack his belongings, making sure he had his wine, his favorite cushions, and his clothes.

While we waited for the mid-day meal to be prepared, Baldwin of Flanders said to Alexius, "We must speak to the troops. Some still do not want to sail to Constantinople and do not see your plight of great import."

Alexius straightened with an offended frown. "What am I supposed to do about it?"

"Show yourself to them." Count Baldwin of Flanders said. He emptied his wine glass in a swallow. "Make a plea. Do something that will win them over."

Boniface, who sat with the group, spoke up. "We shall call for a meeting down by the sea where there is a natural amphitheater. Conon can repeat what the prince says to the crowd as he has the loudest voice."

Alexius stood to pace in front of the pavilion. "What do you want me to say?"

Baldwin shook his head. "Appeal to them on the basis of your father's unfair treatment. We will dress you in royal apparel. Someone found a circlet that will appear to be a crown. I think I have a red robe somewhere. You must look kingly. Noble."

"Pah! This wine is bitter!" Alex flung the cup on the ground. "Get me some wine I can drink, for God's sake!"

Boniface rose and looked at Baldwin with raised brows. Boniface said drily, "Do you think you can begin to have proper manners that befit a king?"

Alexius glared at the two of them. "I am emperor. I will do as I like, and two befuddled barons of Europe may not speak to me in such a manner. Now, go. I would take my rest."

Boniface nodded grimly. I imagined by now he was tiring of the prince's temper. "If I were you, I would think about what I was going to say on the morrow. Everything depends on your speech and your behavior."

Alexius stormed into the tent.

Baldwin got in the last word just before he disappeared. "You are not emperor yet, boy!"

They had their meeting. The assembled men spread out across the beach below the place where the prince would address them. Other speakers, set at intervals in the crowd, would relay the message to those further out.

Alexius appeared amidst much fanfare and pomp, dressed in a scarlet robe lined with white fox fur, and wearing the crown they had found for him. He even carried a scepter. I wondered where they had gotten that.

He delivered his speech with the right amount of passion and fervor, speaking of the unjust usurpation of the throne by his uncle and how his father had been treated. Groans greeted his exclamations. The men closest to us seemed to be in full agreement with the prince.

Yet I noticed those who stood further away. They were not swayed by the young man's speech and stood with arms folded over their chest, an expression of something like disgust on their faces.

The meeting was interrupted by someone yelling in a loud voice, "We should make haste for Acre! Now!"

This was taken up by many. There was an enormous uproar that followed, so much so that the prince could not finish his speech.

The leaders tried to quell the disquiet. Hugh of Saint-Pol bellowed to the crowd, "Listen to me! The journey to Jerusalem is fruitless and will cause injury to everyone. As you know, we are destitute and nearly starving! Our stores have diminished, and we have no money to pay you. We must proceed to Constantinople to..."

But he got no further, for they cried out, "No! We will not go to that city and invest it in war!" They started a chant, "Acre! Acre! Acre!" that was taken up by most of the men.

When they got the crowd quiet again, Alexius repeated his promises. With the mention of the two hundred thousand silver marks, they grew still and most nodded their heads in sullen agreement.

The leaders brought forth parchments and signed them in the sight of the men. This, more than anything, seemed to please the men. The nobles escorted Alexius back to the pavilion where I was waiting.

He was shaken and pale. Guards were posted around his tent. I fetched him wine when he called for it and gave him a little poppy juice in it to calm him.

The feeling in the camp was explosive, and we heard arguments, even fights, throughout the night.

Boniface called for a swift departure from Corfu, hoping, I think, to stave off the worst of the dissenters with action. Yet we were there for several weeks, long enough to run the country dry of food for cattle and men.

Finally, the leaders declared we should sail the next day. As we packed up Alexius' belongings, Villehardouin came bursting into the tent. Baldwin happened to be there, conferring with Alexius and Boniface. All three stood as he entered.

His white hair stood on end, and his face was red. He panted from the exertion of the run. "You must come! At once!"

"Why?" Alexius poured himself more wine. "Are you alarmed because you saw a snake?"

"No, you silly boy! Let him speak!" Boniface laid his hand on Alexius' arm. Alexius shook it off impatiently.

Villehardouin took breath and said, "They are leaving."

"Who?" This from Baldwin who rose slowly.

The count answered, "The French. Odo of Champlitte, Jacques of Avesnes, Peter of Amiens, lords of their people and captains of the host. They said they decided that they would prefer to stay here on Corfu. They plan to sail to the Holy Land as soon as they can. They fear the danger of an attack on Constantinople and do not want to make the journey."

Villehardouin nearly toppled over, so distraught was he. Someone shoved a mug of wine into his hand. He drank and continued, "Some of the other armies, perhaps half, will stay with them. Here. On Corfu."

The reaction of the leaders who gathered in front of Alexius' tent was the same. Shock. Fear. Anger. The emotions rippled across their faces as they reached for the wine the servants brought.

Hugh of Blois recovered first and said, "My lords, we are in a desperate position. If these men leave us, as so many have already done on different occasions, the army is doomed and so is the crusade. We must beg them, for God's sake, to show consideration for themselves and for us, and not disgrace us, nor deprive us of the chance to deliver the land overseas."

They all rushed out and mounted their horses. There were some twenty of them, plus Alexius and his servants. I mounted, too, and rode with Dennis, the physician. A small huddle of men stood in the valley near the sea, the French lords who brought immediate disaster on the crusade by forsaking us.

They saw us coming. Surmising we had come to fight, they mounted their steeds and drew swords.

At fifty yards, Boniface and the others pulled their horses to a screeching halt and dismounted. I followed suit and walked the remaining distance. The leaders of the dissenters, Odo, Jacquis, and Peter dismounted, as well, when they saw no swords drawn and that we came peaceably.

I could not believe my eyes at the scene that followed.

We faced off in the valley – those who wanted to go to Constantinople and those who desired to remain on the island. I was surprised at the number of men and troops they represented. Maybe twenty feet separated the two groups. It had rained in the night, but now the sun shone brightly. A bird sang. The grass was wet.

Boniface, Baldwin, Hugh and the others, including the prince, rushed forward and threw themselves at the feet of Odo of Champlitte. The rest of us watched in stunned silence as the leaders prostrated themselves on the ground, wailing and crying aloud.

"Help! Help! Save us! We beg you!"

I could barely hear them over the wailing. They groveled on the ground, throwing grass and dirt onto themselves. Tears streamed their faces.

The prince was the best of all. He cried so hard I thought he would die of apoplexy. His voice, high and shrill, rose above the others. "I will do whatever you want, my lords! Please save me and my father! I beg of you! Do not leave us! God Himself is watching you!"

Mostly it was wailing. I myself was moved to tears.

The emotional appeal worked. It wasn't long before Odo, a tall blond man with massive shoulders and a regal bearing, wept with them, going down on his knees and raising this one or the other one to their feet.

The others of the dissenters followed his lead. Soon all the leaders of the crusade were on their knees, wailing and crying like it was the end of the world.

"We will not move until you have promised to stay and fight alongside us!" Conon declared in his big booming voice.

I had seen other emotional displays when a bishop or churchman preached a crusade and urged others to take the cross, but I had never witnessed anything of this magnitude or depth.

Boniface pleaded that they might have some privacy to discuss the matter further. They went, then, with the French contingent to the pavilions further back. We waited for maybe an hour before they re-appeared.

It had gone well, I surmised, for they were smiling and patting each other on the back like they were the best of friends. Alexius told me later that they agreed to go with the crusade, fight against Constantinople and set him and his father on the throne. But after that, they demanded that ships be provided for them to sail to Palestine within two weeks of making their request.

A sense of relief flooded the army as we made final provisions to sail from Corfu.

All this time the city of Corfu had refused to open its gates to the crusaders even though it was part of the Byzantium empire. We heard violent encounters with some of the citizens, and at times, the city used their catapults on the walls to send a rain of rocks flying our way.

This discouraged Prince Alexius and the leaders. It seemed that not everyone in the kingdom would welcome Alexius with open arms.

As we met together with the troops on that last day, Prince Alexius was brought forward again wearing his regal apparel. Fuming about the lack of support from the citizens of Corfu, he appeared with face blotched red and wide, staring eyes. I thought he was going to have one of his famous temper fits.

They let him speak, which to my thinking was a mistake, especially in his present mood.

He railed against the people of Corfu and called them every name he could think of. Then he shouted to the troops, "You have my permission to raze this miserable island! Kill them all!

Take their wealth! It will teach them to respect me and my empire!"

I am glad to report that there was little razing done that night. We were ferried out to our ships and made ready to sail. Yet the scene saddened me, for I'd seen what Prince Alexius had become.

He was a despot. Cruel. Unpredictable. Unwise. It seemed he had forgotten everything I had taught him. Now I could only think of getting back to Constantinople and finding Tania.

We took our leave of the island on the eve of Pentecost, May 24, 1203.

The sight of the crusader ships setting out that evening was something I will never forget. Trumpeters announced our sailing amidst much cheering. White sails snapped against a cerulean blue sky as bronze shields hung on the sides of the ships, reflecting the sun's rays.

The sea was full of ships of every description, all bound for my city, Constantinople. Every man's heart was filled with joy at the sight, except for mine. I only dreaded what lay ahead.

It took us nearly a month to reach the city.

As we approached, Boniface, Dandolo doge of Venice, and Baldwin of Flanders entered Prince Alexius' cabin and spoke to him of their plans for our arrival.

The prince would wear the regal garments he'd appropriated for his appearances in Zara and Corfu, including the scepter.

"We will sail close to the walls," Boniface said earnestly. "You will stand on the foredeck while Count Conon with his booming voice will proclaim you as emperor over the empire!"

The prince nodded, his eyes shining. "Yes! The people will acclaim me, that I know, for they cannot love the usurper, my uncle. We will proceed to the palace where we will take the royal throne!"

Baldwin of Flanders, a quiet man with great power, smiled wryly. "Well, I do not foresee it happening that quickly, prince.

We must be patient, no? There are many things to accomplish before you sit on that throne. If I were you, I would say my prayers and hope for the grace of God."

To anyone else, Alexius would have retorted sharply. But he had come to know and respect Baldwin's position. He merely snorted and turned away, shouting at a servant who had the misfortune of being present.

When they left, he fumed to me. "I hate that man! Who does he think he is? I shall be emperor before he can twirl his despicable moustache! Here, Christo. Help me into this robe. I want to practice for my grand debut."

As I obeyed him, I said in a low tone, "It would be wise to heed him, Your Majesty. He knows a lot about the world. You must be patient. What are a few weeks or months if you...?"

"Weeks!" He fairly screeched the word at me. "Months? Christo, you have over-stepped your limit. Leave me! I want to see your face no more! Not until I am indeed on that throne in the palace."

He swirled the scarlet robe and would not look at me.

I left, wondering how this would end.

CHAPTER 14

The Grand Appearance

June 3rd, Year of Our Lord 1203

On the eve of St. John the Baptist's Day, we sailed within sight of Constantinople. As the sun painted the sky with vivid colors of reds and yellows, the city lay in stark outline on the horizon.

I stood on the foredeck behind the prince and the others of nobility as the city came into view. Up and down the long line of ships, I heard the "ohhhhs and ahhhhs" of the men who saw it for the first time.

Fear struck every heart from the lowliest sailor to the highest of the nobles. They murmured, looked to one another and genuflected. But not Alexius. He stood straight and tall on the very tip of the highest deck and lifted his arms at the sight.

It was the second largest city in the world. Baghdad claimed the spot for largest, but since none of us had ever been to that eastern city, or would probably ever travel there, this was the most populated city anyone would ever see.

For me, I could not view it without tears streaming down my cheeks. I thought of my friends, Tania, my uncle on his estate, and Blachernea, the royal palace where I'd lived so long. Would the city and my friends be as I left them, or was it all gone?

The crusaders, led by The Eagle on which I sailed, let down anchors at the abbey of St. Stephen southwest of the city.

Boniface and the others conferred as the ship was anchored and a meal was prepared. They could not attack from the land because of the massive double walls protecting the city from the north.

But they could attack from the sea.

The sheer numbers of the Byzantium army gave the leaders pause for thought, especially after viewing the city and its great defenses.

Spies related to Boniface that there might be close to 30,000 soldiers in the imperial army with five thousand of them the feared Varangian guards. The crusaders, who had estimated that they could gather a force of 35,000 thousand, had been able to gather only 12,000 men. It was almost insane to think they could conquer Constantinople. They would be out-numbered almost three to one, and most of the fighting army in Constantinople had been hired and fetched from allied countries such as Bulgaria, Slovenia, Croatia and Asia Minor.

The Doge of Venice, Dandolo, urged caution at the meeting. He said, "You are now engaged on the greatest and most dangerous enterprise that any people up to this day have ever undertaken. We should act wisely and prudently."

He urged the leaders to find a place where they could gather provisions for the men and horses.

On the next day, St. John the Baptist Day, the men readied the ships. Banners and pennants were hoisted to the ship's masts, and the knights' shields were hung from the bulwarks. The fleet transformed itself into the colorful spectacle that had left Venice almost nine months previously.

A strong wind prevented us from landing on the Isle of the Monks, the intended anchorage. As we drew near the city, and the walls towered above us, the ships sailed within yelling distance of the topmost towers.

Prince Alexius stood on the foredeck, but he did not wear his royal robes. Dandolo had cautioned Boniface against it, urging for diplomacy. To display the prince at this juncture would be a declaration of war.

The whole populace, it seemed, crowded the battlements and peered over, baiting the army who had come to attack their city. In reply, many of the soldiers jeered at them with curses and imprecations.

There was no love lost between these Greeks and the Venetians or Europeans, for that matter. Some of the crusaders shot arrows at the walls. None of them found a mark, though.

We landed on the other side of the Bosporus on the mainland of Asia Minor, making harbor at Chalcedon, the royal citadel of the emperor.

The nobles took their quarters in the palace while the rest of the army made camp on the wide plain. Someone reported that while a corn harvest had been cut, it had never been gathered.

I was among those who went the next day to retrieve the piles of corn the Byzantiums had conveniently left on the ground. We laughed as we worked, for the stupidity of the emperor, Alexius III, was beyond reckoning.

Two days later, the army moved up the coastline to another imperial palace at Scutari. I remembered it well, for it was here that I had seen Tania for the first time after she was taken as a slave.

The army continued to forage for food and fodder for the horses as Alexius III finally moved to repel them. He rallied his soldiers, some twenty thousand, and took his stand with them on the narrow spit of land below the walls across the sea from us.

In late June, the two armies were poised for war. The Greeks and crusaders had sent emissaries back and forth which resulted in no peace, only continued anger and hatred.

I wanted none of it. I'd seen enough war to satisfy me for my lifetime. All I wanted was peace. A home. An occupation. A wife and family.

One day during that steamy month of June, I asked for an audience with Alexis and was granted it.

He had taken control of the palace and set himself up as a ruling monarch. This day, he sat on a golden throne-like chair and listened to his counselors, Baldwin of Flanders and Louis of Blois.

I was announced and given time to make my appeal. I didn't want it to be like this, preferring the conversation to take place in a private setting on the basis of our old relationship.

"Yes?" Alexius rose and stretched his tall, lean body. "Make it fast, Christo. We are discussing many things of great import."

"I ask you for leave," I said after bowing to him. "I would like to visit the city. I have an uncle there and many friends. I will only be gone a few days."

"What? Visit Constantinople?" He stared at me as if I'd asked for the moon. "When we are planning a war? I do not think it is possible. Go back to your classroom, tutor, and learn of the art of politics and diplomacy."

I stepped back, my face burning.

The marquis shifted. "I see no harm in it, Your Highness. He has served us faithfully. Let him go." There was a pause. Then he said, "Why not send him as a spy? He knows the language. He knows the palace."

Alexius snorted. "Him? Besides, whatever you need to know, I can tell you. The army is formidable but not commanded well. You saw that only yesterday when our soldiers routed the Greeks and stole a fair amount of excellent war horses and mules from them. The navy is in shambles. The government is on shaky ground." He paused to draw breath. "What else is there you want to know?"

"I would like to know if I have leave to visit the city, my liege," I said drily, "to visit my family and friends."

Alexius glared at me like he did at times as a child when he trumped my authority with his position. "No. You may not. Now leave us unless we call for you."

I bowed. "Very well, Your Majesty."

He held up a hand empirically. "Wait. We may need you. An envoy is coming from the Greeks. I would have you hear what they say."

I wanted to reply, *you just said I know nothing of politics*, but I did not, for I valued my head, and in Alexius' present state of mind, he might order it taken off my shoulders.

The Greek envoy arrived, and after presenting his credentials, he was asked to speak. He had come, it seemed, to offer a peaceful solution to the stark reality of war.

He read from a paper, his voice echoing off the walls of the palace. "Why have you come to our city and our land in a warlike stance when you have pledged yourselves to fight the enemy and free Jerusalem from Muslim control? You have sworn to deliver the Holy Sepulcher and fight against the wicked in Palestine. If you have come for provisions, the emperor is willing to provide you with food and fodder for your animals as much as is possible."

There was a pause while the man cleared his throat. "If you agree to leave, Emperor Alexius III would be reluctant to do you harm. Nevertheless, if you persist on your course, you may lose many of your men and suffer defeat."

Boniface thanked him and the emperor for the letter. "We will give you an answer in a few hours. Please refresh yourself." He bowed and excused himself.

The leaders of the crusade filed off the dais and retreated to another room. The prince had not given me permission to leave, so I found a window seat with a mug of wine and settled down to wait.

The audience was called in a short time. They had chosen Conon of Bethune to present the reply. He had a booming voice and was as good as any I'd ever seen in public speech.

"My good sir," Conon said, reading from a paper, "you have told us that your lord wonders why we have entered his dominions. Our answer is that it is not his dominion. He has wrongfully taken possession of this land in defiance of God and all the natural laws of mankind. This city and empire belong to his nephew, Prince Alexius, whom you see seated on a throne in this very room. We will give the present emperor a place to live and money to sustain his livelihood, but if he cannot see the way to yield to Prince Alexius and persists to oppose us in our just cause, then he had better not send anyone else."

The envoy bowed and received the written letter. He left quickly without much to say to anyone.

After his departure, the leaders continued to debate their next move. Dandolo decided that it would be a good idea at this juncture, as a last effort toward peace, to parade the prince on the Eagle around the walls and proclaim him as their new emperor.

"It will show the people what we intend to do, and it will help us know how they stand," Dandolo said, gathering his robe about him. "Tomorrow morning. Make it known."

They began leaving, but Alexius motioned to me. "Christo. Here is something you can do that may be within your scope." He had taken to finding great joy in humiliating me before an audience.

I bowed. "Yes, my lord? What is this thing?"

"Take this message to the palace. Spread it among the people wherever you go. Do this before the sun sets."

He handed me a writ. Glancing at it, I saw it was an announcement of what they planned to do with the prince. "Then return here as soon as you deliver the message. Two of my guard will attend you."

I accepted the mission with mixed feelings, for I had little choice. Yes, I would be able to return to the city, but I could not see my friends. I would not even have time to visit my uncle's estate and learn about Tania, whether she lived or not.

They ferried me across the sea and landed at the Venetian quarter, sailing underneath the great chain. The harbor patrol sent out a boat to question us, and when the officer saw the writ from Prince Alexius, he allowed us entrance.

The commerce in the great city flourished as always despite the army perched across the sea. Ships sailed in and out of port, cargo was loaded or unloaded, and hordes of people worked, walked and sold things along the docks. The only thing that I noticed that was different was that the homes near the wall on the side of the sea had been demolished.

When the boat was docked, the two guards and I made our way up the hill to Blachernae. It was past dinner time, so we stopped along the way to buy a meat pasty and orange juice.

The taste of that freshly pressed juice set my heart singing. Yet I had a mission to perform and must not tarry. Everywhere in the city there were papers strewn on the street, in everyone's hand, nailed along the way on the sign posts or any other edifice that would take a nail. I picked up one.

The paper was fine vellum and the lettering was bold. I read it out loud. "To the citizens of Byzantium. I, Emperor Alexius Angelus III, warn you of the coming invasion of Franks and Venetians! Beware! They have with them the pretender to the throne, Prince Alexius! Do not believe them or accept him. I am your true emperor, and I beg you to stand with me against these infidels."

I gathered up two others, thinking I could use the backs of such expensive paper for my own use. Some of the flyers did not have so much information. They merely said, BEWARE THE INVASION! and REJECT THE IMPOSTER PRINCE ALEXIUS!

Shaking my head, I stuffed the flyers in a satchel I carried and continued up the Mese to the palace. My two watchdogs panted behind me as we climbed the hill.

They were asked to stay outside the gate when I showed my letter and gave my credentials. I was escorted in by one of the towering Varangian guards who looked as if he'd like to skewer me with the big axe he carried over his shoulder.

I said to him, "The city is flooded with papers. Like these." I pulled one from my satchel. The emperor has gone to a lot of trouble."

He grunted. "Everyone in the palace who could write was given a pile of them. Even me."

We arrived at a massive door, the Great Hall, I remembered. He entered, was gone for a time, and returned.

"You may go in. The emperor is... indisposed at the time, but his Minister of Trade will see you."

It was Stephen Kastamonities, he who had been Overseer of the Children once long ago. He recognized me immediately.

"Ah. Basil Christopher Xavier! You have taken on a new position. Emissary from the enemy?"

I bowed. "Not enemy. They want peace and have commissioned me to bring this message to the palace. I hope you will give it to the emperor and that he will let his people know what we intend to do."

I handed the rolled script to him.

He rose and accepted it with little grace. I could see a lifetime of ill temper sat poorly on his frame and face. He was a wizened shadow of a man, all grey hair and wrinkles.

He unrolled it and read it through quickly. Then he laughed – long and loud.

Wiping his eyes, he said, "Ah. I have not enjoyed such a good joke for a long time. Not since the jesters came here. Thank God they are gone."

He heaved himself to his feet, his former joviality disappearing into a sneer. "I laugh because your friends have a high opinion of themselves and their army. They are going to parade the prince around the walls and expect the people will clamor for his return to the throne. What poppycock! What lunacy!" He slapped the rolled paper against one hand.

He leaned toward me. "Return now, thou puppy, and tell your friends we will be on the walls. It will be entertainment for our citizens. Tell them that all Constantinople will stand with the emperor, of that I am very sure."

"Is that the official answer from the emperor?"

He snorted. "That is a sufficient answer for you. Be gone now! I have better things to do than listen to you!"

I did not see any that I knew in the palace as the guard took me back to the main gate. As I descended the Mese, I stopped now and then and spread the news of what would happen on the morrow.

I was greeted by stony stares, made worse by the crusader knights who accompanied me. But all were interested, and the news would spread rapidly.

The Fifth Hill stood as it always had, covered with trees and houses. At the top was the Christ Pantocrator Monastery. I looked longingly at the street leading up to it, but knew I did not have time to visit my uncle's estate or inquire about Tania. I had hoped against hope that I would have enough time to make the detour, but the sun was setting as we walked back to the docks.

Preparations for the great day started very early the next morning. Prince Alexius was in a fine mood, for he thought he would be proclaimed emperor that day despite the news I'd brought him of the propaganda the emperor had strewn about the city.

He strutted about his apartment like a glorified rooster, shouting commands and laughing at his own jokes. I sickened of him before long, but as I tried to sneak away, he called me back and said he wanted me near him on the ship.

The Eagle was dressed in regal splendor for her tour of the city.

We set out across the sea at mid-morning with a brisk wind and no rain with four other ships trailing behind us. Alexius had sent other men from the camp into the city to spread the word. He wanted to be sure he had an audience.

He stood on the upper foredeck with a glittering crown on his dark head, a scarlet robe trimmed in white fur on his back, and holding the scepter. It was a sight I will remember all my life.

We drew near to the walls. They were lined with crowds of people, the citizens of Byzantium. I wondered if any of my friends stood there.

As we drew closer, Tantalo, Boniface's troubadour, and Conon of Bethune bellowed out:

"Hear ye! Hear ye, citizens of Byzantium! We bring to you Prince Alexius Angelus, the rightful heir and ruler of this land! Give him your praise, your laud, your love. He comes to free his father and take his rightful place on the throne!"

That, and many other things, were shouted at the crowds on the walls.

The announcement and the sight of the prince elicited no glad response from them, however. Instead, we were greeted with stony silence.

Once in a while, someone would yell back. "Take your baby bimkums back where he belongs! We want nothing to do with him!"

This was followed by scornful laughter, and many others joined in on the same note. Some threw rotting vegetables our way but none reached the ship.

Alexius did not move. For an hour, he stood like a wax figure, head lifted, arms out, scepter up. I could not believe it. Even the look on his face did not waver.

Boniface and the others who ranged near him grew restive and angry. "Turn around," I heard Baldwin of Flanders say at one point. "Let us go back. This is embarrassing."

They persisted, though, on our course around the city as far as the Tower of Eugenius that held the chain across the harbor. Then we headed back across the sea.

It was a total failure. The trip back to Scutari was silent. The leaders of the crusade had clung to the hope that Alexius had a large group of supporters in Constantinople and that they would not have to fire so much as an arrow to put him on the throne.

The fact that none of his family or presumed supporters came to our camp to talk with the prince dampened their outlook about our quest, as well.

Now, I sensed deep disappointment over the turn of events. To a man, no one in the great city had shown even the tiniest interest in Alexius or his bid for the throne.

We landed. Alexius, sullen and ill of temper, stomped to his room, throwing his robes and crown aside like a spoiled child. The leaders met and discussed their plans.

Dandolo shook his head. "I didn't think it would work, but we had to try. The Greeks refused Alexius. Our course is clear."

They were grim, and they were angry. Yes, it would be war, for certes.

CHAPTER 15

The First Assault and The War on the Plains

July, Year of Our Lord 1203

It was about this time that I seriously considered escaping from the prince's service. I had no desire to be part of this war, nor of the new government that the crusaders would create if they were victorious.

But if I left him, I would have no influence over him, nor any place in the palace, and I still clung to the hope that perchance I could save him, could rescue him from the course he had embarked upon to become emperor.

On the other hand, if I did not distance myself from the prince and the crusaders, I would not be free to arrange my own life. I was torn between the two options and waited out the days as war loomed closer.

The weather in July turned steamy hot with intermittent showers and high humidity. On July 4, 1203, the entire crusader army, leaders and common men, attended a mass to pray and confess their sins.

The leaders had chosen to fight, for what else could they do? They divided the army into squadrons according to their nationality so that when fighting, the soldiers could understand commands given. I admired their attention to detail and organization. The first goal was to win that strip of land occupied by the Byzantium army below the city walls.

The plan was to attack the city from the sea. Boniface, Dandolo, and the other leaders discussed at great length how they could land the troops and resist the attack coming from the enemy, a rain of deadly arrows flying at the ships, for they must draw in close to shore to unload.

They decided that archers would ride in the front of the boats and cover the landing of the mounted men.

I did not sail with them. The morning of July 5 dawned cool and clear with a slight breeze from the sea. Before dawn, preparations began. The men, wearing full armor, saddled their destriers and led them onto the ships. They stood beside their horses, ready to mount when they drew near to land.

The moment the ship touched shore, the ramps would be lowered, and they would charge in full battle cry. The leaders hoped that the surprise and shock of this would give an advantage.

The faces of the men, from great to least, were grim as they loaded the ships and started out across the Bosporus Sea. Alexius paced his apartment and the balcony railings, straining his eyes across the water. He wanted to accompany them in a ship from the rear, but they would not let him.

By early afternoon, they returned, jubilant, horns blowing, men shouting at the top of their lungs. The story, told and retold hundreds of times across the camp, was almost beyond belief, another page in the long tale of how far the great Byzantium Empire had sunk.

Dandolo led the attack on the city and faced thousands of Greek archers and cross-bowmen who stood on the land below the walls. As the crusader ships drew close to shore, the doors opened on the transport vessels, and the ramps were lowered.

Hundreds of mounted armed knights splashed ashore while archers on their ships sprayed the defending army with arrows.

The first knights drew up in formation and lowered their lances, ready to charge. But the Greeks, led by the emperor, turned and fled, obviously frightened to see the mass of attackers coming toward them, fierce and warlike.

More crusader troops poured from the ships and gathered in their pre-arranged regional contingents. Baldwin led them to the Greek camp, and they spent the rest of the time gathering rich rewards, for the Byzantium army left tents, provisions, arms and food.

We moved the next day to the area below the Tower of Galata on the north shore of the mouth of the Golden Horn. The leaders of the crusade wanted to take the tower because it held one end of the great chain that had been raised against us.

Now we were closer to the city and less protected. I eyed the high walls and thought of the thousands of troops they had at their disposal.

Having never been near a battlefield, I had no desire to start now in mortal combat, to kill or be killed. But I thought about the danger we were in and wondered what I would do if it were forced upon me.

It was nine o'clock in the morning when we landed not far from the Galata Tower. I helped a half-dozen other servants erect the prince's pavilion near the center of what would become our camp. It was partially up when I heard shouts and the thud of horse's hooves.

A contingent of mounted Greek soldiers charged into our camp. There looked to be hundreds of them. The garrison at the tower joined them, yelling like banshees at the top of their lungs. They were on us in a trice, and our troops were scattered, setting up camp.

"Here! Basil! We must fight!" A servant named Lucas yelled, thrusting a sword in my hand. I grabbed a helmet that was lying on the ground and faced the enemy, my stomach churning and my pulses racing.

We did not have time to mount the horses, which put us to a great disadvantage. Suddenly we were surrounded by the armored knights of Byzantium. They were angry, fierce and furious.

I remember little of my first battle, only that I swung the sword with small skill toward the attackers and screamed until my throat was sore. I think I scored a time or two and saw the men fall, but I was so engaged and overwhelmed with the noise, the dust, and the rage of the battle that I knew little else.

Not even the fact that I was wounded.

The Byzantiums cut a path into the very center of the camp. In our group, Jacques of Avesnes, a Flemish knight and son of a famous warrior of the Third Crusade, led the resistance, his red hair glowing in the morning sun, his cry rallying his troops.

He was struck, a lance wound to his face, and went down. He seemed doomed. A cry lifted the hairs on my neck as the Greeks roared with delight and descended on him.

Spotting the danger, one of his knights, a young man by the name of Nicholas of Jenlain, managed to grab a horse that had no rider. Leaping up, he wildly gestured toward his fallen lord.

"To the task! For God and for country!" he shouted.

He charged into the pack, sending hapless soldiers scurrying. The very impetus of his attack did the trick. The Greeks fled from before the flying heels of his steed and the ferocious knight. Nicholas rescued Sir Jacques and brought him safely back.

Later, the young lord recovered from his wounds and elevated his rescuer to knighthood.

It seemed for a time that we would lose the battle, but then the crusaders were called to arms, and soon the whole area was flooded with knights, foot soldiers, and men at arms.

The Greeks were out-numbered and turned tail and ran, a wild retreat in disarray. Some of them managed to get back to the barges at the shore, but most were cut down as it is hard to run in full armor.

The crusader soldiers ran for Galata Tower, for they wanted that most of all, and it seemed unguarded, its gate left open. If this was the moment to seize it, they would take it.

The Greeks suddenly saw the danger and dashed ahead of them to get to the gate and hold it against them, but they were not fast enough. The crusaders reached the gate, overcame the Greeks in the tower, and by nightfall, we held the tower and a strip of land facing the city.

I mended those who had been wounded, and one of the other medics wrapped up my scratches and scrapes.

"First battle?" The seasoned old man said with a crooked grin as he put the finishing touches to my elbow which had been dislocated.

I nodded. "First, and I hope, last. I am a scholar and not fit for this." I waved my hand toward where the men were burying the fallen soldiers.

He shook his head. "Very few enjoy killing, and if they do, there is something wrong with them. Well, I hope the rest of this war goes this easily. Did you hear that the Eagle took out the great chain?"

"No! Today?"

"Yes, my son. They had a good wind and set double hands to the oars. Getting up speed, the ship crashed through that chain like it was cheese. The Venetians, they know how to make ships, that they do."

He trotted off to help someone else.

I sat on a barrel and rubbed my forehead. With the chain gone, the fleet could sail up the Golden Horn to the very foot of Blachernae.

The Venetians hoped to scale the walls using the ladders built onto their ships, and the others wanted to lay siege with catapults and land mines. Both tactics, I imagined, would be used in tandem to take down the empire that had stood for over a thousand years.

Prince Alexius had cowered near his tent during the attack, commanding several of his personal guards to stand near him and not rush off to fight.

When it was over, we set up his pavilion and set out all his personal gear. It cheered him to drink his special wine, to rest on his chair with his feet up, and to be dressed, pampered and served.

From various vantage points around the camp, I glimpsed the Fifth Hill and what I imagined the monastery on top of it. But I could not see my uncle's estate, nor could I gauge what was happening in the city.

With the emperor's army routed at the walls and the Galata Tower taken, I supposed Alexius III would finally do something to repel the invaders. If he rallied his entire army, they would wipe us out as thoroughly as a person cleans a dish.

The next day, the rest of the fleet sailed into the Horn and anchored not far from the tower. Our camp occupied a narrow spit of land near the sea that stretched from the tower northward about two miles.

The mood was jubilant. I heard many give praise to God for His deliverance of the tower to their hands, yet I wondered if it were God or something else that seemed to hand over land, food, and battles to the men who came against Constantinople.

"A miracle!" Boniface and the other leaders proclaimed one evening to the assembled men. "We must move forward to claim the victory. God is with us, and we are confident we can take this city."

The men cheered, for that is what they were supposed to do, yet I saw many of them look across the strait to those imposing walls, fear glimmering in their eyes. I'm sure they wondered if the next battle would end as gloriously.

On July 11th, the leaders formed their contingents and marched the entire army north to the stone bridge that crossed the strait, the Bridge of the Gods, some called it. Emperor

Alexius III had it demolished, but our soldiers rebuilt it in one day with no opposition from the imperial army.

After that, we moved the main camp to a position opposite the palace, Blachernae, near the abbey of St. Cosmas and St. Damian. Thus, we encircled the Golden Horn on the northeast and presented a serious threat to the palace.

The men spent most of the time in the next few weeks building scaling ladders. The Venetians were busy on their ships, constructing what they called "flying bridges". These marvelous devices were built on the top of the masts, sticking out 110 feet and covered with hides to protect the soldiers who would run across to the top of the walls.

The Greeks harassed the crusading army with daily forays, coming forth from the city gates to fight. Frequently, alarms blared out to rouse the soldiers and engage the Greeks. One time, the Varangians guards attacked our camp.

There was no way possible for me to escape the servitude to His Highness, the prince. I could not return to the city as every avenue was guarded, and no one was allowed out of the camp unless they presented a written pass.

Which, unfortunately, I did not have.

Supplies were running low. Someone said the army would starve long before the citizens in Constantinople felt even the least hunger pains. An attacking army could not blockade the Greeks from getting supplies since the walls encompassed such a vast area.

Boniface spoke to the leaders one day. He said, "We must make our move sooner rather than later. We must bring this siege to an end."

Villehardouin agreed. "There is only enough food for the armies for three weeks. If we were to take the city, why, we could feast until next year."

"What are you saying?" Baldwin spoke up. "That we attack them? How can we? We have only a fraction of their army."

Boniface shook his head impatiently. "We are not cowards. We shall do this or die in the attempt." He straightened and looked around. "I propose that we bring the war to them. We shall have the Venetians attack the walls near Blachernae from the sea, while the rest of the army attacks the city from the north."

He paced the small enclosure. "We will split the armies. Three divisions will be in my command here at the camp to guard it. Baldwin, you and your captains will lead an assault on the walls below Blachernae with scaling ladders. Dandolo will take the third division of Venetians and attack the walls from the sea. Speak to your men. Stir their hearts until they are lunging at the bit. It is either this, or we run like dogs with tails tucked behind our legs."

There were several other brave speeches made, some applause, nodding of heads, and grim looks exchanged.

I witnessed this meeting with utter disbelief.

If rumors were true, the army under Alexius III from Constantinople would make mincemeat of the crusaders before the morning was out. But what could I say? I was merely a servant.

I noted that they did not confer with Alexius. He was present, but he never spoke, and no one paid him much mind. It did not set well with him. He tried to interject his thoughts into the conversation, but they shushed him as they would a child.

I wondered what he was thinking. How could he rule the city and empire with the backing of the hated westerners? As far as I could see, he thought only of getting on the throne and this was the way to do it.

The next morning, the army moved out of the camp. I watched from a knob of a hill nearby. It was like an anthill stirring. Long lines of soldiers marched to the strip of land that bordered the water. The Venetians were already on their ships.

They sailed across the harbor with their ridiculous-looking flying bridges sticking out from the tops of the masts.

The sea-faring Venetians approached the wall of the city below Blachernae while a division of foot soldiers attacked the walls, carrying their scaling ladders.

I watched from a distance, going so far as the shore to see the action. For once, the Greeks fought bravely and fiercely from the walls. The crusader soldiers who mounted the scaling ladders that they put against the barbican gate leading into the palace were pushed off and hurled to the ground.

The Varangian guards presented a strong resistance, and they were joined by the Pisans who battled aggressively, defending their wares, shipping docks and livelihood.

The noise was horrific – screams, shouts, the whine of arrows, captains calling to their men in numerous languages, and rocks thudding into the walls as the Venetians employed mangonels built on their ships. The soldiers below the walls employed a battering ram, which created a constant *wham! wham! wham!* Above all, trumpets blared clear and urgent.

Dandolo had drawn up his ships in a long line along the shore on the northern edge of the harbor. Once again, there was a stern resistance from the Pisans, and the wind picked up. A westerly wind shoved the ships back from the walls.

It was at this moment that the old doge showed his courage. He had been watching from his ship and saw his men retreating from the barrage of arrows and axes. They were thrown to their deaths when the Greeks shoved off the scaling ladders.

He commanded his ship to sail close to land. Then, with some of his crack troops, he deboarded and marched onshore, holding his staff up, yelling at the top of his lungs in defiance to the Greeks.

It worked. His men found new courage. Someone was able to burrow a hole through the wall. It was enlarged, and soon many soldiers streamed into the city.

I learned the rest from the men who returned that evening to our camp. They overcame the Greeks and took three towers and a sizable stretch of the wall.

But the emperor was informed of the danger and sent Varangians to fight them.

The crusaders had to retreat, but they started a fire as they left, giving themselves cover. The fire burned all that night and into the next day, taking out thousands of homes, businesses, and lives in the city.

Now the Byzantiums were roused at last to the gravity of the war. One morning, we were roused from our beds with the trumpets blaring alarms throughout the camp.

The Byzantium army, including those troops they had mustered from Bulgaria, emerged from the gates in a long line. The crusaders formed ranks quickly and marched out to meet them. The two armies would meet on the plain north of the city that was bisected with the Lycus River.

The leaders of the crusade knew it was do or die. We were out-numbered. We would surely fail. I thought they would quail before this, beg for mercy, and leave.

But, no. Grim-faced, the leaders rallied the men and spoke with passion and tears about the soldiers' duty to fight like never before to overcome the heathen Greeks in the city.

I'd had enough of this kind of talk for a lifetime, and at this point, I could think of little else than escape. The enemy they besmirched and portrayed as the devil incarnate were my own people. I was a Greek, although I did not herald it about the camp.

When the crusaders formed ranks, they enlisted everyone from the lowliest slave to the highest ranking noble. All, that is, except Prince Alexius. The cook boys wore pots on their heads instead of helmets and carried iron pokers for weapons. Servants and slaves were hustled from the camp and provided with sticks, staves, anything that came to hand. They were told to make a lot of noise.

I tried to avoid being conscripted, but a captain saw me outside the prince's tent fetching water and motioned me over. It was my second battle, and I pray my last.

The sun smote me harshly out on the plain as I kept step with others of my rank – high placed servants who had no training and no desire for war. I grasped a lance someone shoved in my hand and wondered what I should do with it.

The lower servants and slaves made a lot of noise as we progressed slowly toward the city. Masses of mounted enemy soldiers poured from the city gates, approaching us with maddening sluggish progress. It seemed neither army wanted to fight and held back, hoping someone would surrender or stop this madness.

Sweat blinded me and drenched my clothes. With every step forward, I wanted to run back. I didn't care if someone branded me a coward. This was not my fight, and I did not want to die today on the plains north of Constantinople.

The leaders stayed in the front with their battalions behind them. They were making a good show of courage, yet there were side glances and hesitancy that marked both armies.

We were, as I estimated before, out-numbered by at least ten to one. The Byzantium force seemed to cover the plain. Vallehardouin said, "You would have thought that the whole world was there assembled."

The leaders of the crusade rode in the van. Behind them, in the first line, marched archers and crossbowmen. They were followed by two hundred knights who had to fight on foot because their horses had either been killed, eaten or lost. I marched toward the middle of the crowd, surrounded by Baldwin's contingent of French soldiers on horseback and thousands on foot.

It was a beautiful sight, the crusader knights in glimmering armor, their horses wearing bright silks and the flags from each contingent snapping in the breeze. Armor and shields were polished to brilliance. Our soldiers kept moving forward, undulating with the flow of the terrain.

Prince Alexius rode a fine Arabian stallion at the rear, surrounded by his guard. If it looked bad, he could retreat easily and probably survive.

The Lycus River separated the two armies, yet it posed no great barrier, being not of any depth or width. Like two boxers, the armies shadowed and feinted and drew back, sizing each other up, each unwilling to deliver the first blow. The doge of Venice arrived with his men from the ships, bravely taking up the charge to fight or die.

Suddenly disaster for the crusaders seemed imminent. Baldwin, urged by someone in his entourage who told him it was too dangerous for him to be on the front line, turned back to the camp along with his brother, Henry.

When the men in army saw them start for the camp, they cried out with dismay that he was a coward and would bring shame on the army. Hugh of Saint-Pol and Peter of Amiens rode to the front, thinking to take leadership into their hands and lead the army to victory.

The crusaders' carefully laid plans of attack began to crumble as many of the other contingents saw what was happening and faltered in their march forward. Discipline and order. That's how we would win the day, they said, but now it was disintegrating before my eyes.

I watched in horror as two lords, Hugh and Peter, led a small group of knights toward the Greeks, isolating themselves from the bulk of the army, something they had been warned not to do. The men all around me screamed in dismay, for they knew what this would mean for our attack.

But God was watching out for us, because when Baldwin and Henry realized what their actions looked like to the men, they returned to the fore, riding like the wind to reclaim their place in front of the knights.

"Lords, ride forward now, in God's name, all at the trot," they shouted. They had instructed everyone that the command to "trot" meant to move forward. The command to "spur" meant to attack.

Quickly the crusaders rearranged themselves into one long battle line, now within a crossbow range of the Byzantium army with the river between. The crusaders' indecision and moment of faltering had given the Greeks an opportunity to attack, but they did not, and the crucial moment passed.

When the crusaders reached the top of the hill before the dip down to the river, they paused. The leaders conferred with each other. We were out of sight of the camp, so calling for help from the men there was out of the question. I believe they were going to retreat when something caught their attention from the enemy ranks.

The emperor, Alexius III, rode to the front of the line, then sat his horse and shook his head indecisively. He could and should have made an enormous attack at that moment. We waited with bated breath to see his arm uplifted and his shout to attack.

But we heard no such command. The emperor conferred with his captains. They gestured toward us, obviously urging him to action. But he did nothing.

Time wore on. The sun burned our heads. We waited with our restive mounts and heavily beating hearts. Then, incredibly, Alexius III waved his hand in the air and turned his mount back to the city. His captains and his army followed suit.

We watched in utter amazement as they rode to the gates.

It did not take long for the leaders and the army to respond. The noise was overwhelming as everyone, including myself, shouted, banged swords on shields, and made every other noise-making effort known to man. The horses even got into the act by snorting, whinnying and rearing.

As the last of the great Byzantium army disappeared through the gate, Baldwin gave the order for the crusader army to return to camp.

Amidst the joy and celebrating, I sought a chance to return to the city, but the gates were closed. I would have to walk across the river and the plain to the city and explain to the guards at the gate why I came and what I wanted.

I could not. While all around me the men were leaping and shouting for joy, I walked back to camp in anguish. I was glad I did not have to fight, but it was such an inconclusive ending that I despaired for any kind of positive outcome. Our food was running low. We could not last long as we were.

I wondered what they were doing in the city and imagined the disbelief and anger caused by the emperor's actions. It was an act of utter disgrace. I learned later that a group of leading citizens went to Alexius III and told him that if he continued to act so feebly, they would seek out his nephew and offer him the imperial throne.

We slept uneasily, still fearing another attack and the prospect of a prolonged famine if we could not attain more food.

The morning of July 18th dawned clear. The other servants and I prepared the prince for the day and served him a scant meal over which he complained loudly. I ate only a dry crust of bread.

I went out of the tent to find more fuel to cook the prince's next meal and saw a group of men striding up the hill. Byzantiums. They were flanked by some of our soldiers.

The leader of the group came to me and said, "I am Phillip Diakos, a servant of Philoxenites, the royal treasurer. He has sent me with a message for the prince."

I bowed. "I know you, Phillip. I am Basil Xavier, the tutor for the prince. What would you tell him?"

"Step aside, then, Sir Basil," he said with a twisted grin. "My words are for the prince alone."

"Very well. Wait here, if you would."

I returned to the tent and told the prince about the delegation from the palace. He motioned for his dressers to brush off his costume and comb his hair.

Lifting his chin, he said, "Show them in."

After formalities, the messenger read from a parchment. "I am sent to tell you, Prince Alexius, that the usurper of the throne, he who called himself Emperor Alexius III, has fled the palace and the city during the night, taking with him his daughter, Irene, some of his closest advisors, and over 1,000 pounds from the treasury, along with gold and as many precious items as he could carry."

Prince Alexius stared at him. "You mean –"

"Yes. I mean he has gone. Fled."

"Then, who –"

"Listen." He returned to the script. "I, Emperor Isaac Angelus, request that my son, Prince Alexius, be summoned to me and assume his rightful place at my side."

Phillip cleared his throat and glanced up, adding an explanation. "Last night, hours after Alexius III departed, your father was re-instated as emperor. He now sits on the throne with his wife. He has called for you."

Alexius leaped straight up with such a bellow that we all jumped. Then he tore from the tent and ran to Baldwin's pavilion. I followed, and the palace messengers trooped along behind us.

Prince Alexius exploded unannounced into the tent and yelled the news. Boniface erupted with a bellow of joy, and soon the pavilion was crowded with the major leaders of the crusade. When the news leaked to the army, the noise was deafening. It seemed even the cook boys and the stable hands found something to clang or beat.

When the commotion died to a low roar, Boniface lifted his hands. "We have won our objective, praise be to God!" he said. "Let us bow our heads and thank Him this very moment."

There was still a fair amount of suspicion and fear concerning the Greeks in Constantinople. They were not known to keep their word. What if the crusaders came into the city in good faith only to be cut down mercilessly?

The leaders, included the Doge of Venice, conferred with one another for over an hour about the best way to proceed. Dandolo pushed for sending an envoy into the city to speak with Emperor Isaac and try to get him to sign an official charter that would secure the promises the prince had made them.

They chose four men. Two were Venetians I did not know. The others were a Frenchman named Matthew of Montmorency and Geoffrey Vallehardouin. These left after they received their instructions and prayer for their safety.

They returned as we were eating our mid-day meal. The smiles on their faces and the charter they held out to Boniface, signed by Isaac, told the story of their victory. I heard them say that the new emperor did not want to agree to the terms, lavish as they were, but he had no choice if he wanted to see his son and have him share the throne.

Being blind, he had to have someone co-rule with him.

We packed the prince's belongings while he was dressed and combed. The finest horse in the camp carried him as he made his slow progression from our camp to the city. I will never forget that day. It seemed God's favor rested upon the prince and his reign, and all would be well.

Which shows how little we knew of what was to come.

CHAPTER 16

The Coronation and the Fire

July Year of Our Lord 1203

I lived at the palace in the old apartments reserved for the servants of the children. I did not see Alexius except when he made public appearances, or when I was in attendance on him at one of his many grand feasts. Even then, I spoke not a word to him but was only one of many of his servants.

I had no official duties and did not know my title except servant to the emperor, one of hundreds, it seemed. His chief steward consulted with me on his studies once, and I was called to help find an important document.

One day, the prince called for me. I hurried to his apartments.

He strutted about in the old prideful way of his and spoke of nothing but his upcoming coronation. I think he wanted to show off his position and the splendor of his living arrangements, for he said often, "See, Christo? I am now the emperor, and I can afford such things."

I was embarrassed, especially when he got out his crown and showed me how it fit his head.

"Ah. The crown." I shook my head and frowned in mock dismay.

All his life, he had been haunted by the Empress Euphrosyne's dire prediction about the crown when he was a boy. She had reiterated the curse many times in his presence during the six years of his father's internment, taunting him, scorning him.

He caught my meaning with uplifted brows. "Yes, the curse. That is broken, Christo. The empress is now a captive herself, her husband fled the country, and I am emperor beside my father."

"Yes, Your Majesty. I know. The book of Proverbs in the Bible says that a curse causeless shall fail. Yet, if I were you, I would be careful about... the throne. About the crown. It can be a curse if you..."

"Nothing shall stop me, Christo," he said, leaning close with a sneer. "I am emperor of the world now." He set the crown on its stand as if it burned his fingers. "Leave me. I have much to do."

The coronation, held on August 1st, St. Peter's day, was one I will never forget. The prince was crowned Emperor Alexius IV, co-emperor with his father amidst much pageantry, pomp and ceremony. I had never seen so many jewels, gold, and costly apparel paraded in my life.

The feast afterward fed thousands, yet so much food was left over that the beggars outside the gates felt like kings themselves for a week.

The first problem Alexius had to face was his promise of gold to the crusaders. The staggering sum of two-hundred thousand silver marks astounded everyone in the palace, even Isaac. But my former young charge was resourceful. He and his father concocted a daring plan to raid the churches of precious icons, statues, and plating. They melted these treasures down and gave it to the Latins.

They proceeded with this plan despite an out-cry from the religious orders and the bishops. By this means, they were able to raise half the amount they needed. But more was requires, for the crusade leaders would not let them rest without payment, and so, the raiding went on undeterred. This policy fueled the hatred that was brewing in the city against the westerners camped across the Golden Horn.

Sometime during that month, Isaac and Alexius ordered a portion of the wall torn down to appease the crusaders. The people, angry and feeling betrayed, rallied against the order. The wall was their only protection and security, and to see it lying in rubbish was unthinkable.

But they had no say, and the wall came down.

Isaac became ill at ease as he realized his part of running the government diminished by the day as Alexius grew into his new role and began to assert his authority in every area.

As the summer wore on, Alexius decided to tour his dominion and bring as many of the out-lying countries and areas under subjection to him as he could. This was necessary for any new emperor and was beneficial to the royal purse as he received tributes and taxes on the trip.

All of the major leaders of the crusade went with him except Count Baldwin and Count Louis of Blois who stayed to keep watch over the blind, aging co-emperor, Isaac.

Now that Alexius was gone, I decided it was time to quit the palace and put my own life in some sort of order. To my surprise, Uncle was home. He greeted me as I entered the gate. He was just departing for one of his farms, I suppose.

"Basil!" Dismounting as swiftly as his aged legs would allow, he gave me an earnest embrace and led me to the house, calling over his shoulder to his servant to unsaddle the horse.

He said, "What is this? Why have you come with your baggage? I thought you dwelt in the palace now with our new emperor."

"Yes, I did." I set down my bags inside the door and wondered how this would play out. "But he has gone on a trip, as you probably know, and I am not needed. I decided to come home for a time."

"Oh!" He was all smiles again, patting me on the back vigorously. "I see! I see! Welcome, then, my boy. My home is your home until the emperor returns. You can take your old room. No one has used it all this time."

His good will toward me was so obvious it almost sickened me, for I knew it was based on my position in the palace. He thought I was close to the throne and that I had the ear of Alexius and could bend him to be favorable to my uncle's wishes.

The bottom line of that, of course, was favorable business for my uncle, good custom, and more money into his coffers.

If he only knew what being close to Alexius IV meant these days! Instead of favors, the father and son emperors of Constantinople were stripping the wealthy nobles in the city of their money and properties and taxing the other citizens until they bled. I had long since realized in my association with the politics of Byzantium that it was not healthy to be too close to the throne, and I, for one, wanted no part of it.

In the last few weeks, I'd seen Alexius become what I had dreaded most – selfish, prideful and cruel, the predictable end of those who hold too much power and wealth. I had decided that my days of influence with him were finished.

God was calling me to another task.

I answered Uncle's eager questions about Alexius, our journey, and the final battle out on the plain. I promised him I would resume my duties at his warehouse, but he wanted me to return to the palace.

"I need to hear of events from your eyes, Basil. I want you to tell me when it is a good time to visit Emperor Isaac and Alexius."

I shook my head. "I will return when Alexius comes back to the city. But you must know that he has no thoughts of trade or commerce. He would wine and dine you royally to show off his court, but he will be in no mind to talk of business matters. If anything, he would tax you for the profits you earn in the city, for he only wants to put his government on firm footing and pay his debt to the crusaders. He is having troubles on both accounts. Robbing the churches was not a way to endear himself to the populace, for if the bishops and priests hate him, so will the people. And they do. Most thoroughly."

He grunted, not pleased with this news. "Well, get settled, son. Dinner will be served soon."

I unpacked in my old room, and then went to dinner. After a hearty meal, my uncle led the way to the balcony that overlooked the city.

I had a question for him but had not known how to broach the subject. When he was mellowed with wine and food, I thought I would spring it on him.

"Uncle, I have a question for you."

"Speak, then, son. I will hear you."

I cleared my throat. "Yes. Well, I met a girl last year..."

He snorted. "Ah. A girl. Thought you would never find one."

"This one was different than most. I met her at the Golden Bull, the tavern down by the old palace. Her uncle is the proprietor of it, and she came to help with the business. She wanted... wants to become a physician."

He chuckled. "A woman physician? Who does she think she is?"

I merely shook my head and continued, "We met on many occasions, but she disappeared, and I discovered she had been taken to be a companion to Princess Evdokia."

He leaned forward, interested. "That is fine! She is coming up in the world. From a tavern wench to a lady in waiting to royalty. You should be very happy for her."

I shook my head. "She did not desire this, Uncle. She wanted to escape, and just before I left with the prince to Europe, we managed to get her out of the palace with the help of a jester troupe I had come to know. But she was injured. Your servant, Elijah, brought her here. I was taken back to the prince and had to leave immediately with him. I never saw her again. Do know what happened to her? Her name is Tania."

He leaned back, his face darkened, his brows drawn down. "I want nothing to do with this affair." He strode to the edge of the balcony, staring at the lights in Blachernae. "And neither should you. No, I have never heard of the girl. If she was here, she has long since gone."

"Where is Elijah? I missed seeing him upon my return."

He shrugged. "He left of his own accord. I know not why. Ask the seneschal. Now, if you will excuse me, I must look over the accounts before I retire. I pray to God you do not find this girl. She will only bring you trouble."

I stood. "Then our prayers are at war," I replied, crossing my arms over my chest. "She is not that sort of girl. She is... valuable."

He laid his hand on my shoulder, suddenly contrite. "I am sorry, son. I am tired from a long journey. Go to your rest, and we will talk further on the morrow. Good night."

But we did not talk about it.

Sometime in the night, I awoke, startled. My windows were open, and a breeze lifted the curtains and brought in a strong smell of smoke. Smoke!

It was one thing we feared the most, those of us who dwelt in the tightly packed city. For the wealthy citizens, the fear of fire was especially acute for most mansions were located on one of the seven hills where trees and brush grew in abundance. There was no easy way to stop a fire once it got going.

I threw on my clothes and tied on my boots, hearing shouts in the courtyard. Glancing out the windows, I saw the clouds tinged with a red glow down toward the harbor on the Golden Horn.

The servants were gathered in the courtyard, buckets in hand. Some of them already had doused the perimeters of the estate and returned for more water.

Uncle Alessandro appeared in his dressing robe, hair unruly, eyes distended. "This is a bad one," he said to me after shouting orders to his men who wielded the buckets. "Worse than the first fire. Ten times worse. It may sweep up here with all this brush we have around."

He looked about angrily as if it were someone's fault that bushes grew near his property.

"I'll help with the water," I replied, starting for the well.

"No." He called me back. "I want you to go down the hill and ascertain how wide and far the fire has spread. See if you can tell how fast it approaches."

"Yes, sir. I will do that."

"And be careful. Last time, many lives were lost."

"Very well," I called back as I hurried out the gate, snatching up a bucket.

My first intention was to do as he said and return to help defend the estate. But as I journeyed further down the hill and towards the fire, I could not resist the cries for help as the fire jumped from building to building and tree to tree.

Joining those who fought the blaze, I used my bucket, pouring water on the blaze and using anything else I could grab to defeat it.

"Where did it start?" I yelled to another man who stood in front of me as we waited in the line to refill our buckets.

He told me it started by the wall near the Muslim mosque. Some Muslims and crusaders became involved in a battle. When the Varangian guards and Pisans came to help, and were victorious, the crusaders had to retreat. As before, they started a fire to cover their retreat.

The man said, "They set the mosque and other buildings afire. With this wind, it might take out a fair amount of the city."

"Aye," I replied.

Further talk was impossible as I battled the blaze and moved down the street, away from the path of the inferno as it swept its way through the city, taking out ancient landmarks, businesses, homes and churches with democratic fervor. Nothing was spared.

Sparks flew up to ignite a tree above my head. I found my way back to the Fifth Hill where the fire had burned the lower regions. Homes were ignited even as I passed. Trudging up the hill, the cries of the people wrenched my heart. I was burned and battered beyond belief.

My uncle's estate had been spared. I plunged into the fountain to cool the worst of my burns as the servants, some of them burned, too, fetched him.

"I told you to come back here!" he said, disregarding my sorry condition. "I needed you. Where have you been?"

"Fighting the fire, Uncle," I said. "Can't you see? How could I ignore the plight of the people who lost their homes and lives? I had to help them."

He grunted. "I'll call the physician to see to your wounds. Get some rest, and we will talk later."

The fire lasted for three days, consuming a huge swath of the city, 400 acres, from the Golden Horn to the Sea of Marmara. It reached down toward the harbor and even threatened the Hagia Sophia itself. Fortunately, the winds shifted, and the fire burned back upon itself and died.

It took me a week to recover, and during that time, we heard many tales of the extent of the fire and damage to the city.

It was soon after the fire of August 1203 that the Greeks, without official permission, organized and rebuilt the wall that Alexius and his father had ordered torn down.

As I walked the streets and tended the wounded, I sensed deep anger boiling, exploding now and then to the surface. Everyone, from the servant boy to the lord in his palatial mansion, blamed the fire on the hated westerners.

From that time on, it was unsafe for the westerners to walk in the city, day or night. Many of them fled the city, 15,000 by some accounts, carrying all that they had managed to save from the fire.

They moved to the crusader camp across the Golden Horn. How the crusaders could feed them was a mystery to me, for the money they had previously received from the emperor would vanish with the costs of rebuilding the city and helping the destitute.

Rumors of Emperor Isaac began to flood the city. By all accounts, he was swiftly losing touch with reality. He declared he would combine the western empire, Europe, with Byzantium and become the ruler of all. Influenced by so-called wise men and certain priests and monks, he descended into a world of spirits, ghosts and omens from the dead and lost all credibility with the people.

I did not have the long-delayed talk with Uncle. Every morning he was gone before I arose. Since the warehouse was in disrepair, I helped the new manager, a man by the name of Adolphus, set things right. In this fashion, I kept busy from dawn until night for several weeks.

Alexius returned on the 11th day of November. Riding a beautiful white steed, the emperor seemed jubilant as he rode past where I stood watching his triumphant train pass — his nobles, soldiers, servants and guards. He must have been astounded to see his city in such a state, for great clouds of smoke still ascended. It would smolder for a long time.

The emperor did not call for me, and since Uncle was still off on one of his journeys, I set myself to answer some of my own burning questions.

Foremost was the concern I had for Tania and my other friends, the jesters. Had they been killed or burned? Were they like the others I met on the streets, wounded, sick and cold? I must find them.

One morning, I felt up to walking and journeyed down the Mese, watching the people as I went. The people on the street went about their business as usual, yet the tension in the air was so strong I could almost smell it. Feel it.

Men, in groups of four or five, stood at the squares where smaller lanes met the main thoroughfare, their heads together, casting suspicious eyes to any strangers who would venture forth, especially those with dark skin. Thankfully, my skin was not dark, and my mother tongue is Greek. I passed.

Hatred grew daily against the foreigners, the western crusader army camped on their front porch. They controlled their boy emperor and his father who had made no move to help those in dire straits from the fire. Indeed, Isaac and Alexius continued to raze the churches and ancient sites for payment to the crusaders.

They went so far as purloining dozens of silver lamps from the Hagia Sophia church, tossing them in the fire.

The city was dying. The great Byzantium Empire and Constantinople, the Queen of Cities, that had existed for a thousand years, was rotting from the inside out with its corrupt rulers, angry citizens, and vain nobles whose only desire was more money.

My first stop was the Golden Bull tavern which was crowded, as always. Pushing past a group of soldiers, I entered the dim interior and sat at a table near the wall.

It was not long before an older woman came. A stained apron covered her plain clothing, and an exasperated expression rested on her broad face.

"Yes, sir? What'll it be?"

I gave my order. Mussel stew. Wine.

The stew and wine were as good as I remembered. When she returned to fill my mug, I shoved a coin across the board.

She scooped it up. "Thank ye. I will get yer change."

"Keep it. Thank you for your service." I stood and moved closer to her. "May I speak with the owner, Tassos Kostopoulas? Fine man. Runs a good inn."

She leaned back, glaring at me from unfriendly eyes. "I know no Tassos Kostopoulas. Why should I? My husband, he owns this place now. Tassos, he is gone."

"Gone? Where did he go? Two years ago, he was doing a good business."

She shoved me away. "I know not where he goes. He sells to my husband. I work my feet off. That is all I know. Now go away unless you want to buy something else."

"One more question. There was a girl who worked here. Her name was Tania. Do you know her? Is she here?"

"I know no Tania! Leave me alone, do you hear?"

Her loud voice was raising eyebrows and more attention than I wanted at the moment. "Very well. Thank you." I shoved another coin into her hand as she went past me.

She smiled coyly. "That is more like it, sir."

I whispered, "If you hear of this girl, let me know. I will return."

Next, I found the jester's house and knocked on the door which was now painted dark red. It looked like blood.

A man opened it after my third knock. He was not pleased. "Yes? What you want?"

I tried to smile. "I am looking for a man who lived here two years ago. Horatio, and Patience, his wife. They are jesters, friends of mine."

"Wal, they ain't no friends of mine. I rent this house. Don't know who it belonged to before. Now, if you is through, please move on."

He slammed the door in my face.

It seemed my search for my friends was getting a whole lot harder than I'd thought it would. I bought a cup of ale and sat down at a bench in the square while I watched the house.

It didn't take long. A woman emerged, muffled to the eyebrows even though it was a warm day. Without looking about, she hurried off in the direction of the old palace.

Was she going to report to someone? Was the house watched? Why the secrecy? And most pressing of all questions – where was everyone?

I had no answers and wondered if I should try to find Elijah's brother, Jonah, and his wife, the couple who had lodged me previously.

At my wit's end, I walked to the Great Palace and down to the harbor below it, Buokoleon Harbor or Justinian Bay as some named it years ago, drawn as always to the sea. Ships docked here and unloaded cargo for the government. The area was closely guarded, not like the public piers over on the Golden Horn.

A cold wind picked up and brought a smattering of rain while I watched the ships and the men unloading them. I was just thinking of turning back when something about one of them caught my attention.

He was lithe, tall and carried himself gracefully, so unlike the others. His dark hair blew about in the wind, and I caught snatches of song that he sang while he worked.

But it was killing work. Why would anyone sing? Ah! Only one man I knew would do that.

Horatio!

CHAPTER 17

An Impossible Task

November, Year of Our Lord 1203

I waited for the men to get off work. The rain let up, and a wind tossed about the branches of the trees. The magnolia tree I sheltered under dripped and made me wetter than if I stood in the open.

It seemed to take an eon of time, but finally the men filed to a shack near the quay, collected their personal belongings and walked past my hiding spot.

None of them talked. They seemed bent to either get home or to find a tavern and a mug of ale. Horatio came last. He was speaking earnestly to a young man, one who limped and seemed about to fall.

"Horatio!" I stepped out and revealed myself.

He and the young man stopped, frozen. But it took no more than an instant for the jester to remember me.

"You have returned, my friend." He glanced at the young man and back to me. "I am... busy this evening, but we can talk on the morrow. The Hagia Sophia. Main courtyard. Say about the time of the first bell?"

I chuckled. "You are the same. Early. Yes, I will drag my bones from bed and be there."

"Very well." He nodded and continued on down the lane with the young man.

It was an unsatisfactory meeting, to be sure, yet I knew Horatio helped many people and was busy with his ministry, teaching the Word.

As I made my way north in the darkness, avoiding the Vigla, the city patrol, I stopped to catch my breath just opposite the great Hippodrome. A patter of feet arrested my attention. I swung around, but not it time.

Hands grabbed me, held me. I thought at first it was an assailant and kicked backward but only connected with air.

Someone giggled and released their hold.

"You are slow, Basil," the person said with another chuckle. "You must come and train with me."

I turned. It was a slip of a girl who accosted me in such an unusual manner. It only took a moment before I knew her even though she had changed her hair color.

"Philippa! Where did you come from?"

"I've been following you since you left the house where we lived. Come. It is not safe to talk on the street. My house is right around the corner."

She led me to a humble dwelling on a side street not far from the Hagia Sophia. I was hoping the other jesters would be there, but only an old man and a small boy greeted her when she entered.

"This is Helmut," she said by way of introduction, indicating the old man who did not look at me and seemed entranced by a cup of ale he cradled. "And this young man is Matthew. Say hello to the gentleman, boys. He is my friend."

Helmut glanced up and grunted. Matthew shook my hand in a grown-up manner. "Good evening, sir. Please sit, and I will bring you wine." He was small for his age, for his manners and speech told me he was at least eight.

"Thank you, Matthew. I see you have fine manners." I seated myself on a low bench that was padded with a cushion.

Philippa did not give any reason for the people she roomed with, only that they were friends. I suspected she had taken them in, for the man would have been a beggar on the street had he not this house, and the boy, too.

She disappeared into another room but soon re-appeared, smiling. "Here. I found us a treat." She carried a tray with nuts, wafers and cheese.

Helmut perked up and reached for a handful of nuts, but she nudged his hand away. "Manners, my friend," she said. "Our guest goes first."

I took a few and munched them, washing it down with the poor wine that Matthew brought in a metal mug. I'd heard that drinking alcohol from metal causes illness, but I did not want to offend my hostess, and so I took a perfunctory sip and set it down.

"You are back," Philippa stated matter-of-factly. "I saw you spoke with Horatio. What do you want?"

I sighed. "I want, firstly, to find Tania. And the others. What of your troupe? Why does Horatio work on the wharves like a common laborer? Where is everyone? I was gone two years, and I find everything changed when I come back. All my friends have disappeared."

She flopped down on the floor, crossed her legs, and looked up at me with something that bordered on despair. It surprised me for I had never known her to utter a complaint, and she was seldom sad.

Her sigh matched mine for weight and exhaustion. "Well, I will start with your last questions, for the answer to that leads to the first. Horatio will probably tell you more when you meet with him. When you left with the prince that night, we found refuge at your uncle's estate. But only for a few days, for they came searching for Tania."

She helped herself to the tray of food. "She was not well, as you can imagine, having been shot that way. We got the arrow out and dressed the wound, but she soon fell into a fever. I knew we had to get her to a monastery and in the care of a physician."

"And so, you did?"

She nodded, her dark curls bouncing. "Yes. We heard they were coming, so we escaped at night and carried Tania to the monastery up on the hill. They cared for her for several weeks. I went to see her every day, and when she was well enough, we talked. I hope it was a comfort to her. She wanted to see you, but I told her you had left and would not return for a long time."

She rose and paced to the window. "When she was well enough, we took her to the jester's house, to Horatio's. We thought she was hidden from sight and that those in the palace would have forgotten about her. How wrong we were! We did not know they still searched for her. The princess Evdokia was furious that she had escaped and wanted her back."

"Wanted her back?" I raised my brows. "To discipline her?"

"Oh, yes. The jesters, all of us, fell from favor, for the princess and others detected that we had a hand in her escape. They dismissed us and told us to leave the city. That is why we had to sell the house and disband. Some died mysteriously, yet most of us live on doing what we can to keep alive. We are not allowed to entertain on the streets, and if we are caught, we would be sent away. Or executed."

I nodded. "I am very sorry all this trouble came upon you. It is my fault. If I had thought of some other plan to rescue Tania, you would still be in favor with the emperor."

"No, no. It is not your fault, Basil," she said, anxious to reassure me. "We would do it again even if we knew the consequences."

"That is a comfort."

She turned to me, her dark eyes glinting in the candlelight. "Now you are back, and Alexius, the prince, is the emperor. They imprisoned the empress and her daughter. Do you attend to the emperor?"

I shook my head. "He calls for me occasionally, but I am not required to live in the palace. I never see him except for state affairs when I am on duty. I am nothing more than a servant, one of the lower ones, at that, and so have little influence on him. He has forgotten me with his wealth, position and government worries. Yet I suppose I could try to petition him for you."

She laid her hand on my shoulder. "Do not endanger yourself, Basil. We will do what we can."

"And what of Tania? You never said."

She slumped down on a chair and told Matthew to go to bed. "After she recovered, she found work at an inn down the street. Not the one her uncle owned. She went unhindered about the city until just four weeks ago when she did not return home to Horatio's house. The empress' spies must have seen her and captured her."

"Did they take her to the palace?" I leaned forward.

She nodded. "Yes. They held a mock court and sentenced Tania to hard labor to make an example of her, I suppose. I do not know where she is now, if she still lives."

My heart dropped. This was worse than I'd expected. When I could speak, I said, "Well, then, I will have to speak with Alexius. He must see that such a thing is unjust." I rose to pace the small confines of the room. Matthew and the old Helmut had retired.

I rubbed my forehead. "He will pardon her. He must."

She rose to stand beside me, her hand resting lightly on my arm. "Do not put your hopes in him, Basil. We have petitioned him many times about Tania. There is no response." She shrugged and turned away. "The westerners control him, and I doubt they would give an eyelash worth of concern in such a matter. But do as you wish."

"I wish to find Tania."

Realizing the time was late, I said, "I must go. Pray that the Vigla will not arrest me, for I do not have a warrant to be on the streets at this hour."

Before I could open the door, she moved swiftly and blocked my way. "Then spend the night here. You can have my bed. I sleep most nights out here on that bench, anyway."

"No. I cannot..."

"Yes, you can. No one will know, except for my two friends here, and I doubt they will care. Your secret is safe with me."

She drew near. I thought she would kiss me, but she only patted my cheek. "You are tired. Come."

She led me to her bedroom, and with more assurances that all would be well, left me alone. I did not undress. I merely unlaced my boots, laid aside my cloak, and rolled onto the bed.

I think I was asleep before my head hit the pillow.

With Philippa's strange room-mates, I broke my fast before the sun rose the next morning. She said she had to be at her place of employment early and left as I tied on my boots.

Looking back at me, she said, "Be careful, Basil. Constantinople is not a safe place anymore. Those of us who care about Tania have been either cast aside or killed." She cast me a doubtful look. "Even if the empress and her daughter are in prison, they enjoy royal status and have their spies and agents. And they carry their grudges to Hell and back. I will pray for you. Let me know how you fare."

"Thank you, my dear girl." I solemnly shook her hand. "I will be in touch with you."

It was not far to the Hagia Sophia church. I waited near a fountain in the outer courtyard and watched worshippers, priests and high and low officials pass. No one seemed to note my presence.

Just as the bells rang for the first mass of the day, and the sun topped the horizon, Horatio entered the front gate and strode up to me. I had not seen him without his whiteface, but I knew it was him by his walk and his determined expression.

"Come," he said, taking my elbow. "We will find a place to talk. I have much to say to you."

He led me to an inn and motioned to a table in the common room. The door was open, but no one was about.

"I know the innkeeper and asked if we might be allowed to use this room this morning. I knew no one would be here at this hour, and I have only a few moments to spare before I have to go to work."

Someone had conveniently placed a pitcher of ale on the board and two mugs. I plunked a coin beside it, and we poured our drinks.

"I have many questions," I began, "but I met Philippa last night, and she was able to answer some of them. I would like to hear your version of the story, and why you work now on the docks like a common laborer."

He bent his head. "I would prefer easier work, but this way I keep in shape if I ever am able to return to my real work. Patience and I rent a room in an inn not far from the old palace. She works in the inn, cleaning rooms and waiting tables. Between our two meager salaries, we manage."

He drank his ale and wiped his mouth. "But that is enough about me. You are looking for Tania."

"Yes. Philippa said she was sentenced to hard labor and that none of you know where she is."

He shook his head sadly. "It is a sad story. I blame myself for not watching her more carefully. We search for her, but we have not found her. I suspect they sent her out of the city where there are mines. Slaves work the mines, but they don't last very long."

"No. They don't."

"I am sorry to bring you such sorry news. What will you do next?"

I stood and paced to the window. "I will try to find her. I will also petition the emperor and ask for her pardon and release." I turned to him. "Do you have any idea where she might be in the city? Places where they use slaves for the royal household, perhaps?"

He thought of that for a time and nodded. "You could try the prisons. I'm told they use women slaves to cook the meals for the guards and prisoners. They employ slaves in the palaces, both Blachernae and Buokoleon, in the stables. But I fail to see how you can find her."

"I do not see it yet, either. There has to be a way. God will show me."

He stood. "I must go now, Basil. Thank you for your help. Let us pray."

I bowed my head as he implored the King of Heaven to aid us and give us safety as we searched for Tania. I added a request that she would have strength and hope this day.

After returning home, I bathed and changed my clothes. Uncle had gone on one of his many trips, this time the seneschal said it was to Cyprus.

After much thought and pacing, I decided to pay my old friend, Montage, a visit. His villa was on the third hill not far not far from Blachernae. When I left, he had been employed in the palace, but I did not know where he was at this time.

I did not find him home. A servant told me he was in the palace and would be there until evening.

"Do you know in what capacity he serves there?"

He shook his head. "No. But his office is just off the Silver Dining room."

"Thank you, kind sir." I nodded to him and took my leave.

The Silver Dining room. Each of the rooms was named, of course. I remembered that one well, for it was my favorite with silver everywhere accented by the blue of glass and sapphires.

I found Montage at his desk, his grey head bent over piles of parchments. When I tapped lightly on the open door, he straightened without looking over his shoulder.

"Come in."

"Montage! It is I!"

He recognized my voice and whirled to face me, his wrinkled face alighting with joy. "Basil! Oh, my Lord! You have returned. It is good to see you, son!"

We embraced, and he invited me to sit. I perched on a bench by the wall. He apologized he did not have wine or tea or food to offer me.

"That is well, my friend," I said, chuckling. "I do not need anything."

After we exchanged recent news, and I recounted some of my adventures on my journey, he asked, "To what do I owe the pleasure of your company?"

"Well, sir, I came to ask a favor of you."

"Ask, by all means. If it be in my power, I will do it for you." He leaned back and steepled his fingers.

"You know of my plan to free Tania from the palace before I left."

He smiled and nodded. "Yes, son. And you did."

"She was wounded in a street fight and taken to my uncle's estate. I had to leave to join the prince that night, so I did not know how she fared, or even if she lived. Our friends took her to a monastery, and after that, she lived with them. She worked and lived with Horatio and Patience up until just four weeks ago. Then palace spies saw her and took her back. The empress, or I should say ex-empress, and her daughter held a mock trial for her. They sentenced her to slavery and hard labor. I want to find her and free her again."

"Ah. But it is more difficult than last time, am I right?"

"Yes, Montage, my friend. Ten times worse. When I returned, I learned that the jesters have fallen under the wrath of the government and have been disbanded. None of them know where she is."

He stood and paced to the door. Closing it gently, he returned. "This place gives me no peace of mind. Spies everywhere. Please forgive me, Basil, but I fail to see how I may help you with this task. It is... impossible from my view. I am sorry to say it, but she may not even be alive."

"I know. But I have to try." I regrouped my thoughts. "I guess what I want is a document that would get me into the prisons without becoming one of the prisoners. We have reason to believe that she may be working in the kitchen of such places."

"Which prison? All of them?"

"No, I would guess either the Tower of Anemas or Chalke. If she is in neither of those, we can try others. Can you do such a thing?"

He sat down heavily and shook his head. "If you only knew what I have to deal with daily in this current regime, Basil. There is confusion, intrigue and danger at every turn. I cannot move this way or that way without running into someone who tells me I have made the wrong decision. I wish to God I had never come back."

"Can't you quit this place?"

"It is not so easy. Once you are here and have a position and title, you begin to know things. And they don't let you go when you know things. The only way out for me is to die, I suppose."

He chuckled suddenly. "My, how dark our conversation has become. Let me think on this problem."

He suggested we walk in the gardens. Since he was an official, he had a pass that allowed access to them. I remembered my time with the prince and the hours we spent in the gardens. We had fantastic adventures of hide and seek and other games there.

We followed a winding path that led through tall flowering bushes and found a secluded bench beside a bubbling fountain where a statue in the form of a boy spewed forth a stream of water from his mouth.

"I think I can get you in," he said after a long silence. "There is a man whose job it is to inspect the prisons every month. It is a farce, of course, because who cares how the prisoners fare or if their living accommodations are up to the standard? The man who does it has fallen ill, and I wondered who I could get to do it."

I nodded. "I will do it, of course. How shall we proceed? I am in a great hurry, for I feel she may be ill."

He stood. "I will gather the necessary papers and the pass and will let you know when they are ready." He stretched. "Well, I should return to *my* cell, I suppose."

I regained my feet. "Thank you, good friend. I cannot fathom what I would do without you."

He chuckled. "You helped me once. Now I can return the favor."

CHAPTER 18

An Appeal and An Evil Man

November Year of Our Lord 1203

With a renewed spirit due to the aid of my friends and prayers, I set upon my impossible task.

The letter I wrote to Alexius was carefully worded, appealing to his sense of justice and gallantry if he, indeed, had any of those qualities left. I mentioned our long acquaintance and reminded him that I had always been there for him, even to his escape and journeys throughout Europe in search of support. Now he could do something for me to right a great wrong.

He must see that Tania should be pardoned and released, especially since her two accusers were now held in prison themselves and had no legal power in the city or kingdom. I doubted if he had any affection for his aunt or cousin, yet this argument alone would not win the day.

His main concern these days was the formidable predicament in which he found himself. He must appease the crusaders and continue not only to feed the army but to pay what he promised them. Even with all the lands he and Isaac had mortgaged, and the churches they raided, and the wealthy they taxed, he had accumulated only half of the money owed his friends.

Yet if he continued to raze the city and steal from the churches, his people would turn against him. He already felt the blazing heat of their hatred when he ventured out in the city and doubled his guards on those occasions.

If there was any appeal I could make it would have to be about money. So far, the royal hands had not reached into the pockets of my uncle. I risked his anger, for if I sent the letter, and Alexius realized they had not taxed my uncle, they might very well proceed to do so.

In which case, I would be out on the street, especially when he had told me to leave the issue of Tania alone.

I heard rumors on the streets, not so much about Isaac this time, but about Alexius. It seems he was reveling in his new-found wealth and power. He was wont to go to the crusader camp, to drink until he was silly, and to do undignified things like allow the soldiers to wear his crown.

It was said he had women. And feasts. And much gold and jewels around him at all times. If these stories could be believed, it was no wonder that Boniface of Montferrat, his special friend, complained he did not pay them what he owed.

By early December, the money from the royal coffers dried up completely, and the crusader army was forced for forage for their own food. The soldiers grew more and more restive. Incidents of clashes with the people in the city occurred constantly, and the rage grew.

I finished the missal, rolled it up, and sealed it with Uncle's seal. There. That should give some legitimacy to it. I sent it to the palace by courier and waited.

It was late afternoon when the courier returned. He had no reply, and the tale he told turned my blood to ice.

My letter could not have arrived at a worse time. The crusaders, it seems, had decided to force Alexius to give them the money he owed. They sent a formal delegation to the palace, among them my old friend Vallehardouin, who was their spokesman.

He delivered his speech to a packed crowd in one of the largest halls in the palace. The two emperors with their regal robes were seated on a high platform along with Isaac's wife, Margaret. The hall was filled with every high noble and official in the kingdom.

Into that packed hall came the small group of crusaders. In his true fashion, Valledardouin delivered his speech, ending with an offensive barb, "In *our* country, we do not act with treachery."

Even if Alexius had wanted to placate his friends, he could not at this time, for the place erupted into such a bedlam of noise that he feared for the lives of the envoys. Those worthy men shed their dignity and bolted from the room, glad to arrive back in camp in one piece.

At such a time, the courier presented my letter to a high official close to Alexius as they hurried from the hall to their chambers. Such was the mood among those in attendance, and of Alexius himself, that I am surprised it was not tossed aside and trampled underfoot.

"I will speak with him later and give him this," the official said, tucking the roll into his belt. "Leave us now. As you can see, the emperor is in no temper to hear good or bad, no matter who it is that petitions him."

I went to the warehouse and worked myself to a lather, praying as I did. Would Alexius reply? Send for me? I doubted it very much.

I waited two weeks, up until Christ's Mass, and he did not answer. Having no other options, I went to the palace one day dressed in my finest apparel.

On my declaration that I was Basil Christopher Xavier, tutor to the emperor, I was allowed inside and escorted to his personal apartments. Yet I hadn't counted on the number of officials I had to speak to before I could see him.

One of those was a man I'd seen before. He was so changed from the last time I saw him that I scarcely recognized him. Now he wore fine robes, was well-manicured, and combed. Yet I knew who he was and had followed his career.

Alexius Doukas was his real name. Everyone called him Murtzuphulus because of his heavy, bushy eyebrows. When I saw him in prison with Isaac, I tried to avoid him because of the intense evil that emanated from his personality.

He had been released at the same time with Isaac and rose to the position of chamberlain. In recent days, he had been given charge of the royal navy, which was about a dozen derelict boats down at the harbor. Not a great job, but position and title are everything in the palace.

He stood in front of the doorway to Alexius' room and wanted to know why I sought an audience with His Highness. I think he remembered me from the prison, which was good because I had aided their escape.

"I have an urgent matter to discuss with him of a personal nature, sir. Please allow me to see him for a moment. As you know, I taught the emperor as he grew up and accompanied him to Europe on his quest to regain the throne. I think that amounts for something."

He nodded slowly, searing my face with his intent glare. "Very well. There are two ahead of you. Proceed into his chamber, if you will, but wait quietly until I call for you."

We followed this procedure. I found myself in a large room that was set up like a hall with a throne on a dais and benches along the wall. The room was filled with officials, applicants, couriers, and royal counselors. Alexius sat on a gilded throne and was garbed in his regal robes and crown.

With a bored look on his face, Alexius spoke with a monk who had come to petition him for money or some other such thing. The monk was dismissed with a wave of his hand, and Murtzuphulus motioned for the next in line.

A woman came forward with a gift. She bowed low before him and offered it to him in a basket. He rose and thanked her. A page took the gift and set it aside. Alexius whispered in her ear something that made her giggle. Flushing deeply, she bobbed up and down like a stringed puppet, murmuring her thanks.

He waved her away and motioned to me.

As I approached, I saw no sign of warm recognition on his face. His eyes were cold and his spirit withdrawn as if I were a stranger.

"Basil Christopher Xavier, Your Majesty," I said, making obeisance with a low bow. "How are your studies these days?"

He did not smile. "What do you want, Christo? Cannot you see I am busy?"

"Your Highness, this is a delicate matter. I sent a letter earlier but assumed it was never delivered to you, for I did not receive a reply. Please hear me out."

He nodded and reached for his wine cup and a handful of nuts.

I related the story of Tania as rapidly as I could, emphasizing the injustice done to her and the fact that her two accusers were now prisoners themselves.

"She should be pardoned, Your Highness. And released from wherever they have sent her. Please, I beg of you. Give this task to your chamberlain if it be too small a matter for you. Write the pardon. See that this woman is released."

He stood suddenly and paced the dais. His words, when they came, were harsh. "We are offended that you come to us, Basil, when we did not call for you, nor did we give answer to your letter, which we received, by the way. We have looked into the matter most thoroughly. The girl escaped. She was caught and brought back. Her punishment was light compared to what we do with other slaves who try to escape. You should be thankful we did not have her executed."

"But I can pay —"

He lifted a hand regally. "Silence! This matter is resolved. We are emperor now. We are no longer a child in your care.

What we say will happen. Leave this alone, Christo, or it will go the worse for you. Do you understand?"

"What about the aid I gave you," I said in the heat of the moment, "when you escaped Constantinople from your uncle? I was the only one at your side. Together we traveled Europe and to Italy –"

"Be still, you fool!" When he raised his voice, two Varagarian guards stepped closer. He sat down as if giving a verdict and waved them away. "We are in the midst of troubling times. Yet you bring this matter to us as if it were the most important thing we should think of all day. We have had enough!"

He sighed and beckoned me closer, leaning so he was close to my face. In a low tone, almost a whisper, he said, "I am sorry, Christo, my friend. This is the way I must act as emperor. If I am any less, I shall be deposed. Yes, I am beset on every hand. Will it suffice if I say I will look into this matter again at a later time?"

I nodded, gratified that he had acknowledged me. "Yes, Sire, of course. But she is fragile and may not survive if she is left for long in confinement or ... heavy labor."

"Very well. Go and may God bless you. We thank you for the service you have rendered to the crown, Christo. We may call you soon, for there are matters we need to discuss with you."

I bowed low. "I am at your disposal any time, Your Majesty, and dwell at my uncle's estate. Thank you."

He dismissed me with a weary wave of his hand, and the next person in line was called.

As I left, I chanced to look directly into the eyes of the man they called Murtzuphulus. He pierced me with what seemed a rapier thrust of dislike and contempt.

"Make sure you are available, sir," he said in an under-tone. "The emperor does not like to be left waiting. It would be better if you lived here at the palace. We could make arrangements. Your old room, perhaps?"

I shuddered and took a step backward. Every word from his mouth was menacing, as was the look in his eyes. He wanted to kill me.

"No, my lord. I am well, and I will come when he calls. Thank you." I bowed to him and hustled away like the devil himself breathed down my neck.

I should warn Alexius of this man, I thought as I hurried home. But would he listen? Evidently, both he and his father put trust in him or else they would not have elevated him to such a high position.

Yet I'd seen something in his demeanor and expression when he gazed at Alexius that caused me to quake in my boots.

I shook off palace intrigue and set myself to plan what I should do next. I had to wait for Montage to give me the documents I needed to get into the prison, and since waiting is not my strong suit, I went to the warehouse and spent the rest of the day employed there.

It was cold and rainy the week of Christ's Mass. I joined Horatio's little group of Christians that morning and invited them to the mansion for dinner. Uncle showed up that evening, but he was so tired from his journey that he did not talk.

The next morning, though, we had that long-delayed conversation. He was not pleased with me because the emperor's long arm had finally reached into his purse strings, and he somehow blamed me. I feigned surprise and said I continued to work in the warehouse (of which he heartily approved) and to search for the girl.

He did not make a comment about Tania, thank the Lord, yet he left me with a disturbing statement.

"I can no longer leave this estate for a long period of time," he said as we parted that evening, "and have decided to stay here permanently, or at least until I see which way the wind blows politically. I have a meeting with the leaders of the crusade in the morning. Baldwin of Flanders is an old friend of mine, and I know Boniface of Montferrat, too. They are coming here, so I would appreciate it if you could find yourself absent."

I raised my brows. "I am an embarrassment to you, Uncle? What have I done to displease you? I became well acquainted with Count Baldwin and Marquis Boniface when I traveled to Europe with the prince."

He grunted and set down his glass. "I know. Yet I find your association with the lower classes disquieting. Never bring your friends to this house again, do you understand?"

"Yes, Uncle. Good night."

He did not deign to answer me but stomped off to his rooms.

How he found out about my letter and audience with Alexius is beyond me, except that the seneschal kept close account of everything and probably told him. That he allowed me to stay was something, I guess, but I found his attitude less and less approving, and I knew deep in my heart that I should have to find other lodgings and employment soon.

I packed myself food for a long day at the warehouse the next morning and planned to be gone before Uncle arose. Yet I did not succeed. He seemed in a better mood, even smiling at me, as he entered the dining room to break his fast.

"I will be working all day, Uncle," I said as I rose to leave. "I hope that is pleasing to you."

"Yes. Of course, Basil. They should be gone by evening. We will dine here. I have a surprise for you."

"Oh. Very well. Good day."

I turned to hide my astonishment and left the room. It had been my birth date the day before Christmas, but he had never before honored me in any way or given me a gift.

As I made my way out of the courtyard, my mind on his statement and mercurial change, I almost ran into a courier. In the first glance, I saw he was from the palace, and my heart leaped.

"Basil Xavier?"

"Yes?"

"I have this for you." He handed me a leather packet.

I received it and bowed to him. "Thank you. Was there a reply requested?"

He shook his head. "No. Only that he will be in his office."

I gave him a coin. He thanked me and left hurriedly. Taking the parcel to a fountain where there were chairs and a small table, I broke the seal and opened the packet with trembling fingers.

Inside was a short letter. "Basil. Here are the documents and pass you will need. The job has to be done in the next fortnight. You will need a uniform. The prison is Chalke, as you surmised, but you are required to attend to all four of the prisons in Constantinople under the charge of the emperor. You will need to come here for the uniform. I am working today. Montage."

Four! Oh, Lord. To go into even one prison was a trial at which my heart trembled.

Leaping to my feet, I hurried from the courtyard without a backward glance. Whatever the cost, I was eager to pursue this course of action. I would find Tania today!

CHAPTER 19

A Tour Into Hell

January, Year of Our Lord 1204

A cold wind that brought fitful spurts of rain slanted across the Bosporus. I trotted down the Fifth Hill and back up another one towards the palace.

All along the way, groups of men assembled to parade on the streets in protest against the government, and specifically, against Alexius and his father. They shouted and gestured to the palace like they could rout the emperors from their citadel and bring them down through sheer force of numbers.

I'd never seen anything like it in my life.

I turned a corner and stopped. There, in the square, stood the man I most dreaded. Murtzuphulus! He was making a speech. I drew near and heard snatches of it.

"We must revolt! Rise up against the unholy and unlawful government spawned in the courts of the Angelus emperors! They have sold us, body and soul, to the westerners who want to despoil our fair city and take over our empire, the empire that has stood for a thousand years! Look what they have done to it to pay their debt to the accursed army camped on our shores!"

Of course, it was not as lucid or connected as I put it down here. He paused often to allow the crowd to applaud, shout agreement and add their thoughts. What they said I could not write. It was scathing. Rage contorted their faces. They were ready to tear Alexius and Isaac from the throne that moment.

I was astounded. Here this man was in a high position in the government, given him by the emperors, yet he rallied the men in the street to fight against his liege lord and master! He noticed me, and I thought for a moment he would call out to me, but his attention was taken by someone shouting a comment from the crowd. I slipped away.

I had to see Alexius and warn him. This man was not only evil, but he was traitorous and extremely dangerous. The emperor should have him imprisoned for the words I heard him speak. What was worse was that the people listened to him, believed him and were ready to follow him.

Is he planning a take-over? I shuddered at the thought.

Even though my errand was urgent, I detoured to find Alexius. He was not in his chambers. I found him on the tilting grounds below the palace, but it was not possible to speak with him. I turned away, thinking that after I saw Montage, I would seek him out.

It seemed the fates were against me that day, for Montage was not in his office when I arrived. He left me a note, tacked to the door. "I will return shortly."

Pacing the hall, I wondered if I should return to Alexius and demand he listen to me. But I resisted the urge, realizing I could dash about the palace all day and miss everyone I needed to see.

The time seemed to crawl.

Montage appeared at last, panting with exertion and red face. "So sorry...," he gasped as he unlocked his door. "Had an errand to run and it took longer than I thought. Come in. Didn't expect you quite so early."

I didn't feel like sitting. He took his time to catch his breath and pour two mugs of wine. I perched on the edge of a bench by the wall and waited for him to collect his thoughts, sipping the wine.

He seated himself and drank deeply of his wine. "I have some bad news for you."

"What?" I couldn't keep the sharp tone from my voice. *What else would delay me today?*

"The man who occupies the position I said you could fill, the Inspector of Prisons, well, he came this morning. Early. Wanted the pass and the documents. Said he was well enough to work."

He shot me a disgruntled look. "I think he wants the money. He gambles, and I have heard he is in debt."

"But the pass... you gave it to me."

He nodded. "Yes. I told him he had to take another man along, a deputy he can train in case he is too ill to perform his duties. He did not like it but agreed in the end. I wrote him another pass. You will accompany him." He leaned back.

"This makes my task much harder," I commented, rising to pace.

"I know. But you are resourceful. You can think of a way to get around him. Remember he loves to drink and gamble."

"Very well." I stand. "Pray for me."

He handed me a uniform wrapped in plain white cloth. "You will meet the officer at Chalke gate at first bell tomorrow morning. The reports are supposed to be in to my superior in two weeks, so we must hustle with this. The man you are working with is Cecil Demetriou. Captain Demetriou. You can be assured I will keep you and Tania in my prayers."

"Thank you, my friend." I shook his hand, gathered my things, and left his office.

Alexius was still in the tilting ground on his horse, so I left the palace.

I had hoped I would start today but this delay would give me time to think of my plans and prepare for any contingency. I could not go back to the estate, so I headed down to the docks. Across the channel, I saw the smoldering hulk of a vessel. I inquired what happened.

It seems some hardy Greek lads, who never surfaced to claim the deed, decided to set the Venetian fleet to flames. They concocted a fiery mess of combustibles, placed it on a boat, and set it aflame.

They towed the burning mass out into the current of the Bosporus, releasing it when they figured it was on its course. If all went like they had planned, it would have collided with the Venetian fleet, some hundred ships of all sizes and kinds, and set them afire. If the Venetians lost their fleet, they would be helpless and could be picked off at the Greeks' leisure.

But it did not work. The burning boat sailed toward the Venetians ships, but the Greeks did not take in account how good sailors the Latins are. They had posted guards, and the men saw the floating inferno before it bumped into their flotilla. They lost one ship, and it was reported that a few men were burned, but none died, and there was no great loss to their fleet.

The Greeks were crowing about it, feeling in fine fettle, but from what I could see, they had been defeated in their purpose and had only succeeded in stoking hatred hotter and brighter that burned between the crusaders and the people of Constantinople.

War could not be delayed much longer. I determined to find Tania and flee the city as soon as I could. I knew Uncle would stay to protect his property, but I had no such ties, and wanted only to be away from the city and the impending doom.

I turned to my work in the warehouse and occupied myself for the rest of the day. That evening, I dined with Uncle, listening to his enthusiastic plans for the day when the westerners would completely control the city. I told him of the attempt to burn the Venetian fleet, and he shook his head, saying they should welcome the Latins to our city and submit to them.

"That would be sensible," he concluded, "rather than war."

I did not rise to that bait, only nodded. "Well, Uncle, I am going down to the warehouse early in the morning. We have a shipment coming in, and I should be there to make sure it is taken care of properly."

I promised myself I would make a perfunctory visit to the warehouse to keep my conscience quiet.

He slapped me on the back and congratulated me for my labors on his behalf. Then he presented me with his surprise. It was a beautifully illustrated portion of the Holy Bible on vellum, a smooth yellow paper.

"I found it at a bazaar," he said. "Some monks were selling them. I thought you would like it."

I did and told him so. "Thank you, Uncle. I will keep this as a memento. It is beautiful!" I rubbed my finger across the title page which was embellished with flowers and vines.

He seemed pleased that I liked it and went off to his room.

Early the next morning, I broke my fast and gathered the things I would need this day. No one was about at the warehouse, so I unlocked the door, and inside, in my office, I donned the uniform of the royal army, red and black, picked up my back pack and left.

Captain Demetriou appeared promptly as the bells on the great church pealed. He was an older man, greying at the temples, with a protruding stomach, large neck and head, and red-rimmed eyes. He was carrying a satchel and gave me a cursory inspection as he strode toward me.

His sharp eyes met mine, a rapier glance. "Captain Demetriou. You must be Basil Xavier?"

"Yes, sir. I am to learn from you. We start at Chalke?"

"Yes. Then move on to the Legion Prison, then the prison at the old palace, and then Anemas Prison near Blachernae. Today we will inspect Chalke."

"What do you want me to do, sir?"

"Follow behind me. Listen and take careful note of everything I do. Fetch and carry. Let us begin." He saluted.

I returned the salute, feeling rather silly, and followed him through the gate. He showed his pass, and I showed mine. The guard at the gate saluted but said nothing.

We proceeded to the lower floor. The smell, as always, nearly knocked me over as we descended into what I thought of as a cold hell. We passed several armed guards on our way down the hall but did not see the cells. I looked around for slaves who cleaned, cooked or carried meals, but I saw none.

Demetriou strode to the warden's office, a room the size of a large *necessarie,* and stopped just inside the doorway.

"Proscus! Greetings! Time for the annual."

His words roused a man who had slumped over a table in either a nap or a drunken stupor. He raised his head. He had a long, untrimmed beard and bleary eyes.

He rose slowly. "Greetings, Captain. So glad you could visit us. Please be seated. I will be right back." He gave me a quizzical look and tugged up his trousers as he trotted from the room.

Demetriou took two steps into the office and perched on a wooden table. The room contained, besides the table, two rickety wooden chairs, and a wall of shelves filled with wooden boxes. I ascertained that each box contained parchments. These were the records of the prisoners. On top of the shelves was an assortment of wine bottles.

Demetriou took one bottle and poured himself a mug of wine. He did not offer me one. When Proscus, the warden, returned, he poured himself a drink and they proceeded to talk of everything but the business at hand.

I grew restless and said, "Could I use the *necesarie,* please?"

Proscus nodded. "Down the hall. First door before the cells."

As I left, I heard him say, "You will want to take your deputy around the prison, I suppose. Show him the sights?" They both laughed.

I used the dirty little place and emerged, wondering how I could find out if there were any slaves here, and if Tania did, indeed, live and work here.

When I returned, I saw they had finally gotten down to business. Proscus procured a sheaf of parchments and handed them to my mentor who stuffed them into his satchel.

"Well, let us have us another drink, and then I must be on my way," he said.

Proscus was more than happy to oblige him.

"If you don't mind, sir," I said, "I would like to tour the prison. I thought we were supposed to inspect it to ascertain if it meets the emperor's standard. I read about this job before I came, sir. That's what the official duties of the Inspection Officer entail."

Demetriou groaned. "Oh, very well. I was hoping to avoid that. I've been through this place so many times, I could do it with eyes closed. Proscus, why don't you take him around? Xavier, make notes of anything that does not seem proper according to the emperor's standards. Whatever that is." He sneered at me as he poured himself another drink.

"Go easy there, mate," Proscus said. "That's me best wine, and you have three more prisons to inspect. You'll be doing it on your knees if you keep drinking like that."

He sighed and took his key ring from a peg. "Come along, Xavier. If you must, you must, but I advise you to keep your stomach clamped down hard because this isn't pretty."

I trailed along behind him as he went up and down the rows of cells, keeping a kerchief over my nose to mask some of the smell. But I could not avoid it all.

Some of the prisoners were sleeping, some were awake and banging at the rails, some were just staring off into space. There were three levels. I did not know if I could survive all three, but I did, and I still did not see any sign of slaves.

As we trudged up the stairs, I asked, "Where is the kitchen? Don't you prepare meals here for the prisoners? I should take a look at them, too."

He shrugged. "If you want. It's not much."

We ascended the stairs to the top floor, the entryway. At the end of a long corridor, he opened a door.

He went inside. I followed him.

"The conditions here aren't the best," he said as I gazed at the sorry room they called a kitchen. "But we have to haul all the water we use in and out. There ain't no place to toss garbage. It has to be carried out, too. You seen enough?"

"Are there slaves who work here?" In the one quick glance around, I hadn't seen anyone, slave or free.

"We keep some down below. I didn't take you to their cells. Yes, the slaves prepare the meals, such as they are. Any other questions?"

"May I see the slaves' cells?" I wondered why he hadn't shown them to me before.

He was at the end of his patience. "And go down them steps again? I ain't doin' it, sonny boy. My legs is tired out from running up and down all day like I have. Here. You go down and see. The first key is to the door. Second key, cells. You won't like what you see, but it's the best we can do. Wait. You can't go alone." He called to one of the guards who sat in a cubby-hole at the end of the hall.

"Hey, you! Miklanous. Accompany this man to the slaves' cells!"

The guard muttered a curse under his breath and came to stand beside me. He carried a torch. I received the keys and started down the stairs.

I thought I could out-distance him and have a few seconds to my own, but he kept close to my back, ill will pouring from him with his stream of profanity.

At the bottom of three flights of stairs, I unlocked the door and entered the slaves' quarters. They, too, were locked behind cell doors, both men and women. To my gratification, Miklanous grunted and said he would wait outside. He handed me the torch.

I walked the length of the corridor, peering in each cell as I passed. At the last one, I stopped and bent forward. A girl lay on a pallet. Dirty straw covered the floor. She was young. Dark hair.

"Tania? Is that you?" I called softly.

At first, she did not respond. When I called the second time a little louder, she lifted her head and stared at me.

The girl was not Tania.

CHAPTER 20

A Midnight Meeting and A Revolution

January-February Year of Our Lord 1204

The girl sat up and pushed back her matted hair.

"Tania?" I said again, still hopeful. Surely, this half-starved, filthy girl could not be the woman I loved.

But she straightened and pierced me with a bright stare. Then she came to the cell door, her chain clanking as she moved. She was manacled to the wall. My heart went out to her, whoever she was.

"Yes? Who... who are you?"

It was her voice! I realized she might not recognize me in my guard's uniform. "Basil. Your friend. Do you remember me? Is it you, Tania? Please tell me."

"Basil?" She gripped the rails and nearly fell. "Yes, yes. I am Tania. Or, I once was. Oh, my Lord. I have prayed so hard..." She wept, reaching for me through the rails.

"My darling!" With one hand, for I held the torch in the other, I enclosed her hands in mine, knowing that we had only seconds before I would have to leave.

"I will get you out of here, that I swear." I was crying, but I did not know it then. All I could think was that I had found her.

The other prisoners, on seeing that I paid special attention to the girl, clanged their cups on the bars and set up such a noise that I thought the whole prison would be alerted soon.

"Now?" She reached through for me. "Please, Basil. I cannot... cannot do this... much longer."

I shook my head. "I cannot get you now. But I will come quickly. I promise. Endure a few more days. Many are praying for you."

Miklanous burst into the room. "What is the uproar! Silence! Or you will taste the lash on your miserable hides!"

The slaves quietened but stared with evil intent at the guard. I hurried down the corridor and exited with him right behind me.

After locking the door, I said, "One of them grabbed for me. They all started shouting. I think they thought it was a chance to escape or to kill me, I know not which." I shuddered and handed him the torch. "Remind me not to go there again. It is the place of nightmares."

He grunted. "I could have told you. Well, did you get enough for your report?"

"Oh, yes. More than enough. Cannot something be done for those poor souls?"

He led the way down the hall and up the stairs. "They die in a short time, and you must remember they is payin' for their crimes against the emperor, else they would not be here. The warden, he says there is nothing we can do for them. They work and sleep and work again. And then they die, and we throws their bodies on the garbage heap."

"When do they work? I have to write that down in my book."

"At cock crow in the morning, they prepare food and take it to the prisoners. All is fed and they is back in their cells by the time of the first bells. Same thing for evening. They is out of the cells by the Vespers bell and back in before Matins."

I nodded. He left me at the second floor and resumed his watch with his bottle of ale. I went on up to the office, but before I returned to the captain, I made a detour to the stinking *necessarie,* praying the captain would not come.

There, I drew out a small box I had in a script I carried at my waist. Inside the box was soft clay. It took no more than a few seconds to get an impression of the first and second keys on the ring. I made one of the third key, too, hoping that it unlocked the chains on the slaves' legs.

Back in the tiny warden's office, I nodded to Demetriou and said, "I am finished and can write my report."

He stood and plunked down his mug. "Thank you, Proscus, for another inspection well done. I shall write a good report for you. And your excellent wine."

The warden looked at his empty bottle in distress. "Very well, captain. Keep up the good work."

We left the prison. I was never so glad to breathe fresh air and to see the sun and the blue sky. How would it be to live in the dungeon and never see the sun? To live in darkness? I trembled at the thought and recalled how Tania begged me to hurry. She was sick and could not last much longer.

Demetriou led the way to the Legate Prison which was located in the Old Palace where some of the legions of the Byzantium army dwelt. It, too, was under-ground, and he imbibed deeply of the wine the warden gave him while I toured the place with a soldier.

When we exited the palace and paused in the street, he said, "Well, how did you like the j...job?"

"I cannot say I enjoy it," I said through clenched teeth. I had seen more suffering, grief and pain in this one day than I had all my life, and it sickened me.

He chuckled and taking a step forward, swayed. "Two more... to go, Bashil Tra... Cha... Xavier. You took long time to inshpect the slave's chells in Chalke. Did you find a schweet-heart down there?" He burst into laughter at his feeble attempt at a joke.

I had to remind myself that he was more than a little drunk. "I see you took no pains to inspect the lower levels. Is your sweetheart a bottle of wine?"

He swung at me and missed. Indeed, he nearly lost his balance. I helped him stand, then supported him as we walked up the Mese.

"Where are we meeting tomorrow?" I asked when he said he would leave me for his lodging.

"To...morrow? Oh, no. I do not worksh two days together. Need to write my reportsh. Nexcht week, Bashil. Firsh bell on... shame day, next week. Outside Anemash. You will like Anemash. It'sh worshe than... than Chalke."

I nodded. "I know. Very well, have a good evening."

"You, too." He saluted, almost fell, and staggered off down the street.

I hurried up the street and stopped at a blacksmith's shop that I knew. Bringing out the clay, I asked the man if he could make me the keys. He examined it and nodded.

"If you will give me a few days. I am behind in my work orders."

My heart sank. I wanted it done sooner than that. "Very well. But if you could hurry this through faster, there will be a bonus for you."

He nodded. "It is a small job. Tomorrow, then. About this time."

I stopped at the warehouse and changed into my clothes. By the time I climbed the Fifth Hill, the sun was setting.

It had been a long, trying day, and for the first time in my life, I wanted to drink myself to oblivion and sleep a week. But I could not, not when Tania needed to be rescued, and I needed all my wits about me.

Uncle greeted me as I entered the house. "Basil! There you are! Where have you been? I have scourged the city, looking for you."

"Well, I went to the warehouse. If you will excuse me, I am very tired and need..."

"I need an explanation!" he said, towering over me in his best intimidating way. "I checked the warehouse. They said you had been there earlier but did not stay. Where have you been?"

"I went down to the old city, Uncle. I was…"

"Looking for that girl, I suppose."

"You might say that."

He grunted and turned away. "I thought better of you than that. But, no matter. Clean up and dress in your finest. The emperors have invited me to a dinner at the palace, and you will come with me. I am to be seated on the dais with Alexius himself."

"But, I have to…"

"You *have* to obey me, Basil! Now! We leave shortly."

There was no debate when he used that tone. And I was living under his roof, so I owed him respect and obedience. I hurried to my room, bathed and changed as quickly as I could.

When I reappeared, he was ready for me. We mounted two of his finest steeds and rode with all haste to the palace.

The comparison between the prisons and the palace was almost too much for me. I could hardly bear the noise, the grandeur, the food, the displays of wealth all around me. It sickened me. I wanted to scream and throw something at someone, but I could not.

Uncle was in fine form that evening. He was seated closer to Alexius than I. My neighbor was not charming. It was Murtzuphulus! He grinned and leaned toward me when he recognized me.

"Ah. Basil Christopher. Christo. The great tutor to Alexius." The way he said it made it the worst crime ever committed.

"Yes, sir," I said, drinking my wine. "But now just a humble servant."

He laughed, which from him was a chortle. "I saw you earlier this morning, my young friend. You were on the street. Heading off to your warehouse?"

"Well, it is not mine. And, yes, I went there for a time."

"Not for long, though. I hear you spent some time in the prisons today. Chalke, none the less, where we first met. How did you find it?"

He knew I'd taken the job as inspector. "It was in its usual state of... chaos and disrepair. I was helping my old friend, Montage. He told me he needed someone to go with the inspector on his rounds. I was happy to assist."

"I see." He nodded to the priest at the head table who stood and started the meal with a lengthy prayer.

When it was ended, he said, "I expect you will rise in power and prestige now that your protégé is on the throne. Any young man would want that. What will you do next, I wonder? Become the under-chamberlain?"

I laughed. "You have me wrong, sir. There is nothing I desire more than to be left alone to work at my figures in the warehouse. I have a good life with my uncle. Why should I want to rise with Alexius? He does not want me. See? He never calls for me."

At that moment, a royal servant approached me from the back and said, "His Royal Highness, Alexius IV, would like to speak with you, Basil Xavier."

I cast a glance at Murtzuphulus. He seemed busy talking to the nobleman on his other side, but he gave me a look that said, *I see. Never calls for you, eh?*

Alexius shoved back when he saw me. "You should be seated here, Christo. Beside me. I would honor you."

"No, I do not desire that, Your Highness. I like where I am sitting. Did you want to speak to me?"

"Yes. Afterwards. Watch when I leave and come to my apartments. There is something I would like you to do."

I bowed. "Yes, Alexius, anything." Then, softly for his ears alone, I said, "There is something I would speak to you about."

He lifted his brows as if he wanted to know right then what it was, but I nodded to him briefly and returned to my seat.

The meal was torment. I could not eat. Exhaustion swept over me in great waves so much that I feared I would fall asleep at the emperor's table and that Murtzuphulus would arrest me for disrespect.

At last, Alexius arose and after a short speech, turned and left with his guard and dozens of his attendants. Murtzuphulus and I stood. I told Uncle that I was detained and that he should return home without me. He tried to protest, but I walked away. One does not keep the Emperor of the Byzantium Empire waiting.

I wished the awful man at my side would go away, but he strode purposefully at my side as we entered the emperor's private chambers.

Alexius stood at the windows, staring out in the darkness over the Golden Horn. I could tell he was troubled, for his shoulders were hunched and a frown puckered his brow. His eyes were red-rimmed from little sleep.

He welcomed me and offered me drink. I shook my head. "What is it you want, Your Majesty?" He liked to get down to the matter at hand, and at this point in the day, so did I.

"I... I have an appointment tonight. Down by the docks."

"Tonight?" I could only think it was with one of the women he was rumored to consort with. But the docks were an unlikely place for an assignation.

He nodded. "They are all after me, Christo. After the money I promised them. Boniface was here earlier, ranting on about it, like I could pull the one hundred thousand marks I owe them from my pocket like a magician. It is the curse. The curse of the crown that my aunt used to speak of. Now, this."

He sat suddenly, and two of his serving men lifted his feet to a cushioned stool. Another two relieved him of his cape. A pretty young girl started massaging his neck.

I plunked down on an embroidered stool in front of him. Murtzuphulus haunted the room, lurking in the shadows, listening to our conversation.

"What happened?" I leaned forward, knitting my fingers together.

"The doge. He sent an envoy just before the feast. Said he wanted to meet with me. Just me. Down at the Venetian quay. Said I was to come alone." He lifted his head and glared fiercely. "Well, I won't! Does he take me for a fool? I shall bring a guard. And you."

"Me?" I sat back, shocked. "But, Your Highness..."

"Be still," he barked. "No one will object to someone like you. I want a witness. You will stand in the back near the horses. He will not even notice you." He paused. "Will you come, Christo? I need you."

I nodded. "Of course, I will come. When do we leave?"

He glanced at Murtzuphulus who nodded. Alexius said, "Now. They have the horses ready. Come."

We rode to the wall and approached a small gate in the Venetian quarter. The guards had cleared the area, so no one was about when we dismounted. He nodded to me as I held the reins. I handed them to a guard and followed him through the gate, staying in the rear.

Two Venetian galleys rode the waves close to the shore, and an old man stood on the pier. Each of the galleys contained archers who had their arrows pointed in our direction. Alexius, his robe blowing from the wind, strode out to meet the doge.

"You wanted to see me, Dandolo?" he said, his clear voice ringing over the water.

"I rather doubted you would come." He lifted his sightless eyes to Alexius.

"What do you want?" Alexius' sharp tone reflected his impatience. "Out with it."

"Why do you act with such vulgar ingratitude, my son?" Dandolo's response came immediately with vile scorn. "You know the Franks and my people put you on the throne with your father. You made promises to us. You owe us one hundred thousand pounds of silver. Ships. Soldiers. The church turned to the Roman Catholic faith. Now you must pay."

Alexius snorted, an undignified sound. "We have paid you what we can, and we are working on the rest. We have stripped the city and our treasury of its riches and melted down rare and precious icons for your greedy purse. How much more of this can we bear? Is there no end to your insatiability?"

"I will not bandy words with you. I am not one of your pet courtiers. Either you pay, or we will take what is rightfully ours. What is your answer? Speak plainly."

Alexius raised his voice and spoke each word with deliberate enunciation. "Truly. I shall speak in simple words so you and your friends will understand me. You and your armies must vacate my lands. If you do not leave, we will move to evict you. Is. That. Clear. Enough?"

Silence enjoined the darkness as the water lapped against the dock. Both were breathing heavily. Dandolo straightened. His voice was calm, yet hard and decisive.

"We plucked you from the shit, you miserable boy, and we shall cast you back. I thought once you would make a fine ruler, but you are nothing but a spoiled child. For all I care, go to Hell with the rest of your Greek rabble." He turned on his heel and strode to the boat that had ferried him to shore.

Alexius laughed, but it was a lonely, forlorn sound. He gathered his robe about him and made for the horses. I followed.

He was not talkative on the return trip to the palace. I feared for him and for the empire, for the folly of it all smote me like a slap in the face. He had desired to become emperor at any cost, and now he was turning against his friends, the crusaders, who put him there.

Yet, from his perspective, he had paid some of what he owed and only wanted more time to pay the rest. It all came down to greed, the lust for power, bullying, deception and lies.

If Alexius turned against the westerners to appease his own people, he was in a dangerous position from which I could not save him. Indeed, it had grown beyond me, and I seemed only a bystander, an observer as events turned violent and deadly.

As we parted ways at the palace, I said to Alexius in a low voice. "Sire, there is something I have been meaning to speak with you about."

"Not now, Christo. Save it for tomorrow." He started to rush away, but I held his arm.

He looked down at my hand and stared at me. "Unhand us, you fool!"

"Listen to me, Alexius! For once in your life!" I was panting with emotion. He continued to stare at me, his mouth drawn to a stern line, his eyes flashing with anger. I had only a few moments before he either called his guards or stomped away.

"It is about Murtzuphulus. He speaks to the crowds in the city. I heard him, saw him. He tells them to rebel against you, against your father. He says he can be a better ruler. I am afraid, my lord. Afraid for you..."

He laughed and brushed off my hand. "Old Murtzy? You are jesting. He looks like an ape, but he is kindly at heart and would not harm a hair of our head. He showed his loyalty to our father, as you well know, by spending several years in prison with him. That's what you wanted to tell us? Be off with you! We would seek our bed."

He hustled away without another word.

In the days that followed, my own cares and plans were set aside when Alexius demanded more of my time. I procured the keys for the cells, kept the uniform and pass, and enlisted the help of Horatio to rescue Tania, yet the days flew past in a blink, it seemed, and the conflict between the Greeks and westerners heated to the breaking point.

During the first week of February, the Greeks emerged on horseback from of the city and tried to attack the crusader camp, yet they were beaten back by sheer numbers (they did not bring in the mercenary armies they could have) and the ferocity of the crusaders. Murtzuphulus, in a grand show of support for his people, rode in the van.

At one point, he was cast to the ground and could have perished had the western soldiers been fast enough to get to him, but one of his own soldiers saw his peril and rescued him. The knights hustled back to the safety of the walls.

From the Greek perspective, it was a success and showed the westerners the might of their army. From the crusader side, it was a pathetic attempt to harm them and force them to leave.

Whatever the case, it caused more tension and hatred in the city, and I believe paved the way for the tragedy that was to come.

In the wake of this first clash of forces, unruly mobs in the city took over the Hagia Sophia where the senate, bishops and senior clergy met, demanding they put another man up as emperor instead of Alexius.

After three days, the senate chose Nicholas Kannavos, a young nobleman who was known to be a good warrior and leader. On January 27th, 1204, he was anointed emperor, yet he did not leave the church and did not take possession of Blachernae.

Alexius was appalled at this and appealed to his friends across the strait, to Boniface and Baldwin and the others, for help. He promised that if they drove out Nicholas Kannavos, he would give them Blachernae, which shows how desperate he had become.

It was this decision to bring the crusaders into the city and give them the royal palace that led to Alexius' downfall.

Murtzuphulus promised the people that if they put him up as emperor, he would rid the city of the crusaders within a week.

I was desperate to free Tania, yet these circumstances made it impossible to go anywhere near Chalke prison which was almost next door to Hagia Sophia. I met with Horatio and

Patience, we prayed for wisdom, and for Tania, and delayed our plans yet again to rescue her.

On the morning of February 28th, I awoke to dreadful news, carried to my uncle's estate by the servants. Alexius had been deposed. He was in chains, in prison.

Murtzuphulus was announced as Alexius V, the new emperor.

I hurried to the palace and gained entrance easily for everything was in chaos. Montage was in his office and confirmed the story. He said Alexius had called for me. Two guards appeared at the door.

Montage said, "You must go now. I shall pray for you."

I found him in Chalke Prison, the foulest place on the face of the earth. He had a servant with him in the dark, dank cell, also a small oil lamp, blankets, and food.

He reached his hands through the bars. "Christo! You have come! Praise be to God!"

It seemed I was his last hope, but I did not know what I could do for him. My knees weak, tears flooding my face, I grasped his hands and remembered another time I rescued him from death.

This time, I could do nothing but hear his story and pray for him.

In fits and bursts, tears coursing his cheeks, he related what had happened the night before. It was a tale I could scarcely believe.

"I was sleeping. They burst into my chambers. It seems the guard had already deserted me and pledged allegiance to the... the traitor, that foul fiend, Murtzuphulus. Oh, Christo! I should have heeded your warning! But I thought him to be a harmless old man, a friend to my father and to myself."

I nodded. "I know, Alexius. But it is too late for that."

He continued, "Murtzuphulus awoke me and said they had come for me, that the mobs had broken into the palace, that the guards were trying to keep them at bay, but I must flee at once. I could not take it all in, yet he urged me desperately, and so I fled with him. He took me to a pavilion outside in the gardens where he said I would be safe. Once I was there, though, they threw me into chains. He appeared wearing the royal buskins, the royal boots, you know, and gloated that he would be emperor by morning. They brought me here."

I paced the small space in front of his cell. "He has the favor of the people of this city," I said, knowing it would be no comfort to him. "And he has taken control of the treasury. The Varangian guard has pledged to him. I do not see what I can do for you."

"Go to Boniface, Christo! Go today! Plead with him for my life, for they will kill me, this I know. Tell them I will give them all my gold, the palace, my crown, everything, if they will ransom me."

I nodded. I did not point out to him that at the present moment, he owned nothing, not even the clothes on his back. "I will try, Alexius, but I doubt if they will rescue you."

"What of my father?"

I dreaded the question. "He died. This morning. They say of apoplexy, but I don't..."

"They poisoned him." He threw up his hands and paced his cell. "What treachery! And what did they say of us... of me?"

"That you rebelled, that you were unworthy, and that you are now being held until your trial. Murtzuphulus is riding the current wave of popularity with the people. He is their choice, he says. He will drive the westerners from our shores."

He groaned aloud, weeping copiously. He and his father were not close, yet all hope died for him in that moment.

Silence descended; the only sound was his weeping. I wondered what to say next. When it seemed he had calmed down, I said, "Alexius, are you right with God?"

He lifted his head, his old fiery temper surfacing. "What do you mean? I am a good Christian. I say my prayers. Go to mass. Give to the church. What else is required of me?"

"That you confess your sins to Jesus Christ and have Him cleanse you. A priest will not do. It must be your heartfelt repentance to Christ alone if you are to receive absolution of your sins. Have you done this, Alexius? Are you truly sorry for your sins? Are you ready to die?"

He stomped to the rear of the cell and returned. "I am ready, Christo, for whatever they do to me. Let us not talk of this again. I will survive. Have I not always? My friends will ransom me. They will not leave me to die."

"Very well. I must go, but I will come again to see you. Is there anything you wish for me to bring? If it be in my power, I will bring it."

"Bring my books. My writing. That is all. Thank you for coming. You may go now." He dismissed me as if he were still the emperor.

I bowed and took my leave. When I emerged into the clean air above, I drew a deep breath and wiped my face. My heart broke for him, but I knew it was true. Murtzuphulus would kill him.

But I had other worries, and my thoughts and prayers drew me like a magnet to Chalke, the place of death.

CHAPTER 21

The Prince and the Girl

February Year of Our Lord 1204

While events swirled about my head like a tornado, and the government of Constantinople descended into a vortex of deceit, hatred, greed and murder, I knew I had to free Tania, or she would die.

And I had to do it before war came to the city.

I reported to Montage what happened, and then hurried from the palace. The new emperor was crowned and anointed in the Hagia Sophia, and the crowds, the mobs of the city, filled the streets with celebration. It was with great difficulty that I made my way down the Mese that day, for I wanted to see Horatio and plan our rescue attempt.

Now, with the city in an uproar, might be a good time to do it.

But I could not find my friend and decided I'd better return home to see if Uncle needed my assistance. Whenever there was a change in the administration, he wanted to be on top of the news and find favor with the new emperor as soon as possible. This required much letter writing and fact finding.

I found my assumptions correct, and thus, I was kept busy the rest of the next two days. Murtzuphulus met with the leading citizens and nobles of the city soon after taking the throne. He reorganized the government and dismissed all the old faces, even Niketas Choniates, and put his own men in their places.

In the first week of February, Murtzuphulus ordered the arrest of Nicholas Kannavos, the hapless nobleman the people had chosen as emperor. The guards forced their way into the Hagia Sophia, and the mobs which had so recently called for his ascension to the throne were gone. No one spoke for him; even the nobles and churchmen were silent. He was taken to the Milion where he was beheaded.

I visited Alexius twice while he was in prison, both times bringing him the items he requested. When he heard of Nicholas' execution and the failure of his crusader friends to come to his aid, his hopes fell. The royal guard had come to his cell twice and offered him poison, but he refused it.

Since the emperor closed all markets to the crusaders, they sent a delegation of knights to find food. The knights took a castle on the Black Sea and captured cattle and clothing. But when Emperor Murtzuphulus heard of it, he gathered his troops, 4,000 strong, to attack them.

Murtzuphulus carried the revered icon of the Virgin Mary and his imperial standard as he rode. The crusader forces won the day and took these two items. Murtzuphulus, reeling from his failure, declared that the two missing icons were misplaced, not taken. When the crusaders learned of this lie, they put both on the brow of a ship and sailed around the city, proclaiming the truth.

The emperor asked for peace talks with the doge. Boniface and Niketas Choniates were present when they met on the northern shores of the Golden Horn. The Doge repeated the demands they had against the Byzantium empire and also stated, as one of the conditions of peace, that they wanted Alexius released and restored to his position.

The emperor seethed with rage upon his return to the city, and the war that had loomed over us for so long seemed imminent. I feared for Alexius' life, for Murtzuphulus could not release Alexius, and their demand that he do so told him that the young man represented his greatest liability.

I found Horatio and Patience, and with Montage's help, we finalized our plans.

On the evening of February 8th, just at Vespers, Horatio and I dressed in our costumes – me in the guard's uniform, and he in the dress of an official from the palace. We entered Chalke with a pass from the emperor. No one seemed to notice that it was Alexius, the previous emperor, who had signed it.

The first problem we encountered when taken to the warden's office was that Proscus was not there. The man who accosted us was tall, of broad shoulders, and about the same age as I. He rested one hand on his sword hilt and stared at us as if we were enemy soldiers from the crusader camp.

"Who are you, and why do you come?" He took a step closer.

We introduced ourselves as Demetrius, Inspector of Prisons, and Under-Secretary Phillip Alexopoulus. Both men actually existed. If anyone questioned and sent to the senate for confirmation, we knew they would get nowhere, for the government offices nearby were in disorder with the new regime not even two weeks old.

Eying us suspiciously, the man led us inside his office. It had been cleaned and repainted. New desk. New shelves. No liquor bottles.

"I thought the inspection had been done," he said. "That is what the previous officer of this prison told me."

I nodded. "It was, sir. I accompanied the soldier on that occasion, but there are a few details we missed." I pulled out a parchment and pointed to several unchecked items. "We were instructed to return and complete this survey. It will not take much time."

He shook his head. "I will have to talk with my superior, Captain Manos. There is a new regime, you know. This order was under Alexius IV. It has no bearing on what we are doing now."

I shifted impatiently and felt gentle pressure on my arm, a caution from Horatio who stood behind me. "How long will this take, sir?"

He shrugged. "I do not know. The government is in shambles. It may take a month. More."

"We do not have a month. By that time, this whole city may be burned. We must complete this today, or we will have our fee docked, and the emperor will not receive the report. You, too, will feel the repercussions, for I have heard our new emperor takes care of details. Especially the prisons."

We stared at each other for the space of a few seconds. I could see he would not yield the keys. I had a set for the cell door and Tania's chains, but I did not have the key for the hall doors that led to the cells.

He stepped back and crossed his arms over his chest. "You will have to suffer, then. I will take the risk that the new emperor is too busy to read inspection reports. Off with you! I have things to do."

He turned dismissively to his cabinet of records. I thought to get himself a drink, and I was right, for as we started for the door, I glanced back and saw him withdraw a bottle.

I said, "Oh. I forgot. We brought Proscus a gift. But since you are the warden now, perhaps you should have it."

Horatio withdrew a bottle from his satchel and held it out. It was one Montage had smuggled from the palace – a fine red wine, only what the emperor would drink.

At first, he grunted something in refusal, but then he looked at the bottle. "Ah. This is not something you see every day, is it? Stolen from the emperor's own table?" Something in his eyes told me that our estimation rose with him.

I shook my head. "No. A gift from the emperor. From Alexius, that is. I rendered him a favor, and he gave me this in his appreciation."

"I see." He did not believe me, but he took the bottle, nonetheless. "This... puts a different light on things." He glanced up. "You have until the Vespers bell. No less." He handed me the ring of keys. "I will toss you out myself if I have to.

It was nearly Vespers. We had half an hour. It was not much, but I thought we could do it.

Horatio smiled. "Thank you, sir. Shall we have a drink now?" He eyed the bottle yearningly.

"And share it with you? I think not." He almost put it on the shelf and then brought it back. "Still, it would not hurt to taste."

Pouring a small amount in a tin cup, he handed it to Horatio who passed it to me. We pretended to drink and returned it to him. He quaffed it back in one gulp and sighed.

"That is good. Oh, yes."

We left him while he poured himself more.

"How long until the drug takes effect?" I asked Horatio in an under-tone as we strode down the corridor to the stairs.

He shook his head. "Opium? Not long. We must hurry."

I thought of Alexius on the first floor. I longed to set him free, too, but there were Varangian guards posted at his cell. Four of them. Murtzuphulus was taking no chances with his royal prisoner.

We descended three flights and approached the door leading to the cells of the slaves.

"I will stay and talk with the guard," Horatio said.

Taking a torch from the wall, I went into the darkened hall to the very last cell.

My heart fell. It was empty. All the cells were empty. Then I remembered that the slaves were probably serving food to the prisoners.

I hurried back to Horatio. "I am finished," I said, rushing past. He bade the guard good evening and met me near the stair.

"What are you—"

"The cells are empty. They are serving the meal. Come quickly! We must find the kitchen."

It was on the entry level above the prison. Chalke had been once a grand and beautiful gatehouse to the palace and contained marble floors, spacious rooms off to each side, and frescoed walls.

Sweat beaded my brow as we checked the warden and found him asleep at his desk. This would give us a few more precious moments, but I did not know how we would find Tania and free her if there were guards around and other prisoners.

On the top floor, we hurried to where we heard voices and the clatter of pans. At the end of a corridor, I shoved open a door. We found a group of people bent over hot stoves and ladling soup into pails. Piles of bread were heaped on a counter.

A guard with a whip stood at the door. I showed him our papers and the pass and told him we were there to conduct an inspection which included the kitchen.

"Now you have seen it, go." He folded his arms over his massive chest and glared at us, flicking his whip.

The slaves were chained and left the room in company with a soldier who led four of them at a time below to the cells. They carried heavy buckets of the food.

I did not see Tania. "I must see the food being served," I told him. "For this report." I waved a sheaf of papers under his nose.

"You will leave." He stood obdurate, blocking my way.

I stepped back. "Phillip? Can you help?"

There was no way to avoid it. We did not want to bring harm to anyone, but the guard would not allow me to follow the slaves below to the cells.

Horatio stepped around me. "Come here, big fella," he said, pulling on the man's beard, "I have something to tell you."

Surprised, the guard leaned forward, which gave Horatio an opportunity to hit him on the neck. He fell without a sound. We leaped over his body and before any of the other guards returned, ran out and down the stairs to the cells.

On the first floor, I opened the door, and we entered. A group of slaves came toward us, having delivered their buckets. They were followed by a guard who used a whip viciously. The slaves stumbled, cried out, regained their feet and came forward.

I spotted a small young woman with dark hair in the group. She glanced up and cried out, but threw her hand over her mouth in time.

As they drew near and passed us, I yanked her toward me.

"Come with me! Now!" She was not manacled to the other slaves.

The guard stopped and whirled on me. "What are you…"

I heard no sound, but he, too, fell almost at my feet in a dead faint. Horatio looked about. "Who did that? Come, Demetrius, we must hurry."

The other slaves did not know what to do. Most of them continued down the hall, not knowing their guard had fallen. One or two looked back, and when they did, I shouted at them to keep going, to return to the kitchen, or I would see they were punished.

Sweat was flowing freely down my face. I did not take the time to wipe it away as I knelt beside the girl. "Tania. It is you, is it not?" I looked into her face.

She stared at me through frightened eyes. "Basil? I cannot believe… Oh, my Lord. It is you! Basil, please rescue my friend, the girl ahead of me. She will die if you do not."

I unlocked her chains. "We cannot. All of them will want free."

Against her protests, I lifted her into my arms. She was as light as a feather. "We have to hurry. Horatio, lead the way."

We ran down the hall and up the stairs. But the guard, the big one from the kitchen, had recovered and was standing at the doorway of the kitchen, glaring at us.

"Drop her!"

Thankfully, there were halls and rooms in the gatehouse that was once called Chalke. We dashed down a hall with him in pursuit. Looking back, we saw he had called others.

The corridors made a circuit around the entrance room. At times, Horatio took Tania, and at other times, she ran with us. But she could not keep up. Her strength was so small I marveled that she was still alive.

And still they came. Now the warden, awake from his opium-drugged sleep, joined them. Soon they would call others, mayhap the Varangians who guarded Alexius.

We hid behind furniture, but they found us, and we dashed down the corridor, trying another room, another way. But the corridors all led back to the entrance room. It was a maze filled with the horrors of echoing shouts and heavy feet tramping on the tiles.

They set a guard at the two main doors so we could not escape that way.

The warden called, "Some of you go the other way! We will trap them!"

We knew we were done. Finished. By nightfall, we would all be in one of the cells, awaiting execution. Tania begged us to leave her, to flee, and save ourselves. But I shook my head stubbornly.

"No! We have come this far, we will think of something. Horatio, have you an idea?"

He shook his head. "If we could only pry these windows open, but we have no time. Here they come..."

We bolted again. It seemed a nightmare to which there was no end. But it would end soon. We could not do this forever. They had contained the other slaves in the kitchen. We did not want to descend to the cells, for there they could trap us like rats.

At the end of our strength, we came again to the entrance room. In the hall, I found a small closet we had overlooked before. Motioning to it, I ducked inside and somehow all three of us crowded in.

I shut the door, then opened it a crack.

By now, it was dark. Voices came from outside the prison. Someone pounded on the door of Chalke.

Then I heard, "In the name of Emperor Alexius V, open!"

The guards who stood by the main doors hustled to obey the command. I peeked out. The Emperor and his entourage streamed in – fifty or so of them. The warden and guards who had been chasing us burst from a side room, panting.

Murtzuphulus stood in the middle of the room and glared.

"Your Highness!" The warden bowed. "I am sorry you find us like this, but..."

"Silence!" the Emperor shouted.

One of Murtzuphulus' Varangians stepped forward, his axe menacing the warden. "The Emperor wishes to see Prince Alexius! Take us to his cell! Now!"

The warden bowed again. "Yes, sir."

He turned and with a motion of his hand, waved his guards beside him. They tromped past our hiding place silently, carrying torches. I noticed logothetes, senators, noblemen among them. Servants. More guards.

Suddenly an idea occurred to me. "Let us mingle with them. Tania, can you stand? Walk?"

She pushed back her matted hair and nodded. "Yes, Basil. But I... look a sight."

"It does not matter. No one will notice you. Stay close to Horatio." I glanced at them. "Very well, let us go."

We emerged and joined the crowd. As I thought, everyone was so intently watching the Emperor and his cronies that no one noticed a palace guard, an official and a slender woman with dark hair among them.

As we went down the steps, Horatio came closer to me and whispered over the din, "You know what the emperor intends to do, don't you?"

I shook my head. "See the prince?"

"No, my friend. He... ah, but I do not wish to say. If you would like, stay behind me. Do not look."

We entered the hall and stopped about half-way down the row of cells. Silence filled the area except for the command to open the cell door. A rattle of keys. A squawk as the door opened. The crowd pressed closer.

There was some low conversation. I thought I heard Alexius cry out. I wanted to press forward, to see him. My heart yearned to be with him, to be his friend. But I could not.

Horatio kept a firm hand on my arm, else I would have fallen. Tania pressed her face into his tunic and wept. There were muttered comments around us.

I will always remember the smell of oil-soaked torches, smoke, the putrid stench of the cells, the sound of creaking as if ghosts walked, and, yes, weeping. Perhaps it was myself. I know not.

There was more conversation. I heard Alexius say, "No. No. I will not."

Silence.

Murtzuphulus shouted something. Alexius cried out again, "No, oh, God, no!" he screamed in pain.

I clung to Horatio as I remembered the little boy I taught and loved. I loved him still. But he had gone beyond me. He had changed, and I could not reach him.

The deed was done. Murtzuphulus whirled and marched out.

We flattened ourselves against the cold stone wall as he and his officers and guards stomped past. His face was set grimly, yet he was pleased, and even cuffed one of his officers with a wild light in his strange eyes.

"We are free of him," he said. Someone laughed.

It was all I heard, yet I knew Alexius was gone.

CHAPTER 22

The Way Home

February, Year of Our Lord 1204

They said Alexius died of an accident.

Yes, an accident. He met with Murtzuphulus' fists that held a wire and that wire got tangled around his throat. Garroted. They left his body in the cell like a common prisoner.

I was sick at heart and knew not how I came to be standing outside the prison with Horatio gripping my arm fiercely and Tania weeping at my side.

Horatio gave me a shake and said urgently, "Basil! We must flee! They will come looking for us, and the girl..."

With a sigh, Tania collapsed. I caught her before she hit the ground. "Yes. We need to get her out of sight."

"Come. My house. It will be a haven for a time."

Without further word, we wove our way through the press of people and fled down the street. I carried her. But she was not a burden, and it was not far.

Patience was waiting for us, holding the door. We laid Tania on a bed, and that kind lady did all she could for her. I stepped out as they bathed and dressed her in a simple cotton shift. Then I applied cold compresses and gave her something for her pain.

Yet the girl tossed and turned, and a fever raged in her body. Her face held the grey pallor of death.

"She is very ill," Patience said, shaking her head. "She is exhausted, was poorly fed for weeks and was worked beyond her endurance. It is more than any of us can imagine."

"Will she be all right if she rests?" I stood by the bed, my hands clasped, gazing at her.

"I know not," she said, sponging her forehead "It is beyond my skill."

"Then we must take her to a monastery."

Horatio touched my shoulder. "That would be extremely dangerous tonight, my friend," he said in his deep voice. "We must wait for morning."

It was a long vigil. I sat by her bedside and prayed, sang, and wept through the night. God was with me, for I felt His arms of love and compassion. I believe He wept with me, and it was a comfort to my soul.

Tania survived the night. The next morning, we took her to the Christ Pantokrator monastery on the Fifth Hill, just above Uncle's estate. There she received excellent care.

Murtzuphulus held a grand funeral for the prince. Uncle went to it, but he did not force me to attend. I found my bed and slept the rest of the day. It seemed I could sleep forever, for I knew my beloved was rescued and was safe.

As for Alexius, I mourned for him, but I did not pray for his soul, for he had made his choice, and he must dwell forever with that decision.

The crusaders discovered the truth of Alexius' murder when someone shot an arrow into their camp with a letter attached, telling them he was murdered. This inflamed them. Now they had a noble and righteous cause to attack the city, one in which they could justify their actions to themselves, to the pope, and to other leaders in Europe.

The stage was set for the initial assault of the city. For the next several weeks, the sound of hammers, saws and voices filled the air down by the Golden Horn.

When I went to investigate, I learned that both sides were preparing for war.

The Venetians and Latins constructed defenses on their vessels. They made "cats," structures like small huts covered with hides dipped in vinegar. These could be rolled to the walls to cover the men who would dig under the fortress and pound at it with rams.

The Greeks built high battlements on top of the walls, some said seven stories high, and covered these with hides dipped in vinegar. These wooden ramifications were built out over the walls and were equipped with hatches in the floors so they could dump boiling oil and rocks on the enemy down below.

I visited Tania every day and gave suggestions to the monks for her care. When she was able, about a week after her release from prison, I brought her to the estate. Uncle was too busy with appointments with the new regime and its officers to pay attention to the details of his house.

Yet I had to tell him, for I had plans for the two of us, and those plans included him.

One fine day towards the end of March, I sat with Tania on the sunny patio outside the house. It was her favorite place with her books and parchments, a glass of water, and fruit.

Constantinople lay at our feet. We glimpsed the glistening water of the Golden Horn through the trees to the east. The palace, which sat above us on another one of the hills, brooded in its silent grandeur like a resplendent eagle. Below, the city moved and breathed in its rhythms of life. Hawkers, merchants, priests and sinners, poor and noble blended in its streets, going about their business despite the threat of war and doom.

"It is very beautiful," she said in a low tone. Her color had improved, and she had gained weight, but she would never be the same woman I had met in the Golden Bull tavern.

Now, she was more thoughtful, very frail, and so devoted to the Word of God that at times I thought she was obsessed with it. She had received a parchment from the monks, a copy of the book of Psalms. She read it constantly and derived much comfort from it.

It was, to her, like medicine, healing and restoring her soul.

Her love and life opened like the roses that grew on the estate, bending their fragrant faces to the sun. She, too, lifted her face to the sun and soaked in the warmth like she could never get enough of it. She regarded me with worshipful eyes and followed my movements with utter devotion.

I nodded. "Yes. I love this city, but it is doomed. We must make plans, Tania dear, for I heard the other day that the emperor is going to close all the gates. Traffic in and out of the city will be forbidden. If we do not leave soon, we will be trapped here."

She shuddered and set down her parchment. "I do not want that. Basil, what do you think we should do?"

I stood and paced to the edge of the patio, looking down on the roofs of the houses below us. Then I turned and digging a small box from my pocket, I approached her as she sat on a lounging chair.

I knelt beside her. "This is what I think we should do. Tania Maria Patera, would you do me the honor of becoming my wife?"

She gasped as I held out a ring. The large central diamond was encircled with smaller ones. It was white gold, shimmering like the sun itself. Light and beauty; this she loved so much since her days in the prison.

"Oh, Basil! Yes, yes, of course! I never dreamed..."

I held her close while she cried and laughed, and then I kissed her properly. Or improperly. Does it matter? I kissed her and that is all I can say. Then I slipped the ring on her finger.

We told Uncle. By this time, he was aware of her presence in the house. She had won him over by her acute business sense and aptitude for figures. Indeed, she often did his books for him, working into the night to get the rows of figures to tally. He appreciated that about her, and also that she was related to a wealthy family in Greece that he knew.

When we gave him the news, he laughed, his eyes twinkling. "That is the best thing I have heard for a long time in this dreary place." He poured us wine, some of his best, and made a toast.

"To the happy couple. May they find joy wherever they go, and may prosperity and many children blossom around them like flowers in the garden."

Tania blushed, but I could tell she was pleased.

He went on to say, "This calls for a feast! Yet the closure of many markets and the gates restrict me. What can I do for you?"

"Uncle," I said, "a private dinner would suffice. It need not be grand. I think I can procure the food. Tonight?"

He bowed to me. "As always, I appreciate your resourcefulness. And when is this happy event to take place?"

I glanced at Tania for we had not discussed this matter. "Very soon, Uncle. As soon as Tania feels up to it."

"Well, in that case," she said, laughing and wiping away tears, "next week. Why wait? The war is coming, and we don't want a wedding while there is fighting in the streets."

Uncle nodded, pleased. "And then? Will you stay on here?"

I cleared my throat. "We... uh, we would prefer to return to Greece. May I find some employment on one of your estates?"

He laughed. "Employment? Oh, Basil, you are more than a servant to me. You are everything. But wait. You shall see. I shall make the arrangements, and you shall see."

I could tell he was up to something, but when I questioned him further, he would tell me nothing. Yet the glimmer of joy in his eyes told me it was good.

Even though war loomed, businesses were open and the streets were busy with shoppers and merchants. Tania over-saw the wedding plans, and Uncle paid for it all.

Our wedding took place on March 25, Year of Our Lord 1204 at my uncle's house on the Fifth Hill. I had contacted a priest and invited my friends. When I spoke to Uncle about the guest list, he heartily approved.

"Bring them all, Basil," he said expansively.

The weather that day favored us; a bright blue sky, sunshine, and the scent of magnolia blooms that came on a soft breeze.

Tania appeared, walking down the pathway through the gardens, in blue. I loved her in blue. A veil hid her face and dark hair, but I could see the glimmer of her beautiful eyes when she took my hand confidently.

She had become a lovely woman with a keen mind and a passion for Jesus Christ. What more could I desire in a wife? Tears stung my eyes when I thought of this precious treasure God had granted me, and all the difficulties of our lives seemed to pass away.

The surprise Uncle had for us was an estate in Greece, our own to manage and grow.

"With lots of room for the Xavier clan!" he said, toasting us again.

Besides the estate, Uncle provided us a way to escape Constantinople on his very own ship. I suspect it had involved the bribery of several high-placed officials, but two days after the wedding, we were escorted by Varangian guards and set aboard the *Maria,* an apt name, I thought.

We sailed from port on the 28th day of March as the city prepared for war. I looked back at it with tears in my eyes. It would always be the Queen of Cities for me, although I would never see it again.

I thought of those days with Prince Alexius. Good days. Hard days.

God had given it all to me, and now He crowned me with a beautiful bride, a future, and a hope.

With Tania by my side, I turned from the city to face west. Greece would be our home, where we would raise our children and grow old.

I couldn't wait.

PROLOGUE

Uncle Alesandro survived the siege and occupation of Constantinople. He wrote me that on April 8th, the crusaders attacked the city and were successful in breaking through the wall. Murtzuphulus made a show of resisting the troops, but when he saw thousands of the enemy troops inside the city, he took a page from Alexius III and bolted from the city.

About a year later, he fled ahead of the Latin troops and was finally captured as he sought sanctuary in Asia Minor. He was brought to Constantinople, tried for the murder of Alexius IV, and executed. It was the Doge of Venice who thought up the particular way he would die.

"He always preached about 'high justice'," the doge said with a grim smile. "So, he shall have it."

In November 1204, he was made to mount the column of Theodosius in the Forum of the Bull. At the top, he was shoved off and fell to his death.

Uncle had hired mercenary troops to guard his estate in the city and his farms in the surrounding area. It must have cost him a fortune, but he suffered only minor loss in a city devastated and ruined by the crusaders' three days of sacking, the traditional time allotted to a conquering army to take what they wanted and burn the rest.

Most of the city was devastated and razed. The great Hagai Sophia church survived, but many of its precious, priceless treasures were stolen. Thousands of citizens were killed.

I was content to be in Greece during these events, away from the killing and destruction.

Sometime after the fall of the city, Horatio and Patience visited us, bringing Philippa with them. I greeted them happily and housed them for a time until they journeyed on to Thessalonica and their guild's headquarters in Germany.

Tania and I now have a family of three boys and two girls. We work long, hard hours in our vineyards and farm and spend our evenings around a fire in the back of the house, telling stories.

The favorite story the children want to hear is how I rescued their mother twice from the emperors of Constantinople.

At the ending, she always adds quietly, "And I rescued your father from himself."

We laugh, but it is true. She has rescued me in more ways than I care to recount. She studies her medical manuals every day and treats those she finds in need of aid. She is my right hand. My love. My treasure from God.

I grow magnolia trees by the house, and when their sweet scent fills the air on a balmy summer eve, I think of Constantinople and Prince Alexius, the young man who won the crown but lost so much.

I think of him as the little boy who dangled from a balcony long ago, and the young man who tried desperately to please two implacable enemies. The little boy who called me Christo.

The End

A Note From the Author:

This tale began as a short story written several years ago from the novel, *Mistral, Wind from the West.* The story of young Prince Alexius caught my attention. I felt sorry for him despite the ill reports I read about him from chroniclers of the Fourth Crusade, Niketas Choniates, for one. They said he was "spoiled and head strong, without compassion or reason."

But if one takes into account his blood lines, his home life, if you could call it that, and the culture surrounding royalty in those days, then some pity and regret might be spared him.

I became immersed in the fascinating world of Constantinople before it fell. Much of the beauty and splendor of that ancient city has vanished, but one may still see portions of the old wall, some of Blachernae Palace, and remnants of Buekeleon.

Hagia Sophia church stands, but it is now a museum, much favored by tourists because there remains some of its former opulence and grandeur. Many of the upper windows have been blocked, so it does not have the glowing light inside as it once did.

The Muslim Turks guard it jealously, knowing its imminent place in history and importance to the Greek Orthodox faith.

Recently, a Turkish man was heard to comment to a Greek tourist, "You will *never* get it back!"

The quote goes, "Power corrupts. Absolute power corrupts absolutely." Add unlimited wealth, and you have the recipe for all the ingredients to the downfall of Constantinople: greed, corruption, power plays, murder, slander, and lust.

Prince Alexius was a young man who was thrust onto center stage of the second largest and most powerful empire in the world. He failed to turn from sin and degradation and lost the crown, his throne, his family, his life.

To aid my writing, I studied the book, *The Fourth Crusade and the Sack of Constantinople* by Jonathan Phillips. (Published by Penguin) Many of the details I included in this book are facts. These include the story of the prince's escape from the city, the siege, the Fourth Crusade and its leaders, the royal family and major officers in Constantinople, Prince Alexius and his father.

I hope you enjoyed reading it as much as I enjoyed writing it. I intend to write more stories of medieval times and have titled this series, "A Kingdom Tale".

Virginia Ann Work
Feb. 2020

Other Books Written by Virginia Ann Work

Keys to the Kingdom Medieval Fiction:

Sirocco Wind from the East
Mistral Wind from the North
Zephyr Wind from the West
Lavento Wind from the South

Contemporary Mystery Series: Gina Lindsey

Deadlocked
Deadwater

Young Adult Mystery Series, Jodi Fischer:

The Mystery of the Missing Message
The Secret in the Silver Box
The Curse of the Broken Feather

Devotional with Chris Boelter:

A Fear Not for Every Day (A Daily Devotional on the
Fear of the Lord)